SYNOPSIS

"She was the bane of my existence. Meeting her had been nothing but suffering because it had only left me in a painful need that was never fulfilled." – Law

Law and Zuri met in the most unconventional way, but their connection was one of storybooks. It was genuine, poetic, and undeniable. However, haters will always ruin some shit. Learning what truly sent Law her way, Zuri cut off all ties with the man that had finally reminded her of what truly being unconditionally loved felt like.

Now, she is starting all over. She has divorced her cheating husband and exiled Law out of her life. She's met a new man and is so ready for new beginnings. Yet, once again, haters despise seeing you happy. At a family dinner, her own sister spills some tea that is so hot that it will burn an irreparable hole in Zuri's family and her heart. A family member's unbelievable betrayal leaves Zuri reeling with despair. However, that is only the start of the world wind of treachery, scandal, and drama that's engulfed in this finale.

Is kinship strong enough to birth forgiveness for unthinkable betrayal? Will Law gain his freedom in time to get his girl before she falls in love with her new beau? Those questions and so many more will be answered in A Rich Man's Wife 2!

Ma threw her face into her hands, now sobbing. "He's in ICU. He was in surgery all night. It's not looking good."

I sat down next to Ma and put my arm around her. She leaned on my shoulder, unable to compose herself. "I can't lose my boys," she cried. "I'm so sick of this shit."

I gritted, unable to take this stress that me and Jeezy's street life was putting on her. I had always tried my best to stay out of jail just so that I would never make her feel this way.

Her cell then rang. She jumped for it in her pocket. Looking at it, she stood up. "This is the nurse with an update on Jeezy. I have to step out to take this."

She then rushed out.

Looking at Reese, I asked him, "You good?"

He shrugged a shoulder. Even though me and Jeezy were always at odds, Reese and Jeezy had a better relationship.

"Let me go make sure she good," he told me. As he walked towards the door, he hesitated and looked back at me. "You got this shit, my nigga. Whatever you decide, you know I got your back. Whatever you need me to do, I got you. This should be—"

I shook my head, narrowing my eyes at him and cutting him off. "Gon' out there and see about Ma."

Sighing deeply, he headed out. Whit took Ma's seat, asking me, "What was he about to say?"

"Nothing. That nigga just overly emotional."

Blowing a heavy breath, Whit looked me in the eyes. "Did you decide what to do?"

I had been mulling over what decision to make. I couldn't imagine taking this deal like a bitch, but it looked like the police were doing everything to make me lose this case. I didn't want to be one of those niggas in jail, trying to prove my innocence for the next twenty-five years.

I shrugged. "I don't know."

"You should take the deal," she said softly. "For the kids. It will break their hearts if they lose you. It would be easier for them if they got their daddy back in five years rather than decades. That's a long time, Law."

My heart sank from the pressure to make the right decision. Gambling in the streets had been a breeze. But gambling with my life was the hardest thing I had ever done.

A knock on the door interrupted our conversation. Looking up, I saw Sam and the prosecutor walk in.

Sam looked at Whit and smiled. "Can we have the room, please?"

She nodded. Then, surprisingly, she hugged me. "Think about the kids," she spoke into my ear.

Whit then left the room.

"So, Mr. Woods, what's it going to be?" the prosecutor asked.

The smug, cocky look on her face made my blood boil. Under my anger was a burning desire to be able to be there for my kids as much as possible. Ma had taken me in, but the void of not having my blood mother and father was still felt. I couldn't have that for my kids, especially my girls. Whit had been right; five years was a cakewalk. My oldest would only be fifteen when I was released. They all would still be young enough to grow up with me. I wouldn't be risking Ma dying while I was doing a twenty-five-year bid.

I gave the prosecutor an icy glare. This feeling of loss was fucking unbearable.

I thought for a few seconds. I played the scenarios out in my head. I could lose this case and do twenty-five years. I could be out in five in time to raise my kids. I could also gamble all of that and win this case.

Sighing, I tore my eyes away from her. "Fuck y'all," I spewed. "I'm not taking shit."

Fuck these motherfuckas. Unc hadn't taken that charge for me just to turn around and be a scary-ass nigga.

ZURI TURNER

Ever since my date with Dom, we had been on the phone nonstop. We had even seen one another briefly on a quick lunch date two days before.

"C'mon, let's go," Dom tried to persuade me.

"I'm *sleepyyyy*," I whined. "We were on the phone all night."

The night prior, he and I had been on Facetime until three in the morning. I felt like I was in high school again, talking to my crush. Looking at his face even then made it hard to tell him no. However, I needed to put some space between us. I wanted to be sure that I liked him instead of rebounding *hard*.

"So, you telling me no?" he asked, licking those perfect lips.

I bit my lip, staring into the phone, trying my best not to fall for his sexy aggression.

I had to force myself to say, "Yeah, I'm telling you no."

Dom wanted us to go to brunch, but after staying up with him all night, all I wanted to do was lie in bed until dinner at my dad's house later.

Dom smirked, his eyes leaping with flirtation. "You know that only makes me want you more, right?"

"So, you like a challenge?"

"I like *you*."

Butterflies.

"Do you?"

His eyes lowered lustfully. "Yeah. Sexy ass."

Smirking, I replied, "So, you're just attracted to me."

"Nah, I'm feeling you," he confessed seriously. "I can see myself fucking with you."

That made my heart flutter. It felt so good being courted again. I hadn't felt desired by Rashaad in so long. But this scared the shit out of me. Falling for another man felt like putting my heart in the line of fire yet again. Rashaad and Law had a bitch spooked.

"It sounds like there is a 'but' coming."

"But I know that you are getting out of a marriage and that you've been through a lot of shit."

Sighing, I told him, "True. I'm sorry. So, it's bad timing?"

"Hell nah," he insisted. "I ain't no punk. I'm just willing to be patient."

I grinned. "I appreciate that."

"But you lying there topless is making it real fucking hard for me to be patient."

I gasped, lifting the covers up more. "You can see that?!"

He chuckled. "Nah. I can just tell since your shoulders are bare."

"I could have on a tube top."

"I see a lil' bit of those perfect breasts too," he teased.

At that moment, my Ring doorbell notification went off on my phone. Then the bell rang through my house. Before getting out of bed, I checked the footage on the app.

Looking at it, my eyes narrowed as I sat up slowly.

"Let me call you back."

"You good?" he asked, noticing the change in my expression.

"Yeah," I rushed as I got out of bed. I then slid on my robe and house shoes. "I'll call you right back."

❀ Created with Vellum

PREVIOUSLY IN...

A RICH MAN'S WIFE

ANNAN "LAW" WOODS

The next day was my trial. Sam had told me that it would likely take all day to present both sides' arguments. Sam had an expert to argue that my fingerprint had been transferred to the murder weapon. Their eyewitness was bullshit. I doubted that they even had one.

"Hi, baby." Ma rushed into the attorney-client conference room. Behind her were Whit and Reese. I hadn't expected Jeezy's bitch-ass to come.

Standing from the table, I hugged Ma. Reese dapped me up. Even Whit hugged me. A nigga should have known then that it wasn't looking good for me.

Noticing their solemn expressions, I chuckled. "Damn, y'all look like I lost the case already."

Ma pressed her lips together and slowly sat down. "It's not that."

"What's wrong?" My eyes darted from her to Reese and then to Whit.

Reese cleared his throat as Ma started to cry. "Jeezy got shot yesterday."

Shocked, my eyes bucked as I took a step back. "Word? He okay?"

Ma threw her face into her hands, now sobbing. "He's in ICU. He was in surgery all night. It's not looking good."

I sat down next to Ma and put my arm around her. She leaned on my shoulder, unable to compose herself. "I can't lose my boys," she cried. "I'm so sick of this shit."

I gritted, unable to take this stress that me and Jeezy's street life was putting on her. I had always tried my best to stay out of jail just so that I would never make her feel this way.

Her cell then rang. She jumped for it in her pocket. Looking at it, she stood up. "This is the nurse with an update on Jeezy. I have to step out to take this."

She then rushed out.

Looking at Reese, I asked him, "You good?"

He shrugged a shoulder. Even though me and Jeezy were always at odds, Reese and Jeezy had a better relationship.

"Let me go make sure she good," he told me. As he walked towards the door, he hesitated and looked back at me. "You got this shit, my nigga. Whatever you decide, you know I got your back. Whatever you need me to do, I got you. This should be—"

I shook my head, narrowing my eyes at him and cutting him off. "Gon' out there and see about Ma."

Sighing deeply, he headed out. Whit took Ma's seat, asking me, "What was he about to say?"

"Nothing. That nigga just overly emotional."

Blowing a heavy breath, Whit looked me in the eyes. "Did you decide what to do?"

I had been mulling over what decision to make. I couldn't imagine taking this deal like a bitch, but it looked like the police were doing everything to make me lose this case. I didn't want to be one of those niggas in jail, trying to prove my innocence for the next twenty-five years.

I shrugged. "I don't know."

"You should take the deal," she said softly. "For the kids. It will break their hearts if they lose you. It would be easier for them if they got their daddy back in five years rather than decades. That's a long time, Law."

My heart sank from the pressure to make the right decision. Gambling in the streets had been a breeze. But gambling with my life was the hardest thing I had ever done.

A knock on the door interrupted our conversation. Looking up, I saw Sam and the prosecutor walk in.

Sam looked at Whit and smiled. "Can we have the room, please?"

She nodded. Then, surprisingly, she hugged me. "Think about the kids," she spoke into my ear.

Whit then left the room.

"So, Mr. Woods, what's it going to be?" the prosecutor asked.

The smug, cocky look on her face made my blood boil. Under my anger was a burning desire to be able to be there for my kids as much as possible. Ma had taken me in, but the void of not having my blood mother and father was still felt. I couldn't have that for my kids, especially my girls. Whit had been right; five years was a cakewalk. My oldest would only be fifteen when I was released. They all would still be young enough to grow up with me. I wouldn't be risking Ma dying while I was doing a twenty-five-year bid.

I gave the prosecutor an icy glare. This feeling of loss was fucking unbearable.

I thought for a few seconds. I played the scenarios out in my head. I could lose this case and do twenty-five years. I could be out in five in time to raise my kids. I could also gamble all of that and win this case.

Sighing, I tore my eyes away from her. "Fuck y'all," I spewed. "I'm not taking shit."

Fuck these motherfuckas. Unc hadn't taken that charge for me just to turn around and be a scary-ass nigga.

ZURI TURNER

Ever since my date with Dom, we had been on the phone nonstop. We had even seen one another briefly on a quick lunch date two days before.

"C'mon, let's go," Dom tried to persuade me.

"I'm *sleepyyyy*," I whined. "We were on the phone all night."

The night prior, he and I had been on Facetime until three in the morning. I felt like I was in high school again, talking to my crush. Looking at his face even then made it hard to tell him no. However, I needed to put some space between us. I wanted to be sure that I liked him instead of rebounding *hard*.

"So, you telling me no?" he asked, licking those perfect lips.

I bit my lip, staring into the phone, trying my best not to fall for his sexy aggression.

I had to force myself to say, "Yeah, I'm telling you no."

Dom wanted us to go to brunch, but after staying up with him all night, all I wanted to do was lie in bed until dinner at my dad's house later.

Dom smirked, his eyes leaping with flirtation. "You know that only makes me want you more, right?"

"So, you like a challenge?"

"I like *you*."

Butterflies.

"Do you?"

His eyes lowered lustfully. "Yeah. Sexy ass."

Smirking, I replied, "So, you're just attracted to me."

"Nah, I'm feeling you," he confessed seriously. "I can see myself fucking with you."

That made my heart flutter. It felt so good being courted again. I hadn't felt desired by Rashaad in so long. But this scared the shit out of me. Falling for another man felt like putting my heart in the line of fire yet again. Rashaad and Law had a bitch spooked.

"It sounds like there is a 'but' coming."

"But I know that you are getting out of a marriage and that you've been through a lot of shit."

Sighing, I told him, "True. I'm sorry. So, it's bad timing?"

"Hell nah," he insisted. "I ain't no punk. I'm just willing to be patient."

I grinned. "I appreciate that."

"But you lying there topless is making it real fucking hard for me to be patient."

I gasped, lifting the covers up more. "You can see that?!"

He chuckled. "Nah. I can just tell since your shoulders are bare."

"I could have on a tube top."

"I see a lil' bit of those perfect breasts too," he teased.

At that moment, my Ring doorbell notification went off on my phone. Then the bell rang through my house. Before getting out of bed, I checked the footage on the app.

Looking at it, my eyes narrowed as I sat up slowly.

"Let me call you back."

"You good?" he asked, noticing the change in my expression.

"Yeah," I rushed as I got out of bed. I then slid on my robe and house shoes. "I'll call you right back."

"Okay."

Hanging up, I hurried out of my bedroom, down the hall, and towards the front door.

Opening it, I was met by a stern-faced man.

"May I help you?" I asked, peeking my head out of the door.

"Are you Mrs. Zuri Turner?"

"Yes," I replied cautiously.

"I am Special Agent Derrick Lightfoot." Then the tall, lean, salt and peppered man flashed a badge at me. Reading it, I confirmed that he was an FBI agent.

◌⁙◌

"What in the entire fuck?!" Bianca snapped.

"I know!" I exclaimed.

"Wait a minute, wait a minute, wait a minute," Bianca chanted through my AirPod. "So, Rashaad has been stealing from the prison's budget?!"

I stared blankly into space, still reeling with shock. The FBI agent had only asked me a few questions for about thirty minutes, turned my life upside down, and left.

"Yes. Apparently, the Governor's office had some questions about missing funds from the County's budget, so they contacted the FBI," I explained. "The FBI has been investigating him for the last few months."

"I thought he inherited a lot of money from his mother."

"He did. His ass spent it all. The FBI has been all in his bank accounts."

"How the fuck does he spend that much money?"

Sneering, I shook my head. "Probably on his hoes."

"Hoes don't even cost that much."

"He gambles, cars, trips, and he's been spoiling the fuck out of me and Zoey for years."

"*Woooow*," Bianca sang lowly. "So, why the hell did they want to talk to you?"

"Because I used to work there, and I am married to him."

Bianca gasped. "They think you were involved?!"

"I guess they were making sure that I wasn't. He asked a few questions about my position at the prison, why I quit, etc."

"This shit is crazy. So..." Then Bianca started to sing the viral video, "...*He about to lose his job*!"

"Yep." Sighing deeply, I sat back on the couch, still in pure disbelief. "I'm so glad Zoey wasn't here."

"How is she doing, by the way?"

Thinking of her made my heart ache. "Better. She finally got out of the house today."

"That's good." Bianca blew a heavy breath. "So, what are you going to do? You don't have a job, and you might not be getting alimony if that nigga goes to jail."

"I have savings, and I'll start looking for a position eventually. I want to spend as much time with Zoey as I can before she leaves for school."

"You guys are so sweet," Bianca gushed.

I smiled from ear to ear, so hard that my cheeks hurt. "Yeah, that girl is my world."

My Ring camera notification went off again. I had PTSD from that agent showing up, so I rushed to the app to see who it was. It was only the mailman. Still, I went to check the mail because, though Zoey had already decided what school she was going to, she was enjoying counting the acceptance letters she had been receiving.

"Urgh," I groaned as I stood up. "I feel sick to my stomach."

Bianca scoffed. "I'm sure you do, hell."

Bianca and I continued to gag about Rashaad's scandal as I moped through the house towards the front door. I was able to open it and reach inside the mailbox since it was inches away.

Pulling the mail out, the first letter I saw had the sender and return address written in handwriting. Curious, I read it, and the first thing I saw was Law's name.

I cringed. Yet, I didn't say anything to Bianca. I had forbidden either of us from ever saying his name. I wanted desperately to forget about that naive bullshit I had done.

"Hello?" I heard Bianca call out.

"I'm sorry, girl," I said as I began to tear up the letter into the smallest pieces. "I'm here."

AANAN "LAW" WOODS

For much of the trial, I was in a daze. I couldn't listen to those mother-fuckers ruin the rest of my life. I zoned out, thinking of Ma. I feared the pain that she would feel if she lost Jeezy. It terrified me that I could possibly not be there for her if she did. Whit's words had been ringing in my ears. I hoped that I hadn't been ornery in not taking that deal. The look on her face when the prosecutor announced that I had not taken the deal was devastation and fear.

I was concerned for Reese as well. I didn't trust that he would be able to keep his mouth shut if I were found guilty. He had always said that he would confess if I lost the case. His own guilt would push him to tell the truth. That would only ruin *both* of us because there was no way that I could live with myself if he was in jail for the rest of his life. I was guilty of something. I should have never let him go that day. He had no business there. So, if I had to do time for that, so be it.

The trial had gone on for hours. Yet, for me, it felt like days of watching Sam defend me against lies.

"This has clearly been a witch hunt," Sam said as he made his closing arguments. "They've been prolonging this trial in efforts to construct evidence that doesn't exist, including this imaginary eyewitness that never showed up today."

The prosecution had already made their closing arguments. So, this was it. These were Sam's last words before the judge decided my fate. "In closing, Your Honor, with scientific evidence that the defendant's prints were transferred onto the murder weapon, I urge you to find my client not guilty."

Looking over his glasses, the judge sat back in his chair. The entire courtroom was still in silence. The only noise was the echo of the heels of Sam's Stacy Adams as he walked to his seat next to me.

I couldn't breathe. My life was in these white motherfuckers' hands; the same motherfuckers that kept men like me in jail for fucking sport and then went home to their families like they didn't ruin one with every sentence that they imposed on an innocent man.

Clearing his throat, the judge finally said, "I've combed over this evidence in this trial..."

I blacked out again. I couldn't bear to listen. I thought of my kids, Ma, Reese, and even Zuri, *especially* Zuri. It stunned me that I wanted to be in her life just as much as I wanted to be in my kids' lives. She made my heart lighter.

I wanted that.

I *needed* that.

Without even trying, I had fallen in love for the first time.

I wasn't brought back into reality until I felt Sam put a comforting arm around my shoulder.

The judge's emotionless voice randomly forced its way into my ears. "With that, I find the defendant...."

ZURI TURNER

"Hey, Dad." I kissed him on the cheek, and then he stepped to the side to let me and Zoey in.

"Hi, sweetheart," he told me. Then he smiled at Zoey. "Hey, Grandpa's baby."

She smiled from ear to ear. "Hey, Grandpa."

Luckily, Zoey's bruises were healing. The evidence of her beating, which was still present, was easily covered by makeup.

Hearing the kids in the back of the house, Zoey went to join them.

"Zina and Zadah here yet?" I asked him.

"Zina is."

Just then, I cringed. Since that agent had left my house, I had been literally sick to my stomach. I had been feeling nauseous ever since.

"You okay?" my dad asked.

"I'm fine," I lied. There was no way that I was going to tell my father about Rashaad's thieving ass just yet. My day had been ruined enough. I did not need to hear my father's mouth in addition to all of the bullshit I had already been forced to endure.

Yet, as I burped, I tasted what I had eaten for breakfast come back into my mouth.

"I'll be back, Dad." I excused myself and rushed toward the bathroom.

Once I burst through the bathroom door, I heard my sister squeal. "I'm in here!"

She was simply in the mirror, though.

I forced my way inside and closed the door. Hurriedly throwing the toilet seat open, I fell to my knees and began to throw up.

"Oh my God! Ewe!" Zina exclaimed.

With my face in the toilet, I was gagging as the contents of my stomach spilled out. I could feel Zina rubbing my back soothingly as she made gagging noises.

Finally done, I slowly stood. Zina stepped to the side as I stood in front of the sink.

"What's wrong with you?" she asked, peering at me. "Hungover?"

"No." I found the mouthwash in the medicine cabinet and opened it. "I found out some shit about Rashaad today that has me sick to my stomach."

Zina grunted. "What bitch did he fuck now?"

"It has nothing to do with another woman," I replied.

"Well, bad news doesn't make you *literally* throw up. You pregnant?"

I immediately frowned. "Hell no."

"Why you say it like that? You been fucking, ain't you?"

I shrugged. "Yeah, but I'm on birth control."

Zina sucked her teeth. "People get pregnant while on birth control all the time. You got your period?"

I was about to immediately disagree with her again until I realized that I hadn't gotten my period yet and that I'd most definitely had unprotected sex with both Rashaad and Law.

Seeing the realization come over my face, Zina smirked while leaning her head to the side as she stared at me through the mirror.

Oh shit.

☙❦❧

I was too fucking nervous to even eat dinner. I sat in front of the plate of pot roast, mashed potatoes, corn on the cob, and salad, unable to even touch it. I couldn't think straight until I got to Walgreens and took a pregnancy test. Suddenly, my nausea was worse. But I knew that it was just my nerves since I had thrown up everything in me. My insides were curdling with fear as my promise to God rang over and over again in my head.

"When are you going to have the baby shower, Zina?" my father asked.

Uggh. Suddenly, any talk of Zina's baby irritated me. I had had a lot of nerve judging her for being pregnant by Treyvon when I didn't even fucking know who I was possibly knocked up by.

"In a few weeks," Zina smiled.

Dad reached over and grabbed Zina's hand. "Are you sure you don't want to involve the father, sweetheart?"

My eyes quickly darted over to Treyvon, who hadn't missed a beat, shoving pot roast into his mouth. The nigga hadn't even flinched.

"I'm sure, Daddy," Zina whined.

Zadah chuckled cynically, taunting Zina with a shake of her head.

"You got something to say?" Zina challenged her.

I groaned, immediately annoyed with Zina and Zadah's bullshit.

"Please don't start, y'all," Dad groaned. "Not today. Give us a break."

"Thank you," I sighed.

Zadah sneered at me, shaking her head with disgust. "Fuck both of y'all."

"Didn't Daddy ask you all to stop?!" I snapped. "Gawd damn, Zadah. You are so ignorant sometimes!"

Her brow heightened as her evil eyes zeroed in on me. "Tuh," she spat. "You're always sucking up to Daddy."

"Acting like I got some sense and respecting my father is not sucking up. You might want to try it sometime," I spewed.

Her eyes narrowed as they locked on me. "You're always acting so fucking high and mighty," Zadah kept on. "I wonder would you have your nose so high in the air if you knew that Zoey is the woman that took your husband."

A RICH MAN'S WIFE 2

The Finale

JESSICA N. WATKINS

Jessica Watkins Presents

CHAPTER 1
ZURI TURNER

I immediately bellowed with laughter as Zadah sat back. She was smiling with this smug satisfaction that instantly made a rage grow inside me that wanted to dog walk her ignorant ass. Her arms were folded tightly across her chest as if she had shot the club up with that lie.

The entire table went mute. Even Zoey sat completely still with her eyes as wide as golf balls. She was mortified at that accusation.

I scoffed, shaking my head with pure shame for Zadah. "Are you that fucking ignorant that you will lie on your *niece* just to hurt my feelings?"

Zadah spewed, smacking her hand on the table. "They are fucking! We saw them coming out of the Drake hotel downtown a few weeks ago. Didn't we, Treyvon?"

Treyvon's head slightly lowered. Yet, his eyes peered up at me with so much regret.

"*Didn't we, Treyvon?*" Zadah spit.

"Stop being messy, Zadah," Zina seethed. "You have a fucking problem."

The longer the regret covered Treyvon's face, the harder my heart would pound out of my chest.

Zadah nudged Treyvon on his side. He cringed and then nodded his head quickly.

Inhaling sharply, my head whipped towards Zoey, who was sitting next to me. When she couldn't look me in the eyes - when she looked as sick as I felt - I gasped, clutching invisible pearls.

"Zoey?" I whispered anxiously.

As soon as I said her name, she burst into tears. My heart crumbled into tiny pieces as she jumped to her feet. Her chair scraped across the floor and slammed into the wall behind us.

She took off running through the dining room.

"Zoey!" I screamed as I flew to my feet as well.

I took off after her with the sound of silverware dropping into plates and chairs scraping the floor behind me. I could hear Zadah and Zina's bickering voices grow louder the further I ran through the house chasing Zoey.

"Zoey!" I was now crying as I shouted her name. I was inches away from her as she fled for the front door.

Finally, I was close enough for my fingertips to touch her. I reached forward, clawing at the neckline of her dress. Snatching her back, I caused her to stumble. Yet, my tight grip on her dress kept her standing.

"Zoey, talk to me," my voice quivered.

Now that I was finally standing still, I could feel the presence of others behind me. But I didn't look back. I stared at Zoey as her body shivered in my grip. My eyes squeezed together tightly with regret because I could feel her guilt.

"Zoey," I called softly.

"Let me go, Mama!" she spat, trying to get out of my grasp.

We began to wrestle with one another. She only turned around as she tried to loosen my grip on her dress. But I wouldn't let go.

Holding on even tighter, I insisted, "Talk to me!"

"Let me go, Mama!"

"Zuri..." I could hear my father softly in my ear. He was behind me, his hand supportively settled on my shoulder.

Zoey wouldn't look at me. Yet, she looked behind me, I assumed, at everyone else. Guilt and shame painted her sorrowful face as she tugged on my wrist harder.

"She don't have to answer," I heard Zadah quip. "I took a picture if you wanna see it."

"Shut the fuck up, Zadah!" Zina snapped, sympathy laced in her tone.

"Yeah, fuck you, Zadah!" Zoey spit.

I gasped aloud, stunned at the disrespect she was showing.

"Zoey!" I warned.

"Ghetto ass," Zoey continued spewing at Zadah. "I don't have to explain shit to you. Mind your own fucked up business! You're a hater! Always have been! You just mad because, even with your fiancé, you *still* feel so fucking subpar to Zina and my mama. You'll never fucking have their confidence because you had to *buy* yours and you *still* ain't got shit on them—"

The back of my hand swiftly went up and connected with her cheek before she could say anything else. Her head whipped to the side, and her hand instantly cupped her cheek. The entire room fell eerily silent. Zoey peered back at me with disbelief flooding her tearful eyes.

"Move, Treyvon!" I heard Zadah growl, hurt laced in her words. "I'm beatin' her ass."

"Let Zoey loose," my father insisted softly in my ear. "Just let her loose."

Hearing the disgust in his voice, I obeyed him. No sooner than I let Zoey go, she sprinted out of the front door.

"Zoey!" Zina called as she sprinted past me, chasing Zoey.

Finally, sobs accompanied my tears. I threw my face into my hands, feeling my heart bend and break in ways that I had never imagined it could.

I could feel my father attempting to hug me, but I fought my way out of his embrace.

"No," I cried as I turned away from him.

As I ran into the bathroom, I could see my nieces and nephews discreetly peering into the living room from the dining area. I could hear my father's scolding tone as I rushed inside of the bathroom and slammed the door. I then dropped to my knees as I began to gag and heave. I was so sick to my stomach.

I crawled over to the toilet and put my face in it, dry heaving. There was nothing to come up since my stomach was empty. My sobs echoed inside of the porcelain well. I had thought that there was no woman that Rashaad could have cheated with that would hurt me. I had been through this with him so many times that I no longer feared the other woman. But now, his words echoed in my mind, causing me to reel with literal sickness.

I'm in love with someone else.

The pain was unbearable. It was crippling.

"Zuri?" My father's caring tone accompanied a soft knock on the bathroom door.

He didn't wait for my permission to come in. The door opened slowly. I couldn't face him. I didn't want to face anyone, especially him. Seeing his face would confirm that my daughter had indeed done this to me.

"Zuri, get up, baby. Let me talk to you."

I allowed him to assist me to my feet. Once I was standing, I pulled away from him.

"Daddy, I just want to go home."

"Stay here. I made Zadah leave—"

"I can't be here, Daddy," I cried.

Finally, I looked him in the eye. He recoiled, seeing the hurt in my eyes.

4

Pressing his lips together tightly, he nodded sharply. "Okay."

Lowering my head, I pushed past him. I moped into the living room, thankful that no one was inside. I snatched my purse off of the couch. I was barely able to make it to the front door. My heart was too heavy for my feet to move.

Once at the door, it came swinging open. I dodged it as Zina appeared. As soon as her eyes fell on mine, she reached out for me.

"I'm so sorry, sissy."

"Not now, Zina," I muttered lightly, pushing her away. "Not now."

Surrendering, she stepped aside and let me leave.

AANAN "LAW" WOODS

"My nigga free!" Reese bellowed so loud that his voice ricocheted off of the trees.

I was sitting on Ma's patio smoking a blunt and sipping on some brown. We had finally made it there from the courthouse. I was still wearing the button-up and slacks that I had worn to trial.

I looked up at the sky, absorbing the outside. In the County, our rec time was in doors. I had only seen the sun through dirty, small windows. I had never imagined that I could miss the feeling of the sun and fresh air on my skin until I had been deprived of it. Now, I was able to bask in it.

Since I was released, I had been grinning so hard that my cheeks hurt.

I couldn't believe it. I had won my case. I kept replaying the judge's words in my mind: *The defendant is free to go.*

I was so shocked that I looked at Sam in disbelief. Yet, when I heard Ma's relieved tears, I knew that I had heard correctly. Then Sam smiled and put his arm around me as the judge continued to speak, validating that I was indeed free.

"Yeah, y'all, this a free man!" I looked toward Reese to see who he was talking to. He was putting his phone in my face. Looking at the screen, I could see that he was on Facebook Live. Comments were coming in too fast for me to read them.

"What up?" I said coolly before looking away. I had social media, but I wasn't the type of nigga to be on it.

Just then, the patio door opened. Whit slipped out of it. The aroma of fried fish and greens escaped from the kitchen. Ma was in there throwing down so that we could all have a welcome home dinner.

Looking up at Whit felt so fucking forced. Every time our eyes had met since I was released, her smile seemed fake. Her happiness wasn't genuine. But I couldn't front like we had been on the best of terms before I'd gotten locked up. She had stopped having the willingness and strength to front her happiness a long time ago. I guessed that my not guilty verdict wouldn't change that.

"Where my kids at?" I asked her. I was excited for them to see that their father was finally home.

She looked at the time on her phone. "I'm about to go get them from school and daycare now."

"Bet." I couldn't wait to see the smiles on my kids' faces. There were so many other things that I was anxious to do too. Eating was on the top of that list. Showering alone was vital. Once I had started fucking Zuri, I had gotten so much pussy that I wasn't thirsty for it. And Zuri's presence and pussy were so top tier that my pallet was bougie as fuck for who I gave this dick to now.

"Gawd damn," I groaned with aggravation as I looked at my phone.

It was ringing for the hundredth time. I had had Reese keep my phone on while I was locked up. No sooner than he'd given it to me, and I turned it on, that bitch started ringing and had never stopped.

Ox chuckled as he handed me the blunt. "That's another one?"

Ox had been my most trusted customer before I got locked up. We had done business together for so long that he had become one of two niggas I truly fucked with. The other was Reese. I had always peeped and admired Ox's loyalty and maturity in the game. I also liked how his wife was his right hand. Megan wasn't just the wife of a dope boy who stayed at home all day shopping online and stunting on the 'Gram. Megan was a true hustler who didn't give a fuck about getting her hands dirty. So, when I got locked up, Ox had adopted my entire crew. I trusted only him with them and convinced my distro to do the same. He was the only one I trusted to run my organization the way I had. The hustlers in my network were spoiled with my product and prices, so they were happy to work with someone that I had appointed and didn't give him any smoke. I didn't want his name coming up in the case in any way and had to disconnect myself totally from my dealings in the game, so I hadn't been hitting his line from the County.

As soon as he heard that a nigga was free, though, he came to Ma's crib to celebrate and chop it up, of course.

"Hell yeah. I should beat Reese's ass for putting that on Facebook, man," I said as I handed Reese the blunt.

Ma and I had been too excited to tell anyone that I was free. It was Reese's Facebook post that announced my verdict that had the homies and hoes blowing my phone up. The call I was ignoring at the moment was yet another bitch I had been fucking with before I was locked up. So many of my old hoes had been calling to get their bid in for this good dick that was fresh out.

"My bad, dawg," Reese laughed as he hit the blunt. "I was just excited. But the word was gon' get out anyway."

I was so tired of answering the phone that I had put it on silent. I had talked to everyone that I needed to. I was a popular loner before getting locked up. Besides Ox and Reese, I barely associated with a few hustlas that I distributed to. Everyone else I fucked with was from afar socially. Yet, now that word was out, many of the lil' homies had been stopping by Ma's house to say what up and give respect.

"*Reeese?!*" Hearing his wife call for him, Reese stood. He handed me back the blunt before disappearing into the house.

"Aye," Ox said as he scooted closer to me on the outdoor sofa. "I know you just got out, and you trying to relax. We can talk business later, but I want you to know that you can have all this shit back. We can get right back how we were, my nigga."

"You tired of running shit already?" I smirked, taunting him.

"Hell nah." He grinned as I handed him the blunt. "That money looking real good, my nigga. But you my dawg. It's only right. Whenever you ready to get back in the front seat, I'll be cool with falling back."

As he hit the blunt, I shrugged. "I don't know, man. It felt good getting a break from the hustling and gangbanging shit while I was locked up. I might just chill. I got enough investments to keep my bread up."

Blowing smoke from his mouth, he nodded. "Just let me know."

ZOEY TURNER

"Have a good day."

I clicked my tongue as I opened the door. "Do I look like I'm having a fucking good day?"

I hopped out before the Uber driver could respond. I then slammed the door shut. Since the windows were down, I could hear the female driver muttering what I assumed to be some bullshit in response to my ignorance as she backed out of the driveway.

Thankfully, only my Benz was in the driveway, so my mother hadn't made it home yet. So, I ran up to the front door and put my key in the lock. My hands were still shaking. I was so pissed.

I wasn't ashamed of what I had done. My mother and Rashaad's relationship had been over for years. I hadn't ruined it. I hadn't been "the other woman". I was simply checking a bag. But I did hate that I had hurt my mother. The sorrow in her eyes had been unbearable to watch. That's why I had left my grandfather's house. I had never intended for her to find out. Now that she had, I couldn't face her.

Once inside the house, I ran through the foyer, up the stairs, and into my room. I then hurried into my closet. Dropping to my knees, I first double-tapped my AirPod.

"Hey, Siri, call Rashaad."

I hadn't spoken to him since he'd beat my ass. Though he had been blowing my phone back, I hadn't had anything to say to him. He was a narcissistic, obsessed asshole, and he was lucky that keeping us a secret had been more important than calling the police on his bitch ass.

"Hello?" I was disgusted when Rashaad answered eagerly, like he was waiting for my call like a fucking idiot.

"I need some money," I blurted.

My abruptness caught him off guard and made him stutter. "H-hello?"

"I said I need some money!" I snapped. "I have to get the fuck out of the house. I need a hotel."

Alerted, his voice heightened. "What's wrong?"

"Mama knows," I rushed, voice still trembling.

He fell completely silent.

"Zadah saw us leaving the Drake that night. She took a fucking picture of us—"

"Fuck!" he barked.

"She told Mama in front of everybody at dinner at Grandpa's house today—"

"Shit!"

"I need some money, Rashaad. I can't stay here. I need a hotel."

"I ... I can't help you, Zoey."

"What the fuck do you mean?!"

"My accounts. They're locked. I can't access them."

"You don't have money *anywhere*?"

"I can't get to it right now. But you can come stay with me—"

Disgusted, I hung up on his ass.

"*Uggh*! Fuck!" I spat as I threw everything that I could in two MCM duffle bags.

Luckily, I had been stacking my bread for after graduation. So, I had my own money to get a hotel. I just couldn't and didn't want to spend my own money.

Once my duffle bags were packed, I hurried to my bed where I had thrown my purse and phone. I scooped them both up. I bolted out of my room, down the hall, and flew down the stairs. I prayed that my mother wasn't pulling up when I opened the door. I was ready to avoid her by any means necessary. Luckily, once outside, I didn't see my mother's truck. My eyes darted down the block. I sighed with relief when I didn't see it coming down the one-way street either.

As I stood there, I wondered for a second if I was doing the right thing. I knew that leaving like this, without facing my mother, without trying to explain, was only making matters worse.

But...

"Fuck this shit. He's left her, so the money has left the building. I'm outta here."

I sprinted towards my Benz, lugging my bags along with me. If Rashaad was broke, my mom would be too very soon. There was no need to lie my way into staying in a home that she wasn't about to be able to keep anyway.

Popping the locks, I jumped inside.

I was panicking, realizing that I was now on my own.

I floored it out of the driveway. I couldn't stay in my mother's house anymore. I was sure that I wasn't even invited to. There was no way that I could even fix my mouth to ask my mother for a dime, nor did I think she would ever even offer. I had to make it on my own with what I had, which wouldn't last long with my expensive taste.

Staring with wide, worried eyes out of the windshield, I wondered what the fuck I was going to do now that I was all on my own.

CHAPTER 2

ZURI TURNER

As I entered my home, I knew that Zoey wasn't there since her car was gone.

Walking into the foyer, I felt so empty. My daughter had slept with my husband. And I was now the most alone I had ever been in my life.

Since I was fourteen, Zoey had been my company, my closest friend. She would hug me when I was sad and smile with me when I was happy. For eighteen years, she had been my sidekick. Now, she was the woman that had stolen my husband.

That constant thought had me so numb that I was no longer crying. I felt like I was living someone else's reality. I was disoriented, now emotionless to the fact that the baby she had lost when she was attacked had most likely been my husband's, my grand *and* my stepchild. Climbing the stairs was a struggle. Each time caused a wave of nausea. I was unsure whether I was indeed pregnant or if Zoey and Rashaad were the cause of my constant affliction.

Once inside my bedroom, I padded into the master bathroom. I threw my purse on the sink and dug through it for the Walgreens bag. I fished out the pregnancy tests I had bought and opened all three.

Ten minutes later, I was sitting on the ledge of the Jacuzzi tub, staring blankly into space as I awaited the results and for the three-minute timer to go off on my phone. As I sat, I tried to feel some-thing...*anything*. But there was nothing. I was experiencing something much more than loss. It felt like I was mourning the death of the two closest people to me. They felt dead to me.

My eyes squeezed together tightly as the piercing noise shot through the air, indicating that three minutes were up.

My heart started to beat feverishly.

I stopped breathing.

It took all of the strength I had left to pry my eyes open and peek at the test results.

Positive.

Positive.

Positive.

Shit.

This was the last thing that I needed, but I actually appreciated it because it gave me a more hellish nightmare to focus on. Zoey and Rashaad's deceit was no longer as overwhelming as the constant reminder that I had promised God that I would never kill another baby.

Thankfully, God was a forgiving God. He would have to show me some grace because there was no way that I could have this baby.

I winced as a text message notification sounded off. I didn't want to talk to anyone, not even via text. I peered at the phone, seeing from the preview notification that it was a photo from Zadah.

"That bitch," I hissed.

Gnawing on my bottom lip, I shook my head. I fought the urge to look at the message. I knew what it was that she had sent me. I looked up at the ceiling, praying for the strength to ignore it, but I had none.

I grabbed the phone, unlocked it, and saw the image of the Drake Hotel and Rashaad and Zoey waiting on the curb, hand-in-hand.

AANAN "LAW" WOODS

After a few hours of celebrating with the fam and eating a good meal, I had insisted that Ma go to the hospital and sit with Jeezy. I knew that though she was happy that I was home, she wanted to be with him.

I had no plans of going to see him. He had never been a fan of mine, so it would have been phony as fuck for me to go up there, slow singing and flower bringing as if he was a beloved brother of mine.

So, I took my kids home.

I was finally home.

In *my shit*, versus some small ass, dirty, concrete cell. For a year, I imagined being back in the home that I had made comfortable for them, giving them the security and love they'd needed and deserved. Finally, I was back, and that shit felt good as fuck.

"Good night, Daddy."

I smiled at Serenity as I bent down and kissed her cheek. "Night, Serenity."

"Can we go to the store tomorrow for toys?" she asked.

"What you wanna go shopping for, lil' girl?" I smiled.

"I want more Barbies, an American Girl doll, and a Barbie Dream House," she rambled, barely able to pronounce most of those words.

"I want a new iPhone, Daddy," Willow cut in from the top bunk.

"I got y'all. We'll go shopping soon."

Serenity grinned so hard that her tanned skin turned red. "Yes!"

I shook my head at how spoiled she was at only three years old. I then bent down and kissed her cheek. "Goodnight, Stink."

"Goodnight," Serenity yawned.

"Night, Willow," I said, standing and kissing her cheek as well.

"Goodnight, Daddy."

I was fighting my own emotions as I left their room. It felt like a lifetime that I had been away from my kids.

I had already told August goodnight. So, I made my way towards my bedroom, turning off lights in our three-story brick home along the way. I looked around my crib, taking everything in. This had been the first property I had ever purchased. I was so proud of being a dropout of the hood who bought a three-flat in the heart of Hyde Park. I had completely renovated it and turned it into one six-thousand-square-foot house. The first floor was an open concept with huge living, dining, and kitchen spaces. I had converted the den into a bar area that resembled a club. The second floor was where the bedrooms were. Each bedroom was a master suite. The basement was equipped with a full gym, sauna, and walk-in closets for Whit and I.

As I entered my bedroom, the surreal and genuine happiness ended. I walked past Whit as she lounged across the bed, scrolling through her phone, and entered the master bathroom. We barely shared eye contact. I felt like I was locked up again, imprisoned in a space that I didn't want to be in. But that was how shit had been between me and Whit before I was arrested, and I hadn't expected that it would change once that judge said, "not guilty."

Only now, there was another woman that had my undivided attention. My thoughts were consumed with Zuri to the point that I was underwhelmed with the sight of Whit sprawled across the bed in little to nothing.

Whit wasn't doing anything to make me think of her. Her efforts were nonexistent. Her mind was somewhere else. So many bitches were hitting my line wanting to show a nigga a good time for being at the crib when she hadn't even batted an eye at me. Yet, I was cool with that. This was where we were, where we had been for a minute. She was a real nigga enough not to front like it was anything more than what it had been.

I stepped into the large and luxurious walk-in shower, relieved that there weren't twenty other niggas around me. I appreciated the quiet. I stepped under the rain shower head in disbelief of how clean and hot the water was.

It was as if I had never taken a shower outside of prison in my life.

The relief that I felt since being released was indescribable and unimaginable. The number of times that I thought of Zuri was the same. Along with plans for getting back to life, excitement to be with my kids and giving my mother a little relief, I couldn't wait to fight my way back into Zuri's life.

Thinking of her had my dick rock hard as I showered, dried off, and slipped on a pair of basketball shorts. It was so quiet that it felt eerie. There had never been a moment of silence in jail, not even at night. That was why I didn't want to spend my first night of freedom in a club, turning up. The tranquility that the quiet was giving me was the turn up that I needed.

Walking out of the bathroom, Whit and I caught eyes. She was still lying across the bed, scrolling through her phone. She finally put her phone down, watching me curiously as I left the room.

Any other nigga would be trying to get some pussy right now, but I didn't want any pity pussy from a bitch that wasn't even feeling me. And since Zuri had been blessing a nigga with superb pussy for quite a while, I wasn't so hard up that I had to settle for anything.

Once in the den, I walked over to the bar, grabbing the remote control from the coffee table along the way. As I poured a shot of Clase Azul, Whit caught my attention. She walked slowly into the den, wearing the same curious expression on her face. I admired the curves that she had been maintaining every few years in Miami. Her body was perfect. Her 36 triple d's sat up flawlessly. Giving birth to three kids and a few rounds of fat transfers had perfectly spread that ass and hips. Her cheeks ate up the booty shorts that she was wearing. Her nipples were so hard that their impression was lifelike in the bandeau top.

All of that sexiness... and I felt absolutely nothing.

She stepped so close into my space that her breasts pressed into my stomach.

I dryly chuckled. "What are you doing?"

"I'm about to take care of you," she said, grabbing at my shorts where my dick hung. "What you think I'm about to do?"

I wanted to feel something. This was the mother of my kids, the woman I had spent the last ten years with. But this shit was phony as hell. This was the closest we had been since I was released. We hadn't shared more than a halfhearted hug. Not even a kiss. Her mind had been somewhere else all day. We no longer loved one another, but I knew her like the back of my hand. Her head was elsewhere. Most likely, it was with the nigga that had been fucking her while I was gone. I wasn't sure that she had one or a few, but I wasn't naïve to think that there wasn't someone.

Rubbing my dick was out of obligation, not want, need, or love.

"Stop," I demanded, gently pushing her hand away. To put space between us, I walked away from the bar towards the plush couch that was calling my name.

Aggressively, she grabbed my elbow, stopping me. I turned around and met her lips as she stood on her tiptoes, trying to kiss me.

I turned my face away. "Whit, stop."

She blinked slowly, staring up at me. "Huh?"

"*Stop.*"

"What the fuck?" she asked. "Why?"

"You're just doing this because you feel like you're supposed to, not because you want to." I turned my back to her, making my way to the couch. "I've been around imprisoned people for a year, motherfuckers doing shit because they're supposed to, wishing they could be doing something else. I'm free now. I don't wanna be around that shit no more."

Plopping down on the couch, I could feel her eyes on me. Ten years of taking care of her should have awarded me her respect, at least, of not fronting like what I had said hadn't been the truth.

"I just figured you needed it," she said softly, standing in the middle of the floor.

Her words were filled with so much defeat. There she was, half-naked in front of a nigga that had been locked up for a year, and she was being rejected. Yet, even if I hadn't ever had Zuri, I would have rather hit one of the bitches that was blowing back my phone, not Whit. She felt obligated, but I no longer did. My dick was harder than masturbation for a nigga with no arms, but I wanted my bitch, and that wasn't Whit.

ZURI TURNER

"You've reached the voicemail of Rashaad Turner..."

"Bitch ass nigga," I seethed.

After half a bottle of whiskey, I was now drunk-dialing Rashaad. Yet, he hadn't answered any of my twenty-three calls.

As soon as I heard the beep, I went the fuck in. "You nasty, creepy, bitch-ass nigga! I suggest you find a considerable lump sum to give me with the divorce before I ruin your *precious* reputation! Don't play with me!"

I stabbed the end call button and threw my phone on the bed. There was no amount of money that could take away the pain of what he had done. However, wiping my tears with countless one-hundred-dollar bills was better than nothing.

I didn't have the energy to call Zoey. I didn't know what to say. There were so many questions that I had. I wondered how long their affair had been going on and at what age had it started. My nausea resurfaced when I thought of the possibility of that motherfucker fucking my child at whatever age. I hoped that Rashaad had taken advantage of her rather than my own daughter willingly doing this to me. However, her response earlier that day and her silence told me that she had been a willing participant in breaking my heart like this.

I wanted to go to the police, but since the photo had been taken on her eighteenth birthday and she wasn't willing to admit verbally that they had been fucking, there was nothing that I could legally do.

Just then, the doorbell rang. I was expecting Dom, but I went to the Ring app to look at the camera to ensure that it was him.

Seeing his fine ass gave me the only relief I had felt since the Feds had shown up at my house that morning.

As I made my way through the second floor and down the stairs, I perfected my curls with my fingers. I licked my lips to ensure the hours of throwing up and crying hadn't dried them out. I then smoothed out the mini, fitted tank dress that I had slipped on.

I had attempted to spruce myself up, since I had been crying my eyes out for hours. However, I had been so drunk that I was barely able to hide the bags under my eyes with concealer. I had done the best that I could after showering and slipping into something more enticing than the large t-shirt I had been moping in since coming home.

As I opened the door, I could feel how tipsy I was. I still hadn't drunk enough to forget what had happened, though.

Dom gave me a smile of sympathy as he walked into my house. I shied away from his gaze as I closed and locked the door. Once I faced him, his sympathy deepened.

"Come here," he demanded softly as he took me into his arms.

When he had Facetimed me an hour ago, I tried to look and act normal. He sensed that something was wrong, though. I tried to tell him that I simply got into an argument with Zadah at my father's house, but he insisted that it was deeper. I didn't have the strength to lie, so I told him that I didn't want to talk about it. Yet, he insisted that he was coming over to keep me company. I was down with that since I wasn't feeling being *so* alone so suddenly.

"You want a drink?" I asked as I looked up into his piercing dark eyes.

"What you got?"

"Macallan."

His eyes bulged, and he stepped back. I giggled at his shock as his arms released me slowly.

"The forty-year-old single malt?"

"Yep."

His brows rose. "That's a forty-thousand-dollar bottle of whiskey."

I shrugged, saying, "I know. It's my ex-husband's."

After taking the pregnancy tests, I decided to drown myself in liquor and a little weed. I had gone through Rashaad's stash and stumbled upon a few of his prized possessions of expensive liquors. Considering the level of his deceit, not even killing his most expensive bottle of liquor was enough to feel as if I had gotten revenge, but it was a start.

৩%৩

"I know you don't want to talk about it, but..." Dom was reluctant as my eyes narrowed at him. "Does what happened have anything to do with who was at the door earlier today when we were on Facetime?"

I was too drunk to lie, so I just nodded.

Then Dom nodded slowly and placed a comforting hand on my thigh.

We were in the den. *Really Love* was playing on the projector screen that lined the wall. Dom and I had long stopped watching the courtship of Kofi Siriboe and Yootha Wong-Loi-Sing's characters. As always, we were engulfed in one another as we conversed about any and everything. I was sitting Indian-style on the couch, completely facing him. Most of the time, he had been telling me funny stories about his childhood, and I would just listen, allowing his embarrassing memories to take my mind off of the bullshit.

"You're gonna be okay," he insisted, softly squeezing my thigh.

Those caring words were paired with such gentle persuasion that my insides melted.

"How do you know?" I seriously wanted to know. He had said it with so much confidence that it sounded true. Yet, sitting there, I couldn't fathom that any of this would feel okay anytime soon. I couldn't imagine that my heart would ever stop hurting from this betrayal.

"My mama always says, 'trouble don't last always'," Dom told me.

I smiled as he spoke of his mom. "Your mom must have loved that song."

He nodded. "She did."

"Well, I hope it's true."

"It is," he said with assurance. "And if it's not, I'll make sure it is."

My eyes brightened. "Really?"

"Fuck yeah."

That thug shit and the whiskey drew me to him. I leaned over, slowly bringing our mouths closer to one another's. This was the third time that we had been face-to-face, and we had never kissed. So, I could see the curiosity dancing in those dark eyes as I closed the space between us.

Though I had been the dominant one -taking his lips with mine- as soon as my tongue entered his mouth, he took control. His hand gripped the back of my head. His fingers intertwined with my curls. He closed on them, causing a slight tug, which caused my clitoris to begin to throb.

I was thirsty, but not for dick. I was thirsty for something good in my reality, even if it was just sex.

So, I straddled him, causing my dress to rise above my plump cheeks, revealing that I was pantyless. Our kiss became breathy as the passion heightened. I ground against his bulge like a teenage girl. Feeling its abundant size, I whimpered into our kiss, begging for it to be inside of me.

CHAPTER 3
AANAN "LAW" WOODS

♫ I'm cooking up work on a Thursday (Skrrt-skrrt)
Preppin' my kitchen for a Friday (Friday)
Weekend gon' be rolling (Ftt)
Wraith just waiting on me to drive it (Skrrt) ♫

Yo' Gotti was blaring as I pulled away from the kids' school. The top to my Bentley Bacalar was dropped since it was already eighty degrees. I had always dropped the kids off every morning since Whit wasn't a morning person. Eventually, even if she was awake, I would take them to school because it had become our tradition. I would take them to McDonald's and then school every day. I had never missed a drop-off until I was arrested. They were so happy to hop in the car with me that morning.

As I headed towards the expressway, a call from DC interrupted me spitting the lyrics along with Yo' Gotti.

"What up, DC?" I answered.

"Nothing much, bro. Glad to hear that you're out."

"I'm glad to be out," I chuckled.

"Anything you need, let me know."

"I do need something from you. I was gonna call you once I got settled. I need that address again. I had to get rid of that shit on the inside."

"Why are you in constant need of the home address for the wife of the warden of the County?"

I deeply chuckled at the heightened concern in DC's voice as it came through the Bluetooth. "Don't worry about that."

DC was one of the homies from high school that had become a police officer. Once I was deep in the streets, I reconnected with him. As long as I lined his pockets, he would get information that I needed. He would also let me know anything he found out from Narcotics about possible raids and indictments.

"Don't get me in no shit, bro," he fussed.

"I got you. Trust me. It won't be no smoke."

"Ah ight," he said, though still hesitant. "I'll text you the address right now."

"Bet."

I hung up, sitting up eagerly. I put out the blunt that I had been smoking as the light turned green.

Seconds later, the car was notifying me that DC had sent a text message. It read off the address to me, and I headed in that direction.

I wondered if it was too early in the morning to show up at her crib. But I couldn't wait any longer to go get my baby.

Out of habit, I was up at five in the morning because chow had been that time every day in the County. The entire house was deafeningly still, but thoughts of Zuri were running a fucking relay race in my mind. I knew that calling her wouldn't be enough. She needed to see in my face how apologetic I was and the need that I had for her.

I was willing to do whatever it took to get her back. I had wondered if being out of jail would change my obsession with her, but it had only heightened it. This was our time. This was the moment that I had been waiting on, to show her the type of man that I was outside of the prison garb and walls that separated me from being able to truly pursue her like I was supposed to.

However, the connection between us was only meant to be inside of those cement walls. As I pulled up to the address ten minutes later, I slowed down, creeping up the street as I caught a glimpse of her. She was standing in the doorway smiling into the face of some nigga. Her hair was disheveled. Curls fell into her face. She was holding a short robe closed. My chest tightened when he held her around the waist, brought her against him, and kissed her. The joy on her face was familiar. I had put the same sheepish smile on her face many times.

I gripped the wheel tightly when I realized that the nigga wasn't even her husband. I had seen the warden a few times, and the nigga walking away wasn't him.

Suddenly, I felt like a simp. I had been waiting, holding my breath until the moment that I could see her again, thinking that it was something special between us. Yet, it looked as if she had something special with more than one motherfucker. The smile on her face had been one of satisfaction in getting dicked down all night. Jealousy took over my need to claim her. Clearly, she didn't feel as though she was mine. She had blocked all of my attempts to talk to her. I had sent her a letter that she hadn't responded to. In the letter, I had asked her to call Reese if she was willing to give me another chance so that he could connect us. Every day, I had asked Reese had he gotten that call. Now, I knew why he hadn't. She had clearly moved on to the next nigga.

I was far in her rearview. So, I made sure that she was in mine, speeding off.

WHITNEY PRICE

"Fuck, fuck, fuck, fuck, *fuck!*"

I had been forced to keep a straight face since the moment that Law was released. But finally, he was gone, so I could let all of this pent-up anxiety out.

"Shit!" My breathing was sporadic as I rocked back and forth in the bed. I wrung my hands anxiously. Tears teetered in my eyes.

I didn't know what to do.

Law was free.

I had never expected him to beat that charge. Though the evidence had been circumstantial, Detective Payne had always gone out of his way to ensure that Law paid for what he had done to his daughter. When Law's fingerprints were found on that murder weapon, I knew that Detective Payne had been behind that. And with Law's prints at the murder scene, I was sure that he would be gone for the next twenty-five years.

Now, at any moment, he was going to find out what I had done. Law was always about his bag and his business. He had spent his first day at home with his family. However, it would only be a matter of days or maybe hours before he'd be done getting acquainted with being home and get back to handling his business. Whenever he would find that I had taken those buildings and sold the properties, he *was* going to kill me. There was not an ounce of love for me in Law that would prevent him from doing so.

"Fuck!" My anxieties exploded, causing me to jump out of bed and pace the floor.

I was hyperventilating. Sweat dripped down my forehead. My chest was so tight that I feared I was going to die from a stroke.

Making matters worse, Jeezy was unable to help or protect me. I had to act as nonchalant about him being shot as Law had because I didn't want to get caught up. Yet, I was reeling with panic that he would lose his life. I couldn't even visit him because Law would wonder why since Jeezy had never had a relationship with Law, his kids, or me. And Gloria wouldn't leave Jeezy's bedside long enough to give me a chance to sneak in. I had paid a nurse to let me know if Gloria ever left, and she had yet to budge since Law had sent her back to the hospital.

I loved Jeezy. He got his money out the mud in some underhanded ways, but that nigga fucked with me and put me on. He had taught me ways to get my own by any means necessary. I wanted him in my life. That was difficult now that Law was free, but I was sure Jeezy and I could have figured that out. More than needing him to live to be with me, I needed him to live because when Law found out, I wasn't going to take the wrap alone.

"I have to do something," I muttered to myself.

I felt like I was going insane. My fears were absorbing me. I couldn't think straight. My every thought was how I was going to get out of this and avoid the wrath of ever deceiving and stealing from Law.

ZOEY TURNER

"*Uggh,*" I groaned, slamming my phone down on the table.

"That your aunt again?"

"Yes." My eyes rolled to the ceiling. Aunt Zina had been blowing my phone up since Zadah's snitching ass told on me. She was constantly sending me text messages asking how I was doing and begging me to call her. I assumed my mother had told her that I'd left the house. But I didn't want to talk to anyone in my family about this shit. I just wanted it to go away.

Since leaving my house, I had been at Dior's place. I would have preferred to be at a five-star hotel. Dior's parents had money, but they were hood. My household had been refined, but Dior's was ghetto as fuck. Her daddy was hood rich. His mind was still very much in the projects he had grown up in. So, their house, though nice and big, was in the middle of the hood. Niggas were in and out all day, smoking weed. Music was constantly blaring. It was a nonstop party that I appreciated the first night. But now, I was growing tired of it already. I didn't know what my living situation was going to be, so I needed to save all of the money that I could until I figured it out. Therefore, I had no choice but to stay until I did.

"Your mom call you yet?" Dior peered at me with a smirk as she smacked on the Italian Fiesta pizza that her father had ordered us.

I had only told her that me and my mom had had it out real bad, so I didn't want to be at home for a while. Her parents had no problem letting me stay since me and Dior had been close since we started high school.

I clicked my tongue. "She keeps calling, begging me to come home. She's lonely because Rashaad left. But she should've thought about that before she wanted to go back and forth about dumb shit."

Laughing, Dior continued to eat.

I swallowed relief since it seemed as if she had fallen for all of that bullshit. My mom hadn't called me once. Hadn't even sent a text message. We had never gone this long without speaking, so I knew that she was so pissed that she had nothing to say to me. That fucked my head up. Since Rashaad was claiming to be broke, I blocked him from contacting me. Fucking Rashaad was never supposed to get back to her because fucking him had been strictly about lining my pockets. It wasn't to deceive her or break her heart. I didn't want her husband in any way, so I definitely never wanted to be the woman that he left her for.

"Girl, I can't wait until August. I'm so ready to move on campus," Dior said. Her eyes danced with anticipation. Then, as our eyes met, she pouted. "I wish you were coming to New Orleans with me."

Dior had decided on attending Louisiana State University.

"College ain't for me," I frowned.

Laughing, Dior said, "I can't believe your mom actually fell for those bogus ass acceptance letters."

I laughed as well. "Hey, to her defense, Brit did a good ass job photoshopping those letters."

"Yeah, that bitch is *good*."

My mother and Rashaad had only given me what I'd wanted because I was doing so good in school. Yet, my grades had always been manipulated by Brit. She was a genius with that computer shit. My grades were decent, so there was no need for parent conferences that would have given me away. I wanted my grades to look superb, though, so that I could get anything I wanted.

I had no intentions of going to college. My goal was to be a social media influencer and live off of brand endorsements and ads. For the last year, I had been working on growing my following. That's why the high-end clothes, bags, and trips were crucial. But my mom and Rashaad would have never continued to fund all of that if they knew that I didn't plan on going to college. So, I had Brit falsify an abundance of acceptance and scholarship letters.

I wasn't a stranger to doing what I had to in order to get what I wanted. That obsession had gotten me into a fucked up situation currently, but the same obsession was going to get me right the fuck up out of it.

"Aye, yo', Zoey!" I heard Dior's dad, Mark, bellow.

"*Yeeees?!*"

Suddenly, he ran into the dining room, wide-eyed and seemingly panicked. "Your car is getting towed!"

"What the fuck?!" I jumped to my feet. I sprinted through their house and out onto the porch.

The block on 69th and Aberdeen was cracking. Everyone was outside, especially since it was a nice day. Right in front of the house, my Benz was getting loaded onto a tow truck. I looked to ensure that I hadn't been parked illegally. I knew I didn't have any parking tickets, so I hurried down the steps toward the driver.

"What the fuck are you doing?" I spit.

He chuckled with a sarcastic smirk. "Towing this motherfucking car, what you think?"

"I can see that!"

Still laughing, he quipped, "Then why you ask me?"

"That's my fucking car! I'm not parked illegally!"

"Well, the paperwork says that it *isn't* your car and that the owner reported it stolen. So, you need to get the fuck back and let me do my job, lil' girl."

Grimacing, I turned away. I wasn't about to embarrass myself further by causing a scene.

"Zoey, what's going on?" Dior rushed as she met me on the curb.

I sucked my teeth and started towards the house with her on my heels. "Girl, he said my shit is getting repossessed because the note hasn't been paid."

"Huh? What the hell?" she responded, shocked.

"I know, right? I guess my mama falling off already since Rashaad left."

CHAPTER 4
RASHAAD TURNER

"Good morning, Mr. Turner."

"Good morning, Michelle," I rushed as I stalked by her desk.

Michelle jumped up and scurried behind me, rambling before I could even get inside my office.

"The mayor called—"

"She's always calling," I groaned, unlocking my office door.

"True," she giggled. "But she's called four times this morning, sir."

Entering my office, I told her, "I'll call her as soon as I get settled. Anything else?"

"The budget reports are on your desk. I have a draft for the press release regarding the new housing facility that is being built."

"Great, Michelle. Anything else?" I looked up at her impatiently, waiting for her to give me some privacy.

"That's it."

"Thanks. Please close the door behind yourself."

She nodded quickly and then hurried out of the office. Once the door was closed, I exhaled and dropped my forehead to my desk.

My world was crumbling around me.

The front company that I had created had been visited by Federal Agents Friday. They had questioned the manager about the company's contracts with the jail. Though he was able to give them the desired answers they needed, I had been on edge ever since their visit. I had used that and many other companies to funnel nearly half a million dollars from the prison's budget. I knew that I was being investigated months ago when the IRS froze my accounts and audited me. Though I had kept a tight paper trail, the authorities had apparently been relentless because a former disgruntled administrative employee had whistle blown to the Feds about the mismanagement of funds anonymously. All of my accounts were frozen. I had been able to survive with the funds from the front companies that I had created that had yet to be discovered by the Feds. But I knew that it was only a matter of time that those companies were discovered as well.

Over the years, I had become addicted to getting women to follow suit because of the money that I'd spent on them. But I had gone broke keeping up with the many women that I had been juggling over the years.

Zoey had never been like a daughter to me. I cared for her, but I took care of her out of responsibility. I knew that her well-being was important to Zuri. So, to secure her position in my life, I had to be a father figure for Zoey.

The night that I kissed her, I locked myself in the den and got drunk because the pressure of hiding the embezzlements was getting to me. When she had stuck her pretty face in, I saw a beautiful woman. She had grown into a woman of modelesque beauty with persuasive feminine wiles that drew me in. I kissed her because of the intoxication but soon didn't regret it when she didn't pull away.

Zuri and I had been over for years. I knew that she was only staying with me because her main priority was providing a better childhood for Zoey than her parents had provided for her. Zuri and I were more like roommates than husband and wife. Once Zoey and I started our affair, I had the luxury of living with the woman that I was oblig-ated to *and* the woman that I was falling for.

But I had been played. I felt no remorse that Zuri and her family now knew of our affair. After the shock had worn off, I was relieved that everyone knew so that we wouldn't have to hide. But Zoey wanted nothing to do with me. The money was gone, so she was too.

I groaned as a knock sounded on my office door. I lifted my head, feeling the most defeated I had felt in a long time. This wasn't who I was. I always got what I wanted. Money and women came to me because I took it. Now, they were being taken away from me.

"Mr. Turner?"

I groaned at Michelle's persistence. "I'm kind of busy, Michelle."

"Mr. Turner—"

"Not now, Michelle!" I blurted.

When the doorknob turned, I started to bellow insults in response to her defying me. But I soon heard, "It's going to have to be right now, Mr. Turner," from a male voice that I didn't recognize.

Alarmed, I stood up, wide-eyed, and was met with four men in dark suits entering my office. Michelle was behind them with wide eyes.

"Rashaad Turner, you're under arrest. You have the right to an attorney—"

My heart started to beat out of my chest. I stepped back, glaring at them as one of them rounded my desk. "What the fuck are you talking about?"

"Anything you say can and will be used against you in a court of law," he calmly continued. "You have a right to an attorney. If you cannot afford an attorney, one will be appointed for you." He then grabbed my elbow.

"What the hell is going on?!" I snapped, snatching away. My eyes darted at Michelle, who was standing in the doorway, confusion on her face. "Michelle, get my attorney on the phone. Now!"

She jumped out of her skin, nodded quickly, and scurried away.

The agent behind my desk insisted, "Put your hand behind your back, Mr. Turner."

"I'm not doing shit!" I barked.

"Mr. Turner, let's not make this difficult," one of the agents urged as he put his hand on his gun.

"This is my job," I insisted. "You're going to do this here?"

One of the other agents smirked. "Isn't this where you committed your crimes?"

Chest heaving, my narrowed eyes bore into his.

"Put your hands behind your back," the agent next to me urged.

Grimacing, I stood down. Lowering my head, I put my hands behind my back and turned them towards the agent.

This was it. This was happening. The end of my life and career was beginning. The reign over my own destiny was being snatched from me. I wanted to blame Zuri for being so bullheaded that my presence in her life wasn't enough to make her shut the fuck up about the other women. I wanted to blame Zoey for being so fucking beautiful that I wanted to spoil her with anything in the world as long as she let me inside of her. Yet, as I was being led out of my office, I was man enough to realize that my greed had brought me here. I hadn't only been taking money to splurge on Zoey and Zuri. Every bitch that I put my hands on had experienced the life of luxury that was financed by my crimes. My ego had been the ultimate beneficiary, though.

As I was led out of the admin suite, I was met with a slew of gasps and murmurs. I lowered my head, hiding from the questioning, shocked, and even amused eyes of the personnel and correctional officers that we passed as they led me out of the building.

Amongst the whispers, my ego swelled.

I refused to go down like this.

ZURI TURNER

Zina gasped so dramatically that it made my eyes roll.

"So, you aren't going to your own daughter's graduation?!" she snapped on the other end of the phone.

"No," I groaned with the covers over my head. I had *the worst* hangover migraine.

"Are you serious, Zuri?!"

I winced, her constant nagging making my stabbing headache even worse. "Don't I sound serious?"

"You don't even know if what Zadah said was true."

I scoffed. "You can't be that naive."

"That picture could have meant anything. Daddy holds my hand all of the time."

I had sent Zina the picture last night since she had been texting me with this same save-a-hoe bullshit in defense of Zoey.

"Zina, stop," I urged with a groan. "She lied to me that night, saying that she was in Houston, and he was supposed to be at Mastro's. Why would they both lie to me unless they were fucking?"

"But it's your daughter's graduation," she insisted.

"And I don't give a fuck."

Zina blew a heavy, defeated breath. "This is all so crazy."

"Don't I know it," I said, clicking my tongue.

"Maybe he took advantage of her."

"She didn't look in distress in that picture."

"He could have been doing this to her for years, maybe even since she was little. She could be a victim of sexual abuse."

I laughed dryly. "Something is telling me that she isn't."

"You aren't going to ask her?"

"I don't have anything to say to her. If she were younger, this would be different. But that girl is smart, and she is eighteen years old."

"There are so many sexual abuse victims where the abuse continues for years after they are adults."

"True. But Zoey isn't a victim."

"You don't know—"

I threw the covers from over my head, shouting, "I know, Zina!! I fucking know! When the lil' bitch left my house, she said, 'Fuck this shit. He's left her, so the money has left the building. I'm outta here'! I heard it on the fucking Ring camera!" Even repeating it brought tears to my eyes.

Inhaling sharply, Zina asked, "She said that?"

When I woke up this morning, I prayed that the day before had never happened, that it was just a nightmare that I had to wake from. Especially when I had woken up in Dom's arms with him kissing my forehead. The night with him had been heaven and much needed. The dick was so good that no matter how drunk I was, I remembered every stroke and every lick. He was masterful at eating pussy. And he tastes like good energy and obsession.

Once he left, the butterflies flew away, and my hellish reality set in. Even though she had broken my heart, walking around my big house alone made me miss Zoey. I wondered how long she was going to hide from me. That's when it dawned on me that she probably had run away. So, I checked the Ring app and saw her leaving with her bags and had heard what she'd said as she was bolting away instead of facing me like the grown woman she *thought* she was.

I was so enraged. That's why I had an associate of me and Rashaad's who had a tow truck go get her car since *I* was paying the note.

"Yes," I answered Zina, hating to admit it. "So, no, Zina, she was not taken advantage of or abused. If anything, she probably took advantage of Rashaad."

My other line rang, so I pulled the phone away from my ear and saw that Bianca was calling. I appreciated the chance to end this call with Zina to stop talking and thinking about this bullshit for just a few minutes.

"Let me call you back, Zina."

"Okay," she said sadly.

Even amongst my own heartache, my heart went out to Zina as I clicked over. No matter the constant drama between me and my sisters, we loved each other and our family in our own crazy and chaotic way. I knew that she was genuinely concerned for me and Zoey.

"Hey, Bianca," I answered.

"Bitch!"

My eyes widened, hearing her excitement. "What, girl?"

"Rashaad got arrested at work!"

I sat straight up, head spinning from the sudden movement. "He *what?*"

"*Rashaad got arrested at work!*"

I gasped. "Shut the fuck up."

"I swear to God!" she insisted as she bellowed with laughter.

A slow smile spread across my crusty lips from ear to ear.

"The Feds walked up in the admin office and hauled his bitch ass out in cuffs! Right past other correctional officers and inmates. The whole fucking jail is talking about that shit."

I lay back on my pillow, grinning so hard that my cheeks hurt.

Bianca continued to ramble so fast that I could barely understand her amidst our constant laughter. None of the personnel had been able to find out why he had been arrested, but the entire jail was talking about the warden being taken out of his office by Federal agents.

Karma was such a bitch, and I appreciated her.

AANAN "LAW" WOODS

Now that I had been released and given my family my time, it was back to business. Out of habit, I was ready to get back to the grind. I had been honest when I told Ox that I wanted to chill on flipping bricks. I knew the hustle. I didn't know life any other way. And after seeing Zuri with that nigga, I had a fire in my soul that wanted to put all of my efforts into the game. That's how I dealt with life's disappointments before getting locked up. Every time I felt locked in my dry-ass relationship with Whit, I made more money. When I got shot at, I made more money. When niggas tried to rob me, I made more money. When loyalty was broken, I made more money.

So, after leaving Zuri's crib, I headed to the property management company that was managing my properties while I had been away.

"Good morning, Aanan." The receptionist, Linda, jumped to her feet as soon as she saw me coming through the door. "Oh my God," she smiled. "It's so good to see you."

I snickered inwardly at the way she arched her back, sticking her breasts out as I entered the office in the South Loop.

I bent over the desk and gave her a quick hug. I had only held her for two seconds, but I could feel her body exhale just as quickly. Linda had always had a crush on me. She was an older woman, but she had never spared a moment to flirt with me when I came into the office.

"It's *so* good to see you," she swooned as she licked her lips.

"Good to see you too, Miss Linda."

Her eyes shied away. "Please don't call me that. You're making me feel old."

To fuck with her, I gently grabbed her chin and brought her eyes back to mine. "I apologize."

She swallowed hard, blushing as I released her chin.

"You don't have to be sorry about a thing, sweetie." Her words were breathy as she seemed to lose herself in my eyesight.

"Is Debra in?" I decided to release this old lady from my trance before she had a fucking heart attack.

She was flushed as she stuttered, "Y-yes, she's in."

"She busy?"

"Not too busy for you. Go ahead and knock on the door."

I nodded and strolled a few feet away to the closed door. I knocked lightly and quickly heard, "Come in."

I opened the door and peeked inside. Debra slowly looked up from what she was reading on her desk. Her eyes widened as soon as she saw me. "Oh!" she exclaimed, standing up with a bright smile. "You're out!"

I chuckled as she rushed from around the desk with her arms opened wide.

Debra had been managing my properties since the moment that I had purchased them. Because she was the liaison between me and the tenants, maintenance, and contractors, we had gotten to know each other pretty well. She knew that I was a street nigga that had been trying to legitimize my bread by investing in legal businesses such as real estate. She was really proud of me and loved my relationship with my kids since they were often with me when I came into the office. So, she was disappointed and sad to hear that I had gotten locked up.

We met in the middle of the floor, hugging each other. As she rocked me slowly, she asked, "When did you get out?!"

"A few days ago."

She pushed back, looking up at me, grinning. "So, you're free? You beat the case?"

"I did."

"Yes!" she exclaimed, softly smacking my arm with her tiny hand. "Congratulations."

"Thank you."

"Have a seat," she urged as she rounded her desk. As she sat back down in her seat, I sat comfortably in the leather seat in front of her desk.

"So, what can I help you with?" she asked.

"I was just stopping by to get an update on my properties. I know that I could have called, but I'm taking every opportunity to be outside."

She looked at me with a confused stare, causing her brows to curl. She was so quiet that I started to become nervous.

"You good?" I asked.

"Are you?" she returned with a nervous chuckle.

"Yeah, what do you mean?"

"We're no longer managing your properties, Aanan. You sold them."

My eyes ballooned. "What?! Sold?!"

Her eyes batted rapidly. "*Yes*. What's going on right now?"

"I didn't sell shit!" I barked. "Who the fuck bought them?!"

Her lips pressed into a tight line. "I wasn't privy to that information. I simply received a call from a real estate attorney notifying me that this company's services were no longer needed to manage the properties."

"Do you still have this lawyer's information?"

She nodded quickly. "I'm sure that I do."

She spun around to her laptop and started typing quickly. I could see that her having to deliver this news to me was heightening her anxiety. As she typed, she looked nervously between her laptop and the concern and confusion etched on my face.

Taking my phone from my pocket, I pulled up Chrome and went to the Zillow app. I typed in the addresses of my buildings and saw that they had, in fact, been sold recently.

"What the fuck?"

⚬⚬⚬

As soon as I stepped into the offices of the real estate attorney, Avery Hayes, the receptionist's head popped up from behind the computer. Her eyes narrowed as she immediately saw the smoldering anger dancing in my eyes.

"May I help you?" she asked, standing.

"Nope," I barked as I walked past her desk towards the hallway, where I saw office doors.

"You can't just go back there!" the receptionist urged behind me.

Ignoring her, I stalked towards the wooden door that read "Avery Hayes" in vinyl lettering.

"Excuse me, sir?!" the receptionist quipped.

Bursting through the door, I could feel the receptionist on my heels.

The door suddenly opening caused the lawyer inside to sit back on high alert. "May I help you?" she asked, brows deepening.

"Mrs. Hayes, I tried to stop him," the receptionist rushed. "I am *so* sorry. He's not on your calendar."

"I don't need to be on the fucking calendar, bitch," I barked, causing them to recoil with wide eyes.

"I'm calling the police," the receptionist announced as her skin began to turn red.

"Call them so I can explain to them how this sus-ass firm sold my fucking properties without my permission!"

Avery's brows curled even tighter. She leaned forward onto the desk, telling the receptionist, "Mae, I'll take care of this. You don't need to call the police. Just give me a few minutes."

As the receptionist inched out of the office, I closed the space between me and the attorney's desk. "You were the real estate attorney on the sales of properties that I own. I didn't initiate or authorize those sales."

Her eyes widened more with confusion. "So, how were they sold?"

"*You* fucking tell *me*!"

Her eyes ballooned even more as she attempted to calm me down. "Okay... okay... What were the addresses?"

I rambled off the addresses and waited impatiently as she began to type feverishly on the keyboard.

࿐

♫ I'm seein' her lookin' like Keisha, like
"Do you love me, do you love me not?"
Damn, you hit the spot
Taste like candy (candy), sweet like fruit (ooh)
Wet like water, can I love on you? ♫

"You made me wait all this time for you to party with me again just for you to get out and act like a bitch the whole night?"

I gave Ox an icy glare and then tore my eyes away without saying a word. I put my attention back on the bottle of D'Ussé that I had been drinking from the neck as we sat in the VIP section at Clutch. It was bitches all around us who had been invited by Ox to show me a good time. They were twerking and popping pussy to "Wockesha", but my mind wasn't anywhere near on their phat asses. Ever since I had left Avery Hayes' office, I had been in my head; plotting.

Just then, my eyes landed on a woman making her way through the dense crowd below the VIP sections. As if she could feel me, our eyes met. She stopped in her tracks, frozen as she stared up at me as if the vision of me was an illusion. Then, she smirked and rolled her eyes. She began to make her way up to the VIP section.

She had been the first woman to garner my attention since I'd gotten out. All of these other hoes had been so thirsty and simply didn't measure up to Zuri. But Persia was cut from a different cloth. Her banana-coated skin was smooth like butter. She was a ripe twenty-five with the ass and invisible waistline of an Instagram model. She had her own bread, so the labels and diamonds that she was draped in were bought with her money. And she was always draped in them. She was as fashionable as Cardi B and Nicki Minaj. When we were fucking, she was riding in an Ashton Martin and a Ferrari. But her money didn't come from other men. She was a hustler with multiple streams of income, one being from brand ads, since she was a popular influencer on TikTok.

"Oh shit," Ox said with a chuckle as soon as he'd seen her. "What up, Persia?"

"Hey, Ox." Then her eyes cut to mine. "Law."

"What up?" I grinned.

Immediately, Ox scooted over to give her space to sit. The sweet aroma of her perfume swept over me. The women shaking ass and popping pussy around us started to glare at Persia, wondering who the fuck she was. But they could all go to hell because Persia was shitting on them.

"You're out, huh?" she asked softly, staring up at me.

"Yeah."

My dick was rocking up. I found it funny that I hadn't even considered getting pussy since I'd gotten out because my mind had been so consumed with Zuri. But it was as if my dick knew that top-notch pussy was in its vicinity.

Persia and I had been fucking consistently for a few months before I was locked up. She had been the closest I had been to another woman besides Whit. I was feeling her, and she had potential. But she was such a successful woman and a good girl that I didn't want to have her waiting on a nigga to see if I would beat my case or not. So, when I didn't get bail, I never called her. Reese had told me that he had seen her in the hood one day shortly after I was denied bail and had told her what was going on.

Leaning over, she gave me a telling look. "You could have told me that you were getting locked up, Law."

I shrugged a shoulder. "I didn't want to put you through that."

"Why not?" She then started to smile teasingly. "Because you care about me?"

I shrugged again. "You a'ight."

She smirked as her eyes softened. "Mumph. I'm drinking with you tonight?"

I raised a brow, interested in that look in her eye. "You came here alone?"

"Nah. My girls are here but fuck them. I'm here with you now."

I chuckled cockily. "Bet."

Persia was the perfect thing to take my mind off of the bullshit. We sat there chopping it up, getting back acquainted. Eventually, the hoes left because my attention was elsewhere, and Ox knew that he couldn't get away with fucking any of these bitches without his girl finding out.

Persia sitting next to me with those thick thighs and big titties on display had almost made me forget the bullshit until she'd excused herself to the bathroom.

"Bro," Ox said as he took Persia's seat. "You good?"

I finally decided to tell him what was what. "Nah."

"What's going on?" Ox asked, leaning towards me from his seat.

"Whit went behind my back and sold my properties."

Ox's eyes blinked rapidly as the words I'd said settled. He then sat back, dumbfounded with a loss for words.

Looking at him had finally made me chuckle for the first time since I'd left that attorney's office. He looked like I'd felt when I'd forced the attorney to show me the sale paperwork.

"She sold and owns every last one of them. I ain't got nothing."

I couldn't believe it. After investing most of the bread I had saved into those properties and turning them into seven figures of prime real estate, they were gone. Over three million dollars of properties had been snatched away just like that. I had nothing except the bread that I had given Reese to hold down for me while I was gone.

I couldn't wrap my mind around Whit's disloyalty. Our relationship had been dead for years, but I had always been loyal to her. She had never needed for anything, even when I was locked up.

"How the fuck did she do that without you knowing?" Ox barked.

"Somebody with a fake ID in my name signed them over to her."

"You don't know who?"

I slowly shook my head. "Nah."

"Did you kill her yet?" Ox pressed.

"She won't answer the phone. I went to the crib, and she's gone."

No sooner than I'd seen Whit's name on the paperwork, I had started to blow Whit's phone up as I sped to the crib.

"Gone?" Ox asked with a raised brow.

"*Gone*. A lot of her clothes are gone out of the closet. Her toiletries are missing."

Nothing much had changed in the crib we shared since I was locked up. Whit had the same routine. Her clothes had been in the same place. She had been using the same side of the sink. But that afternoon, as I looked around the house, I noticed that a lot of her stuff was missing, including the Louis Vuitton suitcase set that I had bought her for Christmas a few years back.

She hadn't even taken the kids with her. She had dropped them off to my mother, telling her that she was taking a trip to get away from me because we had gotten into it.

I had to look away from Ox. I couldn't take the sympathy that my homie was giving me. That shit made me feel even sorrier for myself.

"What about the kids? Where are they?"

"When I called August, he told me that Whit had picked them up from school and dropped them off at my mother's house."

"You think she split?"

"Hell yeah. That girl ain't stupid. She's gone. And so is my money."

"So, that's something else we gotta take care of," Ox told me, giving me a knowing look.

"It is."

"Taking care of Detective Payne is a priority, though. He's not going to stop fucking with you until he gets what he wants."

I took a deep breath. I had wanted nothing more than to get out of prison, but I was suddenly missing the peace that I had when I was inside. My only worries then were beating my case.

Finally, I nodded. "Yeah, I was trying to let that nigga breathe, but I see that I can't."

TWO MONTHS LATER

CHAPTER 5
AANAN "LAW" WOODS

"**Y**es, daddy!" Persia's breathy persuasion made my dick grow harder inside of her wet walls. "*Yes*, daddy! Yes! Shit!"

I had her in her favorite position. She was lying on her left side. I straddled her left leg while holding her right one up on my shoulder, giving me the deep penetration that she liked. She loved for this big dick to be deep in her guts.

"Aargh," she growled softly, digging her long nails into my arms as I drilled that pussy.

I had been fucking with Persia heavy since bumping into her at Clutch. We had gotten right back on track, not missing a beat. Whenever the kids were at school or with their grandmothers, she was at my side. Her essence had been a good distraction from my life, not going nearly as I thought it would when I was released.

When I had been fantasizing about getting released, I saw myself relaxing with Zuri, showing her the man that I really was, while making up the year that I lost with my kids and making more investments to ensure that I would never be in a position that a motherfucker could put me in jail again. However, I was back hustling. Ox had gladly given the network back to me. However, I had insisted that instead of going back to being a hustler, he be my right hand since he had held my crew down while I was away.

Because of what Whit had done, I was forced to start all over with preparing to leave the game. I was back at risk of dying in these streets or going back to jail.

Zuri was still an obsession but a memory as well. Being with Persia showed me even more that I was in love with Zuri. When I looked at Persia, there was no real need for her in my life. She was beautiful and made my dick hard on sight. We got along, and she knew how to be with a nigga like me. But when I looked at Zuri, I felt more than attraction; I felt like I had found what was mine, what was my future. I didn't want to share her with anybody else. This was why when I saw her with someone else, I felt so deceived. I couldn't shake her from my thoughts. I still fantasized about her. No matter how thick and beautiful Persia was, I couldn't get that chocolate beauty off of my mind. I had so much to focus on to keep my mind off of her; my kids, hustling, and rebuilding. Nevertheless, Zuri still invaded my thoughts, stalking and crippling me.

◌◦◌

Twenty minutes later, I was chilling in the living room, smoking a blunt while Persia cooked breakfast. She loved to do wifey type shit for me, but she never pressed that I commit to her because she was used to that not being an option because of my relationship with Whit. When we reconnected, I hadn't told her what Whit did because it wasn't her business, and that shit was embarrassing as fuck.

As I puffed on the blunt, Ma called.

"What up, Ma?"

"Hey, baby." The sadness in her voice pulled at my heartstrings.

"Still no good news?" I asked her.

"No." Hearing the sudden onset of tears, I sat up.

Jeezy had been in a coma since surgery. His prognosis hadn't improved. Ma had been by his side every day. I feared that her health was going to start to deteriorate along with Jeezy's if he didn't get any better.

"He has fluid on his lungs. He has to be put on a vent. One of my nurse friends told me not to ever let them put him on a vent because he'd never get off of it, but they are saying I don't have a choice. I don't know what to do—"

"Ma," I called softly to stop her rambling.

"Oh gawd," her voice curdled.

"Ma," I pressed. "Just calm down. I'll call around to get some advice to make sure you're doing the right thing."

She sighed, relieved. "Thank you."

My line beeped, indicating that another call was coming through. Seeing that DC was calling from his burner phone, I quickly ended the call with Ma. "I gotta take this call, Ma."

"Okay," she cried.

"Try to stay positive."

"I'm trying."

Then I clicked over to DC.

"What up?"

"Yooo'."

"Tell me you got some good news for me."

"Yeah, she finally slipped up. She has a cell phone in her name in Palmetto Bay, a suburb outside of Miami. I got an address on her from the company."

Rage overtook me as weed smoke poured from my nose. Fury had been festering inside of me since I realized that Whit had not only run away but had left her own kids behind too. They had finally gotten both parents back, and now they were missing the other. Every time they asked me where their mother was, it broke my heart that she would leave them behind like this. But I understood. If anyone knew my wrath, Whit did. She knew if I had ever gotten released and found out what she had done, her life would be over. There was no love between us to keep me from killing her. It now made sense why she had been trying to convince me to take that deal. She never wanted me to get out so that she could continue stealing from me.

"Text me the address."

"Will do—"

"*Baaaabe*, your plate is ready," Persia called out from the kitchen.

"Is that Mrs. Warden?" DC asked, excited.

I withdrew in response to the reference. "Nah. That's Persia."

"What the fuck, man?" DC quipped. "What happened to Miss Warden?"

"I went over there, and it looked like she had more going on than I thought."

DC scoffed. "I bet. You know her husband got arrested."

My eyes widened. "Damn, for real?"

"Yeah. The Feds arrested that nigga at work."

"Gawd damn. For what?"

"Some money scandal shit."

"Umph." Figured. That nigga always looked sus as fuck to me.

"So, you ain't gotta worry about that nigga," DC told me. "He's facing some real time."

"Shit, she don' moved on from him. It's some new nigga now." Even though it made me reel with jealousy.

"And?" DC pressed. "You ain't no soft ass nigga. When you ever let another nigga stop you from getting what you want."

"How you know I want her?" I tried to argue.

"I'm smart as fuck, nigga. You had me check into her, so I know that she was the counselor at the County. She ain't got no street ties, so if you have me getting an address on her, you want her for different reasons. I'm assuming you spent some time with her while you were locked up." I grimaced, hating that he was right as he continued, "You want her, go get your girl, my nigga."

ZURI TURNER

"*Stoooop*, bae." Though I was pushing away from him, I was giggling. I thought it was so cute how Dom adored the way that my body was changing.

To dodge his advances, I rolled over on my side, turning my back to him.

I could feel his soft grip on my waist as he turned me over onto my back. "Why? Let me see."

I cringed as he pushed my sleep shirt up above my stomach. "Why?"

"I like it." He even then bent down and kissed it.

Recoiling, I muttered, "Ewe. I look fat."

He looked up at me with adoration dancing in his eyes. "You look pretty. That pregnancy glow shit is real."

By then, I was four months pregnant.

I had made the appointment to get the abortion shortly after everything had happened. Yet, as the appointment approached, my promise to God kept ringing in my mind. Since I had made that promise, my life had been so blessed. The recent pain and heartbreak I had experienced didn't hold a candle to the perfection that my life had been since making that promise.

There was no real reason not to have my baby. I would be able to take care of it alone. I had raised Zoey without her knowing her father. And considering that I had gotten pregnant despite being on birth control and after all these years with Rashaad, I figured that God had given me this child to make me not so alone.

Dom and this baby had come into my life just in the nick of time. I wasn't as alone as I could have been had it not been for the baby and Dom. Surprisingly, when I confessed to him that I was pregnant, he didn't run. He said that he felt a connection to me that he didn't want to be broken because I was pregnant. So, he had never left my side and had seemingly become as attached to my pregnancy as much as I had.

However, I hadn't told him that I didn't know who the father of my baby was. Out of embarrassment, I told him that the baby was Rashaad's. Yet, I had no idea who the father was. The number of weeks I was meant that the baby had been conceived the one week that I had had sex with Rashaad and Law. So, there was no way for me to figure out who the father was. Regardless, I didn't want to tell either one of them that I was pregnant. Both of them were criminals that had broken my fucking heart. I still thought of Law and even missed him. Dom reminded me so much of him that it was painfully apparent that he wasn't him. He was close, but there was no replica of Law. There was only one Annan "Law" Woods. I had no idea if he had been released or not. Bianca knew to never bring him up to me. I had no interest in finding out how his trial had gone. Though I still craved him, I still felt that he had been a complete fraud the entire time of our entanglement.

I stretched and yawned, forcing myself to wake up. Dom and I had spent that afternoon in bed after he had come over and fucked the shit out of me.

"You hungry?" he asked.

"Hell yeah," I giggled.

"Fat ass," he teased.

I immediately pouted. Because I was older, this pregnancy was taking a completely different toll on my body. I was feeling every symptom and craving. "See? I told you I was getting fat."

Dom clicked his tongue. "Babe, stop it. Get your fat ass up and put some clothes on so that I can feed you."

I blushed, loving the way that Dom took care of me. He was so unreal. Life had dealt me such a bad hand when it came to men that it was very hard to believe that Dom's intentions were pure. But every day, he proved my reservations to be unnecessary.

I climbed out of bed and went to my vanity for my toiletries. "Where do you want to go eat?"

It was silent for a few seconds, so I turned to see Dom staring at his phone. The light from his phone was blinking, highlighting his irritated expression. His phone must have been ringing while it was on silent.

I sighed, sucking my teeth, and leaned against my dresser. "It's her again?"

Dom reluctantly looked up at me. He blew a heavy breath and then set down his phone. "Yeah."

I scoffed, shaking my head.

"I'm sorry."

"It's not your fault."

"I'm not going to answer."

"You should. Tell that bitch to leave you alone."

He easily did. "What, Miesha?"

He'd even put the call on speaker, which he did every time she called to assure me that Miesha's obsession was one-sided.

"Can we talk, please?" she begged.

She sounded so fucking pathetic and desperate.

Dom's forehead fell into his hand. "There is nothing to say. It's over, Miesha."

"I just don't understand. Why her?"

"It being over between us has nothing to do with her. I stopped fucking with you before I met Zuri."

"Bullshit!" she angrily spat.

I scoffed quietly, shaking my head at this bitches' delusion.

"Miesha, you gotta stop calling me. You gotta let this shit go," Dom insisted.

"We were so good together, though, Dom. *I love you.* I can't stop thinking about you."

"Miesha, stop calling me. I have to go."

"Dom—"

"I'm literally in bed with Zuri." As she inhaled dramatically, he told her, "Stop calling me." He then hung up.

The moment that Dom posted a photo of him and I at a restaurant in his stories a few months ago, Miesha's stalking became relentless and scary. He had shown me text messages of him cutting her off before he'd even met me. I had also seen how she was obsessed with getting him back, though they were never together, ever since. Yet, when she found out about me, it made her infatuation with him swell. I applauded Dom on how he handled the situation. He was always open and upfront with her about me. The bitch was just delusional.

Seeing the irritation on my face, he climbed out of bed. The vision of his naked body made all irritableness scurry away. Dom was fucking perfection wrapped in chocolate. I could barely see his skin in the dimly lit room as he strolled toward me.

Closing the space between us, he took my waist, brought us chest to chest, and leaned down, causing his long locs to cascade over me.

"Don't let her fuck up your mood. I can't handle if she's fucking with you too. Okay?"

Pressing my lips together tightly, I said, "Okay."

As I walked away towards the bathroom, he lightly smacked me on the ass. I looked back, smiling at him, and then padded through the bathroom door.

I was trying my best not to fall in love with Dom. Not because he didn't deserve my love. I just feared that this surge into admiration was a rebound. So much in my life had changed so drastically, so fast, that I was forcing myself to focus on now being single and pregnant. I was officially a single woman. The divorce was final. Because of Rashaad's legal troubles, he had agreed to everything in the divorce and finalized it quickly. I had been given our home and an investment property that I quickly sold. I planned to live off of that money for a while so that I could enjoy this pregnancy versus stressing and the drama that I had with the last one.

Zoey and I still hadn't spoken to one another. Her constant silence and distance were only further proof of what she had done. I wondered if she was with Rashaad, and the fear of learning that she actually was with him pushed me to stay away from her.

So, I had a bunch of shit to deal with rather than falling in love with a man that I'd met just a few months ago. But the butterflies and infatuation were indeed there.

ZOEY TURNER

"Damn, Zoey, can you get your shit, please?"

I gritted, gnawing on my bottom lip as Dior stomped through her room. After two months of living with her, things had changed. She was snappy and irritated. I knew that she was tired of me being in her space.

I gathered my things from the floor and put them on the pallet in the corner of her room that I had been sleeping on. That pallet was an example of how low I had been feeling. Life had not been the nonstop party that I thought it would be now that I had graduated from high school and was no longer living with my parents. Things had really gone downhill. My money was running low. I no longer was in contact with Rashaad. His broke ass couldn't have helped me anyway. Each day that Dior said something snarky to me, homelessness was feeling nearer and nearer in my future. Worse, the only person that had come to my graduation was Zina. I had hoped that that being one of the biggest days that my mother had been waiting for anxiously that she would show up with open arms and forgiveness in her heart. But I hadn't heard from her. That right there told me that she truly hated me and that if I wanted her help, I would have to grovel my way back into her life.

I wasn't cut like that, though.

Sighing inwardly, I swallowed my pride and asked her, "You need some help?"

Dior was packing to leave for college in a few weeks.

"Nah, I'm good," she muttered, not even making eye contact with me.

Tired of being treated like I was a soft-ass bitch, I stood, grabbed my cell phone, and left out of the room. This was one of the few times that Dior's house was empty. Her parents had gone out with their crew to celebrate someone's birthday. Yet, it was one o'clock on a Friday night, so the block was cracking outside of the living room window.

Just as I was about to step outside to get some air, there was an explosive thud coming from the kitchen that made me scream and jump out of my skin.

I spun around with wide eyes as Dior appeared, flying down the stairs.

"What the—" Suddenly, Dior's words were lodged in her throat, unable to escape. I stood in the living room, feet planted, unable to move as I stared at the three men that were charging toward me. Their faces were covered with masks and hoodies. But their guns were right in my fucking face.

"Where the money at, bitch?!" one of them barked at me.

I cringed as he raced toward me. The barrel of the Nine stabbed into my forehead so forcefully that I felt blood. Piss ran down my leg. A puddle formed at my bare feet as tears instantly overflowed from my eyes.

"I-I-I-I-I don't know," I cried.

Out of my peripheral, I saw Dior takeoff up the stairs. The other two niggas took off after her.

I squeezed my eyes shut and started to pray. All I could hear were my prayers and Dior screaming. I shook feverishly, fighting to catch my breath. I saw death coming. It was right there in my face.

Suddenly, I felt my body being rushed. I gasped, crying out, but I never opened my eyes. I was too scared to. Then I was being forced to the ground. The barrel of the gun was now on the back of my head.

This was how I was going to die, like many young girls in the hood; in places they had no business. Dior's house had never been an environment that I was used to. They had money, but it came with a lot of threats of danger because her father was a hood nigga.

I should have left a long time ago.

Then heavy footsteps could be heard tumbling down the steps.

"We out!" I heard one of them bark.

Then the pressure of the gun on my head was relieved. I finally breathed, but I didn't open my eyes. I continued to pray, begging for my life until I heard nothing, no footsteps, no voices.

I slowly opened my eyes. I looked back into the kitchen and saw that no one was there. I was still shaking violently as I attempted to stand. My head was still spinning. My breaths remained unsteady.

I inhaled sharply when I realized that I didn't hear Dior upstairs. That's when I finally found stable footing. I took off up the stairs.

"Dior?!" I shouted. "Dior?!"

Finally, I found her in her parent's room on the floor. Her head was bleeding. I looked around the room and saw that dresser drawers were opened chaotically, and her parents' belongings had been pulled out of them.

When Dior began to groan, I sighed with relief, gasping for air as I slid down the wall behind me.

CHAPTER 6
ZURI TURNER

The next morning, my phone was ringing at an ignorantly early hour.

Groaning, I reached over on the nightstand for my phone. Since it was Zina and she was due any day now, I answered, "Hello?"

"Zuri!" she spat.

My sleepy eyes ballooned. "What?"

"Zoey finally called me."

I was initially relieved that she wasn't in labor so gawd damn early in the morning. But I held my breath, waiting to see what I would feel now that someone had gotten in touch with my daughter. Zina had been calling Zoey ever since all of this had happened. I had been hoping that Zoey would eventually call her back so that she could have some kind of contact with an older family member that loved her. I wasn't sure if I wanted to be there for her, but I knew that she needed somebody. On the one hand, I wanted the best for her, and I missed my daughter so much. Yet, the shit she'd pulled had me seriously regretting *not* swallowing her hoe ass.

"Okay?" I pressed.

"She's been staying at Dior's house," Zina rambled so dramatically that she was short of breath. "There was a home invasion last night."

I sat up slowly. "Is she okay?"

"Yeah."

Relieved, I let out a sigh of relief.

"But she left, and now she's staying in some motel."

"Okay." I stared into space, wanting to feel more, wanting to go rescue my baby girl.

But I could no longer do that. Spoiling her had only awarded me her disloyalty and disrespect.

"Okay?" Zina repeated with surprise.

"Yeah. Let her stay with you."

Zina sucked her teeth. "You know I can't afford nan 'nother mouth to feed. Zuri, stop acting like this. Are you fucking serious?"

I laughed psychotically. "Did she seriously fuck my husband?"

"She's your daughter."

"I know!"

Zina had been getting on my fucking nerves with this sympathy for Zoey. But considering that she was having a baby by her sister's fiancé, I guessed hoes stuck together.

Zina then inhaled dramatically and cried out. "*Ooooh*, God!"

"Stop being dramatic, Zina," I laughed.

"Zuri!" she cried.

"Zina, it's hard enough to deal with my own sadness. I can't deal with your dramatics too—"

"Zuri, shut the fuck up!" she spat. "My water just broke!"

I COULDN'T KEEP MY EYES OFF OF TREYVON. THEY KEPT BOUNCING over to him as we all sat in the waiting room of Labor and Delivery. I had been staring at him so much that Zadah almost caught me.

It wasn't a surprise that Zadah and Treyvon were there. As always, after all of the explosive drama, Zadah and Zina were back on speaking terms. It was as if the catfighting was their love language. However, I had had very little to say to Zadah since she had chosen to wait to tell me about Zoey and Rashaad at the most embarrassing moment. I knew that she was so spiteful that she was waiting to throw that in my face at the moment when she needed to redeem herself or win an argument. Zina was wrapped in this love/hate relationship with her. However, I had been on the outside looking in for years. Zadah's insecurities were turning her into a jealous, vindictive, and spiteful bitch. I was now only cordial with her when we were all with my father to make things easier for him.

"Zuri, Zadah."

I looked up when I heard my father's voice calling our names from the door of the waiting room. His elated expression was so adorable. His eyes were wide and bouncing, and his smile was so energetic and contagious that I had a smile as well.

"You all can go in to see her and the baby now."

I stood eagerly. "What did she have, Daddy?"

Zina had decided not to learn the gender since she had two girls and a boy. But she had told me that she was hoping for a boy since Treyvon didn't have any.

Again, my eyes went to Treyvon, watching as he looked eagerly at Daddy, waiting in anticipation.

"It's a boy," my dad smiled.

It was hard for me to discreetly watch Treyvon as he tried to hide his satisfaction. There was a light in his eyes that he tried to hide behind Zadah. It was obvious that Treyvon was okay with having this child, as long as its father remained a secret.

As Daddy led the way to Zina's room, I followed him out. Zadah was right beside me, but then she suddenly stopped, causing me to pause and watch her. She stared at Treyvon questionably.

"What?" he asked, raising his brows dramatically.

"Where you goin'?"

Oh my damn...

Treyvon blinked slowly as my heart began to beat thunderously with anticipation. "I wanna see the baby."

Chile...

"Why?" Zadah quipped.

"Why not?" Treyvon shot back. "Stop being a bitch, Zadah."

And I oop!

Treyvon pushed by Zadah, frustration blanketing his face as he followed behind my father.

I ducked my head as I shuffled down the hall, trying to hide the smirk on my face from Zadah.

"He's been acting like such a bitch lately," Zadah grumbled.

"Yeah?" I dryly asked.

When Zadah scoffed, I looked over at her. She looked at me with narrowed eyes.

"You still mad at me, huh?" she quipped with a frown.

I huffed, saying, "Zadah, I'm not talking about that shit here."

"I thought I was helping you out, letting you know what was going on."

I stopped dead in my tracks, glaring at her. "You knew exactly what the fuck you were doing, and it wasn't *helping* me. Ain't nobody stupid enough to believe that bullshit but you, so, like I fucking said, *drop it.* I'm done fucking with you."

Zina got a kick out of arguing with Zadah, but I was over that shit. I was prepared to be cordial only enough to please my father, but that was it.

I then spun on my Pumas and hurried away from her messy ass to the room where I had seen Daddy and Treyvon go in. I was excited to see the baby, but I was also really excited to see Treyvon's reaction.

As I hurried into the room, Daddy was taking the baby from Zina's arms. Zina was still perspiring from a thirty-minute labor.

"You pushed that baby out quick, girl," I teased her as I

approached her bed. "You a professional." She blushed as Daddy handed me the baby. "What's his name?"

"Tremere."

Before I knew it, I was choking on my spit. Zina's nerve had me fucking gagging. She had named that baby after her and Treyvon. Her middle name was Merelynn, after our mother.

"Unt uh! Don't be coughing all over that baby," Treyvon fussed. "Let me see him."

Then as he took the baby from me, my choking became uncontrollable. As I fought to keep my composure, I caught eyes with Zina, who was snickering.

"This bitch trying to give the baby Covid," Zadah muttered.

I had to laugh at myself, which caused Zina to begin cracking up. Only she and I knew the true joke, but the way that we couldn't keep ourselves together had the whole room laughing.

For a second, looking around that room, we looked like a happy family. As I laughed, life felt so pleasant and normal.

Yet, under the surfaces of our smiles was deceit and betrayal that was beyond measure. Looking at Zina's baby and feeling my own gave me hope that normalcy was coming to stay. Yet, the turmoil had only just begun.

RASHAAD TURNER

"You should take the deal, Rashaad."

I grimaced, sitting back at the table in the lawyer's office. Since he was also a friend, we were talking about my list of federal charges over shots of Jameson.

"Fuck no," I spit.

After being arrested, I had bonded out the next morning. Since this was my first time being arrested and facing charges, I hadn't been put on house arrest, and they didn't consider me a flight risk. My connections in the city and the fact that all my accounts were frozen had helped as well. Because of my financial and social status, I knew a lot of attorneys. However, many wouldn't work with me because of their own connections to the politicians in the city and state. Then those that would take the case weren't saying what I wanted to hear. All of them were suggesting that I take the deal of twenty years that the prosecution was offering.

That was bullshit, however. Motherfuckers went to the Feds every day for financial crimes and were doing two to five years.

I knew that I was guilty. But I wasn't going to let them treat me any less than every other official that had stolen from this state.

"There is too much evidence against you to fight this," Will insisted.

"Just say that *you* can't fight this," I scoffed.

"Nobody can," he chuckled dryly. "Not even OJ's lawyers can get you off for this shit!"

I sat back, taking a big gulp of my Jameson. "Motherfuckers get away with lighter sentences all the time!"

Will frowned, glaring at me as if I was being an idiot. "You *ain't white*, motherfucker," he reminded me with a condescending laugh. "You a *nigga* that was blessed enough to have a position that any of these White men wanted, and you fucked that up. You stole from them. They ain't letting your Black ass get away with this shit!"

Will wasn't just a lawyer; he was one of the homies. We had grown up privileged, with successful parents in the same suburb outside of Chicago. We had gone to the same grammar and high school. We had shared a lot of women. So, I knew that he wouldn't steer me wrong. Looking at him, I didn't see encouragement or positivity. I saw disappointment and confident surrender.

My shoulders sank. My ego evaporated. Reality was setting in. I could feel concrete walls closing in around me, the same ones that watched so many other Black men like me get locked behind unjustly. I had done my crime, but because of my skin color, I would be given much more time than a White man that had done the same.

"If I take this to court, I'll lose?" I asked.

Will nodded confidently. "And they'll give you more time."

I gritted. "Fuck."

"What did you think was gonna happen, man? You stole—"

My shame cut him off. "I know what I did."

"Then why would you do it, dawg?"

I blew a deep breath, tightening the hold on the rocks glass. My whole life, I had only focused on establishing myself with money. My parents had only taught me that as a Black man, I would be defined by how much money I had, not the type of man, husband, or father that I was. I had never been interested in learning how to be a good man or good father. That's why I had been a terrible father. I hadn't felt real affection for any woman until I naively fell for Zoey. When the divorce was finally over, I didn't flinch. Ten years of marriage was over, and I had no ill feelings about it. I had never established a relationship with God or an emotional connection with women. All I knew was money and buying what I wanted with it.

This was the only time in my life that I felt any heartache, and it wasn't because I had torn my family apart. It was because I was now broke and out of control of my destiny.

"Greed," I answered. "That's my best answer, man; fucking greed."

Shaking his head, Will finished off his whiskey. "Take the deal, bro." He then looked at his watch. "I need you to roll out, though. I have some important people coming soon."

I discreetly grimaced. "Damn, it's like that?"

"I can't have them see you in here. It's going to affect my business."

I cringed inwardly but didn't let him see that shit on my face. I figured that was coming. He hadn't been the first to out me because word of what I'd done had spread through our professional and social scenes. Lots of people weren't fucking with me, and more were being added to the list daily.

"Appreciate the meeting," I said, extending my hand to shake his.

But Will only nodded and put his attention on making a call.

Feeling the sudden frigid change in the atmosphere, I tucked my tail and got the fuck up outta there.

ZURI TURNER

"You was dumb as hell for laughing that gawd damn hard," Zina said, quietly cackling all over again.

I shook my head, snickering. "You the one dumb for naming this baby Tremere. You bogus as hell."

She shrugged playfully. "I can name my baby after his parents."

Daddy, Zadah, and Treyvon had left the hospital about an hour ago. Now, Zina and I were free to spill the tea.

"But all your kids' names start with 'J'. You knew what the fuck you were doing!" I started to crack up again.

"Shut up before you wake my baby up," she warned, still laughing.

I quickly quieted, remembering that I was holding Tremere. He was a beautiful baby, but he didn't look like anyone since he was only a few hours old.

"Treyvon looked so happy," I admitted.

"He did."

Watching her smile, I was envious. Though this baby had been conceived with deceit, he had both parents that wanted him and loved him unconditionally. I couldn't say that for the baby that I was carrying. At that moment, I decided to stop judging Zina and to let her handle this situation as she saw fit. Ever since Zadah had turned her ignorance against me, I no longer felt bad for her or for keeping Zina's secret.

"I guess I should go so you can get some rest while he's sleeping," I said. "You want me to get you something to eat before I leave?"

"That's okay, sissy. Treyvon texted me and said that he was coming back up to see the baby and would bring me something to eat."

Nodding, I stood to put Tremere into the bassinet.

"Zoey texted me," Zina said hesitantly.

"Mumph," I grunted as I gathered my purse.

"She's really fucked up. She asked me for money."

The sympathy that she had in her eyes for Zoey was so fucking annoying.

"She needs a place to stay," Zina added.

"She should be at school," I said. "She was supposed to be moving on campus by now. Why isn't she?"

Zina only shrugged.

Frustrated, I shook my head and pushed the bassinet next to Zina so that she can reach it when needed. I then bent over and kissed Zina on the cheek. "I'm gone."

"Think about calling her," Zina pressed.

"Mmm humph."

ૡૐૹ

Once in the car, I couldn't stop wondering why in the hell Zoey wasn't at school. I realized that she hadn't even come home to get her things that she had been gifted at her trunk party. I knew that she had been able to save a few dollars over the years, but that couldn't have been enough to get her all new things for her first year at school.

Listening to my gut feeling, I dialed her school and followed the prompts to talk to admissions.

"Hi. Admissions office. This is Cate speaking. How may I help you?"

"Hi. My name is Zoey Turner. I was calling to confirm my move-in date."

"Sure. I can help you with that. What's your date of birth, correct spelling of your name, and student ID number?"

"I don't have my student ID on hand at the moment. I'm sorry. I'm driving. But I can give you my birthdate."

"Okay, great. Go ahead."

I rattled off the information as I got on the expressway. I could hear her tapping rapidly on the keyword as I sat in silence. Something didn't feel right. Zoey had been too excited to move on campus. Nothing would or should have stopped her from doing so, not even being scared of my wrath.

"*Ummm*, what is the spelling of your name again?" Cate asked with a weird tone.

"Zoey. Z-o-e-y. Turner. T-u-r-n-e-r."

"I don't... see any registration for that name."

"Did I miss registration?"

"I don't see that you were ever accepted at all."

A wave of disappointment hit me so hard that I squeezed my eyes together. But I quickly opened them, remembering that I was driving.

"O-okay," I stuttered quietly. "Thank you."

The entire ride home, my gut feeling grew. Zoey had already disappointed me to the utmost. There was nothing else that she could do to hurt me anymore. But realizing that her lies didn't start or stop with Rashaad was frightening.

Once I got home, I went to my computer desk. I fished through the drawer for the folder that I had kept all of Zoey's acceptance and scholarships in.

I spent the rest of the afternoon calling every school that had accepted her and every organization that had awarded her a scholarship.

Each of them had no records of ever contacting my daughter.

⚜

"So, when we gon' kill her little ass?" Bianca spit, pacing the floor.

As soon as I called her, crying my eyes out, she came right over.

An hour later, tears were still teetering at my eyelids. I couldn't believe that I had been this bamboozled by the people that I had loved and respected the most. I had been completely deceived by the people that I had catered to most of my life.

"Just give me the word," Bianca snapped. "You can't beat her ass, but I can dog-walk that little lying-ass heifer. So, all that shit was fake?"

"Every last one of them. I actually scanned and emailed one of the letters to the school for verification, and they confirmed that it wasn't real. She probably had one of her smart, techie friends do it."

"Oh. My. God. Why lie about that shit? Wasn't she like a fucking genius?"

A sadistic laugh accompanied my tears. "No. I called her high school and got a copy of her transcripts because I couldn't understand the need to lie either. She was faking her grades too."

"Gawd damn!" Bianca was so pissed that her face was beat red. "Where she at? I'm whooping her ass for you."

I cringed, remembering that I had been too embarrassed to tell Bianca about Zoey and Rashaad. But I was too weak, at the moment, to give a fuck about the shame that I would feel now if she knew.

"She doesn't live here anymore. She hasn't for two months now."

Bianca stopped pacing. Her head tilted dramatically to the side as her arms folded. "Why the fuck not? Where she at?"

I stared off into space. I was so fucking numb.

"Remember when I told you that Rashaad left me because he said he was in love with someone else?'

"Yeah."

When I simply stared at her, she bucked her eyes, signaling for me to go on. But I had no words. My tears spoke for me as they rolled down my cheeks.

Bianca gasped aloud. Her hand went to her mouth. She then slowly sat beside me on the couch.

"Nah, wait," she said, jolting back up on her feet. "I need a fucking drink for this shit."

She walked over to the bar and went behind it. As she made her drink, she said, "Please tell me you are fucking lying."

I barely shook my head. "I wish I was."

"That R Kelly, pissing on young bitches, child molesting, Woody Allen motherfucka!"

CHAPTER 7
ZOEY TURNER

"Hi. This is your Uber Eats driver. I'm outside with your order."

"You aren't coming in?" I asked him, devastated.

"No, ma'am," he insisted, sounding weak and white. "This doesn't look like a really safe environment."

"Uggh. Fine," I snapped, hanging up.

I climbed out of bed and slipped into my Gucci slides. I then grabbed my room key and hurried out of the room. Once in the hallway, I kept my head down to avoid the losers, dirty niggas, and prostitutes that littered the hallway. Every time I was forced to leave the room, I was brought to tears. It was nothing like the five-star hotels and resorts that I had been used to.

The lobby was even full of niggas and bitches partying and smoking weed like they were in a fucking club.

"Aye, what's your name, shawty?" I heard some ignorant motherfucker say behind me.

"Not interested," I quipped without turning around.

"Damn, you rude as fuck," the same voice said.

"She look like a bougie bitch anyway," another one replied.

I cringed and sped up my stride.

Once outside, I saw the chaotic, blue eyes of my driver.

Then the window rolled down, and he eagerly asked, "Zuri?"

"Yeah."

I walked up to the passenger window, and he literally threw the McDonalds' bag at me before speeding off.

I then hurried back into the motel, hating my fucking life.

"Excuse me, pretty lady?" I heard as I felt a tug on my arm.

I snatched my arm out of this dirty nigga's hands. I could feel my skin crawling from his touch.

"Ewe, nigga! Don't touch me!" I spit.

Suddenly, all eyes were on me. Lustful eyes filled with deadly threats glared at me.

Too many women had gotten shot and killed because they had rudely rejected these niggas, so I hurried down the hall, praying that I wasn't followed.

I put the key into the door with a shaking hand. I didn't know shit about surviving like this. I had been spoiled and sheltered. Suddenly, I was on my own, clinging to the little money that I had left while eating off of the dollar menu at McDonald's.

I didn't have a car. I didn't have a place to live.

I was ready to buckle.

I couldn't take it anymore.

I had been too ornery to speak to my mother, but I needed her.

ZURI TURNER

"Uggh!" I groaned, kicking my feet. I hadn't even opened my eyes yet, but I knew that it was too fucking early in the morning for my phone to be ringing.

Along with the piercing ringing of my phone, I heard Dom in my ear chuckling deeply since he was spooning me.

"It's not funny," I whined.

"Answer that shit so I can go back to sleep."

Sucking my teeth, I reached down on the floor where my phone was plugged up. Looking at the name calling me, I gasped.

"What?" Dom urged as I sat up, staring at the screen.

"It's... It's Zoey."

"Answer it."

"No," I insisted, shaking my head. "I don't know what to say."

I had told Dom everything. I had to. He couldn't understand why the daughter that I loved so much and couldn't live without when we'd first met had disappeared from my life. He had supported me in not contacting her, but he always hoped that we would reconnect.

"Just say hi," he said.

"Hi?!" I spat above the continuous ringing. "I don't want no casual greetings with this little heifer. That's the *last* thing I wanna say. I wanna know why she fucked my—"

Suddenly, Dom took the phone out of my hand. I gasped as he hit the "answer" button and then put it on speaker. He then put the phone up to my mouth. But I closed my lips tightly, sucking them into my mouth.

"H-Hello?"

Hearing Zoey's voice softened all anger in me. She sounded so scared and fragile, like the little girl that I used to protect.

Dom's eyes bulged at me as he softly nudged me in the side.

Grimacing, I forced, "I'm here."

And Dom shook his head at my orneriness.

"Ma? I need some help."

"What's wrong, Zoey?"

"I was staying with Dior, but I can't stay with her anymore—"

"Zina told me."

"I've been staying at this hotel, but it's not safe."

"Where is the hotel?"

"In Harvey on 169th and Halsted."

"Okay?"

"Can you send me some money?"

"Can I send you some money?" I quipped. "Are you fucking serious, Zoey!? That's the only reason why you called me?"

Dom's back straightened. He started to wave his hands, trying to stop my oncoming ranting.

"You haven't spoken to me in two months after fucking my husband, and you got the audacity to call me and ask me for some money?!"

Her "grown" ass didn't have shit to say then.

"You'd have a very safe place to stay if you were in school, Zoey. Why aren't you in school? Huh?" I taunted her.

Silence.

"Because your fraud-ass was lying about that too," I spewed, causing Dom's forehead to go into his hand. "Clearly, I spoiled you too much if you can't last a few months in the hood. I lasted there and in worse situations just fine and lived. You want a fucking handout because it's not comfortable where you sleep, princess? Suck it the fuck up! Welcome to fucking adulthood. You wanted to be grown so bad. Well, enjoy!"

Fuming, I hung up. Feeling my heart ache, I cringed and flung myself back on the pillows.

"That is *not* how the fuck I intended for that conversation to go," Dom said.

"You shouldn't have made me answer the phone."

He leaned over, kissing my cheek. "Sorry, baby."

"I cannot let her make me feel bad." I was speaking to myself more than Dom. I was talking myself into giving this tough love to Zoey that she needed. "I spoiled her too much. I gave her too much. She needed to get out into the real world. She needs to grow up before she ruins her life."

"You're right, baby."

"Then why does it hurt so bad?" I burst into tears.

I threw my face into my hands, sobbing. I could then feel Dom hold onto my waist and turn me over. He had rolled me over on top of him. His muscular arms held me as he kissed my forehead.

"It's gonna be okay."

I cried in response."

"You hear me?" he urged.

I could only nod.

"You want your favorite Alfredo Shrimp Omelet from Truth?"

Still sobbing uncontrollably, I nodded eagerly, and he laughed, still pressing those soft lips so lovingly against my forehead.

"I'm going out tonight, but I can come to your crib afterward."

Dom and I were holding hands as we left out of his house. The sun was shining so bright that my eyes squinted as they tried to adjust. Dom and I had been laid up in his bedroom all morning. He had even had the breakfast that he had offered delivered to his house instead of us having to go to the restaurant.

"You don't have to," I told him. "Chill with your friends. You haven't in a long time."

Dom and I had been up under each other a lot. He was taking full advantage of me not having a nine-to-five. It was like I was at his beck and call. But I wasn't complaining.

"I want to," he told me.

"I might be knocked out," I warned him.

"I won't stay out late then."

Smiling up at him, I noticed a woman marching up the driveway. Dom followed my eyesight and immediately cringed.

"Nah, Miesha! We ain't doin' this shit!" he barked.

Dom's demeanor changed from the large, loving teddy bear that I was used to, to an enraged beast.

"So, this is her," she sassed, folding her arms, leaning against the trunk of his car.

"Bye, Miesha," he said. He then literally put his hands on her and started to push her down the driveway.

"I just want to talk to you!"

"It's nothing to fucking talk about!" Dom was so irritated that he was shaking the girl. "We were just fucking! *For a few months.* Now it's over. Gawd damn! Let it go!"

"But why?"

"BECAUSE!" His roar was so powerful that it echoed between the brick houses surrounding us. Fearing that he would hurt this woman, I started to inch down the driveway towards them.

"I can't..." he said, putting his hands to his forehead. "You 'bout to fucking make me hurt you."

He then walked away from her. But when he felt her following, he started to jog back up the driveway. Along the way, he grabbed my elbow and brought me along with him. I scurried next to him, struggling to follow along with my short legs.

"Just let me talk to you, *please!*" Miesha begged. "We had something."

Her words were so needy that it was scary.

Groaning, he popped the locks on his car and hurried me inside. He then slammed my door and hurried around the front of the car. Miesha had sense enough to plead her case from the other side of the car. She continued to beg as Dom hopped inside. Looking at her, I saw a woman that was truly delusional. I saw confusion and wonder in her eyes. Every time we made eye contact, it looked like the sight of me made her die inside.

"This bitch is crazy," Dom grumbled as he started the car.

"Dom, please?!" Miesha shouted over his engine turning.

Shaking his head, he backed out of the driveway at high speed, almost hitting her.

"What the fuck, man?!" he snapped. "I'm sorry, baby."

"You don't have to be sorry, Dom," I told him sincerely. I had always known that she was obsessed, but seeing it for myself had confirmed it. She looked like a maniac.

"Have you considered getting a restraining order?" I asked him, reluctantly watching his anger stir.

"I can handle her," he said, shaking his head. "It's not that deep."

"Yes, it is, clearly," I laughed sarcastically. "Women are just as crazy as men are."

"She just needs to get it through her head that I didn't choose her. Her ego is bruised. She'll get over it." He was trying to act like it wasn't a big deal to spare me. As he drove away from his house, I could tell that he was trying to smother his anger in order to keep me calm.

"I know about a bruised ego. But I'm not at Rashaad's door begging him to take me back, nor am I filling his inbox with hundreds of text messages and voicemails. You really need to consider a restraining order."

"That's a piece of paper. That shit don't keep a motherfucker away that don't wanna be. I'm just gonna have to put my hands on that bitch."

"And then your Black ass will be the one locked up. Is that fair?"

He sighed, admitting, "You're right."

"You shouldn't have given her all that dick," I joked, trying to lighten his mood. As he laughed, I asked, "You fucked her like you fuck me?"

"Never," he said, slipping a hand on my thigh as he bent corners. "I didn't lead her on. I promise."

"I know. I read the messages with my own eyes. But people have feelings. You can't be laying up with random people giving them that good ass dick and expect them to have the sense to walk away. People are crazy out here."

"It's your fault," he laughed.

My mouth dropped. "How?!"

"She was only calling and sending messages at first. As soon as I posted your fine ass on my social media, she went crazy."

He then gazed at me with so much love that his cute ass looked heavenly.

I guessed that I must have been gazing at him because he then asked, "What?"

"Why me?" I asked him genuinely.

I couldn't understand why a man as fine and established as him was so willing to be beau'd up with a woman that was pregnant with someone else's baby. If he was just showing up after midnight to fuck, I wouldn't be questioning him. Yet, he was the complete opposite. His attention and presence were so consistent that I felt so kept and like I was his.

His eyes squinted as he bashfully smiled. "What you mean?"

"You're so handsome. You have money. You've got your shit

together. You don't have any kids. You can be beau'd up with any woman in this world. Why my pregnant ass?"

His smile deepened. "Because I wanted you the moment that I saw you. When I looked at you, I knew that you would be someone special in my life. I thought that would change for me when I found out that you were pregnant, but it didn't. So..." He then put his eyes on me quickly, winked, and then put his eyes back on the road. "Here we are."

I literally got teary-eyed. I had to put my attention out of the passenger window because I didn't want him to see me getting emotional. This wasn't pregnancy hormones. These tears were of appreciation for a godsend.

AANAN "LAW" WOODS

"*Laaaw!*" Stacy's six-year-old daughter screamed my name with such excitement that my smile pierced through my thick beard from ear to ear.

I dropped the bags of toys and clothes that I was holding and then bent down and picked her up.

"Hey, baby girl," I spoke into her big, thick ponytail.

"I missed you!" she exclaimed.

"I missed you too."

"Where you been?" she sassed.

"I was away for a while."

"You bring me something?"

Putting her down, I laughed, along with Stacy's caregiver, Gabriella, who had let me into the two-story home out in Oak Park.

Stacy's son must have heard the commotion because he came into the living room with wide eyes.

"What up, my nigga?" I greeted him with a grin.

He had been able to keep his seven-year-old cool. He ran up to me, throwing his hands around me and hugging me tightly.

I reached down, giving him the same love.

"What's up, Law?" he finally greeted.

"Oh, Lord. You about to start spoiling my kids again. Where the fuck you come from?"

Hearing Stacy's voice, I looked up and saw her rolling into the living room. I felt some relief leave my chest. She and her kids had been one of the responsibilities that I had left hanging when I was locked up. Though Reese was taking up the slack, I knew that nobody could do my job like I could. I worried about her and her kids just as much as I had worried about my own.

She glided towards me in her powered wheelchair. I bent down and gave her the longest, tightest hug.

"I missed you," she said into my stomach.

"Missed you too," I told her.

Before I chopped it up with Stacy, I gave the kids the toys and clothes that I had bought them. They opened that shit up excitedly like it was Christmas morning. Then I gave them a hundred dollars each. After that, Stacy sent them to their rooms while Gabriella cooked them dinner.

Since I had cut off communication once I was locked up, I sat down on the couch, and we caught up with each other for hours.

"I'm so sorry for what my father did to you," she insisted eventually. "I can't believe he's this obsessed with getting you back."

"You ain't got no business apologizing for him," I insisted, laying a comforting hand on her arm. "Besides, I understand him. He's a father. So, am I. I would kill a nigga and everyone he loves if a fucking hair is misplaced on my daughters' heads. I can't blame him."

"But you've made amends. You continue to every day."

"I think that's what pisses him off even more," I said cockily. "I'm doing a better job of taking care of you than he is."

Her shoulders sank as she sighed, staring up at me.

"What?" I asked.

"Don't kill my father... Please?"

I smiled slowly. "I can't make any promises."

Her head lowered, but she didn't argue with me because she knew how the game went.

"How is your family?" she asked, changing the subject.

"The kids are good. Ma and Reese are going through it. My brother, Jeezy, got shot."

"I heard about that. One of my girls from the neighborhood he runs in told me. I heard he wasn't doing too good."

"He's not. They had to put him on a vent."

"Damn," Stacy sighed, giving more sympathy to Jeezy than I had been.

I was more so worried about Ma and Reese than anything. Day by day, Ma was crumbling, trying to hold on to faith that Jeezy would make it.

"What's wrong? Something's on your mind. I can tell," Stacy said. "And it ain't your brother."

I chuckled since Stacy knew me and Jeezy's history.

I needed a woman's opinion, so I was cool with opening up to Stacy. "Honestly?"

"Please," she said with a smile.

"I've been thinking about this woman I met a while ago."

I paused, waiting for Stacy's reaction. After a few months of me visiting and taking care of her after she was shot, I could sense that she was crushing on me. I was taking care of her and was the only man that was visiting her besides her father. Her kids' father had abandoned them the moment that she got pregnant with them. And though she was a beautiful woman, because of her condition and our situation, I would never take advantage of her feelings for me. She knew that, so she never spoke about her feelings. But I could sometimes sense some disappointment when I spoke of women.

I watched as she pushed past her feelings and nodded, insisting silently that I go on.

"I wanted to get up with her when I got out of jail, but when I bent down on her, she was with another nigga."

"And?" she pressed.

"I tried reaching out to her while I was locked up, and she never responded. When I saw her with that new nigga, I couldn't take the rejection."

"Why wouldn't she respond? What did you do?" she asked, giving me a knowing look.

"I fucked up," I admitted.

"So, you fucked up, *and* you were locked up and wasn't sure if you would beat your case. You expected her to sit at home and just wait for you?"

I thought for a second, knowing what the smart answer was. "Nah."

But honestly, the chemistry and bond between Zuri and I had convinced me otherwise. I just knew that she would wait on me; that once she was no longer upset that she would come back to me.

"She had feelings for you?" Stacy asked.

"She never said it, but I know she did. I felt it."

"But you know you have feelings for her, right?" she asked, leaning her head to the side.

"Yeah."

"Feelings strong enough to let her go without a fight?"

Her eyes were checking me. I pulled mine away from her just as Gabriella began to shout from the kitchen.

"Stacy, c'mon and eat now! It's been too long since you've eaten!"

Rolling her eyes, Stacy hissed, "I'm firing this bitch. She thinks she owns me."

I chuckled. "She's been taking care of you for years. She's like a mother to you."

"I got a mama. She's dead."

I shook my head and slowly stood. "C'mon. That shit smell good back there."

She looked up at me with eager eyes. "You're staying for dinner?"

"Yeah. I need a good meal before I catch this flight tonight."

Her eyes brightened. "Where you goin'?"

"Miami."

"*Oooo!*" she smiled. "That sounds fun."

As I followed Stacy through the house towards the kitchen, I listened to her go on and on about wanting to go on a vacation. I had assured her that she had been able to continue to do everything that she used to before I'd shot her and more, so she had been on vacation a few times. But it had been a while since she'd been on one without her kids.

I let her think that I was going there on vacation, but this trip was personal. I had purposely waited sometime before rolling up on Whit. I wanted her to get comfortable and think that I wasn't coming so that she would be vulnerable and waiting when I popped up on her ass.

CHAPTER 8
AANAN "LAW" WOODS

♫ 'Bout to go stupid again
She out the roof of the Benz
I'm 'bout to do her to get her
I'ma fuck two of her friends
Just made a flip off the wop
Fuck the Frank Mueller, I jump out the jeweler again ♫

I had had important business to attend to in Miami. However, a nigga had been locked away from the party for some time. So, when Ox suggested that we hit the strip club, I was game.

Ox and I were in VIP with naked bitches around us of all flavors and sizes twerking to "Stupid Again".

"Gawd damn, these bitches out here *pressure*, my nigga," Ox said, salivating at a beautiful bitch that was playing with her pussy in front of him as he rained a thunderstorm of bread on her.

I smiled, watching as his wife, Megan, was next to me, doing the same. Ox and Megan's look and energy reminded me a lot of Gucci Mane and Keyshia Ka'oir. Whenever they stepped out, they were always dripping in diamonds and high-end labels. And Megan always wanted them matching to a T. They were often photographed in the most expensive seats at sports events. Megan was perfect from head to toe. What had not been perfect naturally had been modified by the best doctors. Ox loved a redbone, so she was just that. But he was black as midnight and a big nigga. He had to be damn near two-eighty. But that shit was solid because he stayed in the gym.

Since he was now my right hand, I had been spending more time with Megan and Ox. I admired the way that they loved each other. She was his right hand in every way. She appeared to be the perfect spouse, with the mind of a hustla, the heart of a gangster, and the face of an angel. Unfortunately, spending time with them only made me think of Zuri even more. Megan and Ox's bond was a lot like me and Zuri's, so being around them had me craving my baby even more.

A thick, chocolate stallion walked in front of me. Her curves were so massive that they were obviously bought. But these hoes down here had been going to those doctors in the Dominican and Colombia that were more skilled than Bob the Builder. Ox had been right; these hoes down south was pressure. Everything about their bodies was exaggerated and perfection.

Yet, I knew Zuri had my soul when the stripper bent over in front of me, and her ass fell to the side, causing her pink pussy to open, and all I could think of was how much her appearance reminded me of Zuri. Zuri was just a more pure and natural form.

I still threw some money on her, adding to the carpet of bills at our feet.

I noticed Ox checking his phone. He was reading a text message. As he read it, his nostrils flared more and more.

"What's up?" I asked him.

Clicking his tongue, he locked the phone and tossed it in his lap. "That nigga, Vaughn, on dummy shit. His head don' got big. He too busy spending his bag instead of checking his crew. Them little motherfuckers out there acting up. They just killed somebody."

Scoffing, I shook my head. Vaughn was a hustla that I served out

West. He had been slowly getting money until recently. That nigga had scammed his way into a PPP loan and copped major weight with the bread a few months ago. Ever since, he had been wilding out and not being the boss that he needed to be. His crew was running amuck because the money was trickling down to them. It was getting to their heads, and his crew was much younger, so they were getting unruly.

"Them niggas supposed to be on corners, not shooting ma'fuckers."

"We gotta go holla at that nigga when we get back."

Nodding slowly, my phone rang, so I tapped on my AirPod and answered it.

"Yeah."

"What's up?" It was Persia.

"Out. What up?"

"Oh okay. I didn't want anything. Just wanted to talk to you before I went to bed. When you coming home?"

"Soon."

"Okay." Then she sighed. "I miss you."

"I'll holla at you."

She clicked her tongue. She wanted more, some loving sentiment that I didn't feel for her, and I wasn't about to stunt.

I hung up on the sudden tension.

Persia was cool, but she wasn't my soulmate. She didn't feel like the one. Before getting locked up, I wouldn't have known the fucking difference. Zuri had made me feel that highest level of admiration and need that a nigga could feel for another woman. That feeling was more addictive than drugs, and I was well aware when the next bitch wasn't giving me the same high.

ZURI TURNER

I stared up at Dom's beautiful brick house, hating the women's intuition that had sent me driving over there at nine in the morning the next day.

"Calm down, Zuri," I heard Bianca insist softly through my AirPod.

"I can't," I whined as I began to pace. "I'm telling you; something is wrong. He never came over last night, and he didn't call. That's not like him."

I hadn't known Dom for long, but he had been so consistent since I'd met him. So, when he hadn't shown up last night or answered any of my calls, I knew that something was wrong.

"Maybe he got drunk. You said it'd been a while since he went out with the guys. Maybe he went overboard," Bianca suggested.

That sounded plausible. I only wished that I believed that.

Something didn't feel right.

I stared at his house, gnawing on my bottom lip nervously. "He ain't so drunk that he isn't answering the door."

"You're over there?!" Bianca spat.

"Yes!"

"Girl, get your ass from over there," she gritted.

My arms flailed as I insisted, "I'm worried!"

Bianca groaned as if I was being fucking ridiculous. "Is his car in the driveway?"

"No," I answered reluctantly.

"Then why the fuck are you ringing the bell?" Bianca laughed. "Get your ass in the car before he catches you being a damn stalker."

I huffed and puffed, unable to get rid of the bad feeling in my gut. I could feel sweat beginning to pool on my forehead, between my thighs, and under my arms.

Pouting, I moped to my car. "I knew he was too fucking good to be true."

"Girl, stop trippin'. He could be anywhere."

"Yeah, anywhere in some bitch pussy."

Bianca laughed at my nerve. "Says the chick that's knocked up by some other nigga."

I pouted so hard that my bottom lip touched my chin. "That's probably why he's done fucking with me."

"Oh my God, girl. Get your shit together! Your pregnancy hormones are irritating."

As Bianca continued to fuss at me, I popped the locks and flung the driver's door open. I then plopped into the car, hating the sinking feeling in the pit of my stomach. I let Bianca rant as I turned the air conditioning up to the max. It was nearly ninety degrees that morning already.

Bianca was still calling me all kinds of stupid bitches for showing up at Dom's house. Yet, as she got in my ass, I still continued to stalk him. Dom was the only good thing in my life at the moment. Though I knew that he was too good to be true, I wasn't ready for the fantasy to end.

I went back to our text message thread to see if I had missed any messages.

I hadn't.

He still hadn't called me back either.

Desperate, I went to the Facebook app to stalk his page to see if he had posted anything on his timeline or story recently.

"You know what I'm sayin', girl?" I heard Bianca ask as I typed in Dom's name in the search bar on the app.

"Mmm humph," I grunted, though I hadn't heard a-, "Oh my God!" I had never heard my own voice riddled with so much pain.

"What's wrong?"

I stared at his page, rereading the barrage of posts over and over again that were flooding his timeline.

"No, no, no, no, no," I chanted in disbelief.

"*Zuri*!" Bianca shouted.

"*Nooooo*!" I screamed as tears immediately began to stream.

"Zuri, what's going on?!"

I could only cry as heartache washed over me. I leaned over, resting my head on the steering wheel as I sobbed.

"Are you still sitting in front of Dom's house?" Bianca asked.

Hearing his name made me begin to sob even louder and harder. My chest hurt so bad. I felt waves of nausea and lightheadedness crashing into me like violent waves.

"Zuri?" Bianca's voice was so soft and timid. "Talk to me, please."

I was getting too overwhelmed. I could feel myself getting sick. Thinking of my baby, I took deep breaths, trying to calm down.

"Zuri?"

"Yeah," I finally was able to say as I sat up.

"What's wrong? Why are you crying?" she asked.

Swallowing hard, I looked down at my phone, which was still in my hand.

"Dom is dead," I whispered in disbelief.

"What?! When? How?"

I began to scroll his page again, fingers trembling uncontrollably, continuous tears making it so hard for me to even see. "Most of the posts on his page are just condolences. I'm trying to look at the comments to see what the hell happened."

I finally saw a comment under one of the posts that had a link to an article.

Gasping, I told Bianca, "There is an article."

Hands shaking violently, I clicked on it and unknowingly began to read out loud. "Two were shot dead in a murder-suicide at Bar 72 lounge right before closing. Witnesses say that the four men had been at the establishment all night and were closing their tab when the woman, now identified as *Miesha Green*..." My eyes bulged as I sat straight up, and Bianca gasped. "... when the woman, now identified as Miesha Green, approached the three men from behind as they sat at the bar and began to fire. Dominic Samuels was killed immediately. Witnesses say that Miesha Green then turned the gun on herself, committing suicide. Investigators have reported that a search at Miesha Green's residence recovered evidence of Miesha's obsession with Dominic Green, which included words scrawled on the wall that read, 'I won't let you do this to me.'"

ZOEY TURNER

I moaned as my stomach began to turn. I was so hungry that I was becoming sick on my stomach.

I had fifty dollars to my name and needed all of those dollars to continue renting the room at that dirty-ass motel for as long as I could.

I couldn't ask any of my friends for money because I was too ornery to let them know that I was broke. Those bitches would have the whole internet talking about me, and I couldn't have that shit. My dumb ass had been up under Rashaad too much to meet any other niggas with some bread to get money out of, but I was on a hunt.

I couldn't live like this. I blamed Rashaad for ruining everything. He was supposed to be my sugar daddy, but that nigga wasn't anything but salt and headaches. Every time I asked him for some money, he asked me to be with him because all of his money was tied up by the Feds or with him trying to fight his case.

"Argh!" I groaned aloud as I jumped out of bed, feeling something crawling on my arm. "What the fuck?!"

I began to swipe repeatedly at my face and body, suddenly feeling as if bugs were crawling all over me. I used the light on the back of my phone to inspect the bed and saw a bed bug.

"This is fucking gross!"

Beginning to cry, I realized that I couldn't take this shit anymore. I got my phone off of the nightstand and called Zina. She was the only person in my family that had been reaching out to me besides my grandfather, who I was too ashamed to talk to.

"Hello?" Zina answered.

"Hey, Auntie," I pouted.

"Hey, boo. What's up? Are you crying?"

"Yes." Hearing her concern made me begin to bawl. I felt so helpless, especially after my mother had hung up in my face. I had never heard her sound so pissed. I knew that I had hurt her, but I thought her love for me would eventually soften that anger over time. Yet, two months later, it seemed as if her rage had only multiplied.

She was done with me.

"You okay?" Zina asked.

"No," I insisted. "This hotel is fucking disgusting, auntie. I need some money."

Sighing, Zina replied, "I told you that I couldn't afford to give you any money. Whatever I give you is only going to keep you in that raggedy motel another night."

I frowned, groaning.

"Just come stay with me, Zoey," Zina insisted. "You can have the basement. At least you'll be safe, and I ain't got no bugs," she tried to joke, but I didn't find anything funny. Hearing the silence from my end, Zina sighed. "Okay, sorry. But seriously, Zoey, just come stay with me until you find a job and can make it out here on your own. It's not safe there."

Hearing that only made my frown deepen. Staying in Zina's struggling ass house with all of her fucking kids was no better than this buginfested motel. Living with Zina would catapult me to a new low.

But I didn't have a choice.

AANAN "LAW" WOODS

That night, me, Ox, and Megan met up with one of the homies, Cookie, on Opalocka Boulevard in front of Crabman 305. Ox and I were sitting on the hood smashing some chicken and shrimp and crab rice when she pulled up in her Range Rover.

"That nigga, Law, free!" she sang as she threw her truck in park and hopped out.

I chuckled as she ran up to me and threw her arms around me. "What up, Cookie?"

"Hey. How you doin'?"

She sucked her teeth. "*Shiiiit*, I'm here. Can't complain."

Cookie was an OG who I supplied. She was bringing a lot of my product down to Miami, so Ox and I fucked with her heavy.

"Hey, Ox. Where is the misses?" Cookie asked.

"She in the restaurant getting some more food to go, with her phat ass."

Cookie laughed, gloating, "I told y'all this shit was good."

"Hell yeah," Ox nodded, finishing off his to-go tray.

Cookie then went into the backseat of her truck and pulled out a book bag. I sat my to-go tray on the hood of our rental and took it from her when she handed it to me. Opening it up, I saw a few hammers.

Laughing, I said, "Damn, Cookie, I'm not going to war. I only needed one."

She shrugged. "Aye, I was just making sure y'all was straight."

I laughed, pushing the bag of handguns behind me, and resumed killing my food. "Thanks, Cookie."

She, Ox, and I fell into some casual conversation as we waited for Megan to come out of the restaurant. The parking lot was cracking with other customers that were either waiting for their orders or were too impatient to get to a table, so were eating on and in their cars.

Fifteen minutes later, Megan came out of the restaurant with three to-go trays. Me and Ox hopped down off of the hood and got ready to roll.

"You need me to roll?" Cookie asked with a raised brow.

I chuckled at her old ass still being so willing to be a gangster. Cookie was in her mid-fifties, but she was still out here being a trap queen. I had heard that she was definitely a force to be reckoned with in these streets.

"Nah. This some personal shit. I don't need nobody else involved," I told her.

She nodded, giving up.

"You sure these straps are clean, right?" I pressed as I threw the bag in the car.

"Serial numbers filed off," Cookie said. "And they fresh. No bodies on them."

I nodded. "Well, there will be one now."

"This the crib?" I asked, looking up at the house on SW 83rd Avenue in Palmetto Bay.

"Yep. Cookie said she saw her coming out of here a few days ago, so this it," Megan said.

Looking up at the crib, I was thoroughly impressed with how Whit was living. The large house was sitting on an oversized corner lot, adorned with mature oaks and fruit trees. That shit looked almost majestic. Through the floor-to-ceiling windows, I could peer in and see the vaulted ceilings. The neighborhood looked so family-friendly. It probably had the best schools and parks. This shit was perfect for my kids, but she hadn't even called for them.

Since meeting Whit, she had never had this much initiative. I had made the money, found the cribs, and made the investments. She had never taken any initiative besides shopping and raising her kids. Which was why I hadn't trusted handing my properties over to her to begin with. I had faith that I would win my case, but if I hadn't, there was no way that I was going to sign my net worth over to her.

So, she took my shit.

Feeling my rage boiling over, I threw the driver's door open. "Let's do this shit."

Before I could climb out, I peeped a car approaching. We all sat back as it pulled into the driveway. We waited as a woman climbed out while keeping the car running. Peeping the bag of food in her hand, I figured she was an Uber Eats driver.

We all watched closely as she rang the bell. Then the door opened, and Whit appeared. Her smile was so bright that it could be seen all the way to the curb. She had not a care in the world while spending my fucking money.

I was fuming as Megan hissed, "This fucking bitch."

Megan was peering out of the back window, fuming at the mouth like a killer ready to attack.

Once the driver had gotten back to her car and pulled away from the house, Megan was already climbing out of the ride.

Laughing, me and Ox hopped out. Megan's short legs were damn near running up to the front door. As me and Ox met her on the stoop, she began to beat on the door like the police.

"Chill, bae," Ox told her.

She inhaled, nodded, and stepped back away from the door.

Suddenly, the door flew open, and Whit appeared. At first, she was pissed, as if she were expecting the Uber Driver. Then, she became baffled. She only saw Megan and Ox at first, so her eyes batted with confusion. I then forced my way between the two of them, revealing myself. She gasped and then tried to slam the door, but my body was in the doorway, and my massive hands were around her throat before she could shut it.

I could feel her esophagus crushing in my hands as she fought to get air in her lungs. I forced my way inside the house, dragging her along with me by the throat as I heard the door closing behind me. Once in the living room, I threw her stupid ass across the room, causing her body to crash against the glass coffee table. Shards of glass went everywhere as her body crashed onto the floor. She gasped for air, coughing violently.

Just as she caught her breath and was about to try to run, Megan pulled the hammer out from behind her waist, cocked it, and put it to her head.

"I just wanna know who helped you do this shit," I said calmly.

Whit glared up at me as if she despised me. There was so much hate in her eyes that I wondered what I had done to her to make her despise me this much. Sure, our relationship was dead, but we both had a hand in that. I hadn't made her stay, and she hadn't tried to leave. But many people have fucked up relationships. This level of deceit wasn't warranted, in my opinion. Yet, I still struggled to do this, knowing that I would be leaving my children without a mother, something that I never wanted to do to them.

"You gon' kill me, Law?" she asked, still fighting to catch her breath. "I've been with you for all these years, and I can't get this? I'm not worth this?"

"I would have given you anything you wanted," I told her. "I *did* give you anything you wanted. You never needed for anything. I was taking care of you."

"I wanted *more*. I didn't want to have to need you for shit. You wouldn't sign them over to me," she griped.

"Because I wasn't fucking convicted yet!"

Seeing the disgust in her eyes, I realized how she had been feeling for the past year. She wanted me to be in jail. She wanted me to lose that case. She didn't have the balls to leave me, but she didn't want anybody else to have me. So, to her, the best place for me was to be in jail.

I scoffed, shaking my head. "Who helped you, Whit? You know that nigga gotta die too, so who had the fake ID?"

"You really gonna kill me?" she asked with tears pooling in her eyes. Her face and limbs were bleeding from the shards of glass that had stabbed her skin during the fall. "You're never gonna get your money back if I'm dead."

Smiling, I told her, "My kids are gonna inherit those buildings and everything in your name if you're dead because you at least had sense enough to look out for them. And since they're under eighteen, I'll be the trustee of all of it... and your life insurance policies."

Gritting, her eyes lowered.

"One more chance: Who the fuck helped you, Whit?"

Defiantly, she kept her head lowered, not willing to snitch.

I looked over at Megan and simply nodded my head.

I turned, taking long strides towards the door just as the loud blast of the gunshot ricocheted amongst the walls surrounding us. I couldn't watch as Ox and Megan cleaned up the mess. I wasn't hurt that Whit was now dead. I was only hurt that my kids were now motherless, just as I had been. I had wanted more for them, which was why I had stayed with Whit all of these years. Obviously, she had thought that my presence was a curse, but it was really a blessing meant to make life better for our kids.

As I opened the door, my cell rang. I took it out of my pocket, saw that it was August, and answered, "What's up, son?"

"Dad, when are you coming back?" he rushed, sounding annoyed.

"What's wrong?"

"Grandma won't let me play Call of Duty because it's a school night."

"She's right." Approaching the rental, I leaned against the hood.

"But I did my homework. I wanna go home," he pouted.

"I'll be back in the morning."

"Okay," he said, sounding relieved.

"I'll talk to you later."

"Love you, Dad."

"Love you too, Son."

CHAPTER 9
RASHAAD TURNER

"Finally, Motherfucker," I grunted as I rushed to answer Will's call. I had been blowing his phone up for the last few days to get updates on my case. He had been distant since our last meeting, just like everyone else in my life. My friends and associates were dropping like flies. No one around me wanted to be associated with me or my case.

"Will, man, where you been?" I answered.

"Busy," he spat.

His tone made my eyebrows curl. He sounded like I was bothering him, rather than like I was the motherfucker paying him five-hundred dollars an hour to work my case.

However, I stopped myself from checking his ass because he was literally the only lawyer in my circle that was willing to take my case.

"I was just calling to get an update on my case. The next court date is coming up."

"There isn't an update," he scoffed with a cynical chuckle. "I told you to take the damn deal."

I stood from the bed in the hotel I had been staying in since leaving Zuri. I started to pace the carpeted floor. I was heated that Will was being so fucking nonchalant about my freedom.

"And I told you that I wasn't taking it," I said.

"You did." Then he took a deep breath. "That's why I can't take your case anymore."

"Are you fucking serious?" I barked.

"*Real* fucking serious. Your reputation is shit, and my other clients are threatening to stop doing business with me because of my association with you and this case."

Wincing, I begged, "*Will*, c'mon, man."

"I'm sorry, bro," he insisted. "I can't represent you."

"Will—" The dead end stopped my embarrassing groveling. I tore the phone from my ear and looked at it. He had hung up.

"Fuck!!!" I barked, throwing my phone across the room.

It hit the window, causing it to shatter. The many pieces of the screen hit the floor as I started to panic.

I paced, feeling my chest tighten as I fought to breathe.

My life was over.

With no one willing to take my case, I would be forced to work with a low-budget, inexperienced attorney who would tank my fucking case, giving me even more years than the prosecution was offering me.

"Fuck this." I stalked over to the dresser. I hadn't wanted to go this route. It was so fucking extreme, but with everyone turning their backs on me, I didn't have a fucking choice.

I retrieved the passport and cash from the drawer. I stuffed them into my back pocket. I then ensured that I had my cell and wallet. That was all that I was taking.

I rushed into the bathroom, flipped on the light, and found my razor and shaving creme. I went to work on shaving off my beard and mustache.

My hands were shaking. I couldn't believe that life had turned out this way. But I couldn't argue with God about it. I was reaping what I had sown. For years, I had taken away from my wife. I had hurt her and the women on the side that I played with. And God never gives it back how you give it. I didn't give a fuck about love, so he didn't get me back in that way.

He got me where it would hurt me the most, where it would crumble me: in my pockets and reputation.

But I wasn't going to just take this shit. If they wanted to give me time, they would have to find me.

ZURI TURNER

"Here are your discharge papers. Please take it easy. Because of your pregnancy, it is critical that you avoid any stress. You can have a stroke or lose your baby. It's important that you be very careful."

I scoffed, not seeing how I could avoid stress with the hand that life was dealing me.

The nurse looked at me with sympathy spilling from her eyes. I could barely look at her. Since learning of Dom's murder a few days ago, I had been a wreck. I hadn't known him long enough to be in love. I hadn't even been important enough in his life to be notified by any of his family of his murder. I had only met his best friend, who had hit me up on social media about Dom's death and funeral arrangements, once he remembered that no one else would have known to contact me. I was in utter shock that he was gone and that Miesha had done this. But honestly, my suffering was very selfish compared to his friends and loved ones that truly knew him.

I was so tired of dealing with the barrage of heartache and loss that I had run my blood pressure up sky high.

That morning, I had a prenatal appointment. My blood pressure was at stroke level, and my OBGYN had sent me to the emergency room.

"Here is your prescription for amlodipine. Please take it every day as prescribed and call your OB/GYN if you feel sick again."

I nodded weakly, feeling Bianca's sympathetic eyes on me. She was sitting close by, next to the bed, rubbing my leg soothingly.

The nurse pressed her lips into a line as she watched my sad eyes fight back tears. She laid a loving hand on my shoulder and then turned to leave the room.

"You want me to help you get dressed?" Bianca asked softly.

I thanked God for her. She had come to the emergency room with me since she had come to my prenatal appointment as well. She hadn't really left my side since I'd found out about Dom's murder.

"I got it." My voice was so weak that it was at a whisper.

I slowly threw my legs over the side of the bed and pulled myself out of it. Bianca jumped up to get my clothes from the closet and quickly brought them to me.

"Here you go," she said.

I hadn't needed her help, but she helped me into my maxi dress anyway.

"You're going to be okay," she tried to assure me as we dressed me.

"I'm sorry, but I don't believe that, Bianca," I scoffed. "Everything around me is crumbling. My daughter is a fucking whore. My husband is a whore and a criminal. Dom is gone. And, shit, the person that put the biggest smile on my face is locked up."

Bianca's eyes darted away from mine. She then lowered her head, pursing her lips together.

Then she took a deep breath, saying, "He isn't locked up, Zuri."

My eyes batted slowly. "Huh?"

"Law isn't locked up; he was released a few months ago."

Right then, even in my sadness, I felt relief and hope. I felt safe, and joy pierced through my pain. A small smile crept into my tears as I thought of him being free.

And that's when I knew I had been in love with Law and still very much was.

ANNAN "LAW" WOODS

After coming home from Miami, thoughts of Zuri were even more invasive. I couldn't think of anything else.

That afternoon, I finally drove over to her crib. This was going to be a challenge that I had to boss up, face, and win. Fighting for another chance with a woman had never been something that I had to do. Yet, DC's words kept replaying in my mind. I wasn't the type of weak ass nigga to let another man keep me from the woman that I wanted.

That afternoon, I was sitting a few feet away from her house in my trap car. I hadn't rung the bell because her car wasn't in the driveway. So, I sat, waiting for her to return from wherever she was so that I could get my woman.

Just as I was growing impatient, my phone rang.

"Hello?"

"Hey, Law."

I gritted, hearing the sadness in Ma's voice. She hadn't been the same since Jeezy got shot. She only pried herself away from the hospital to help me with the kids because being with them took her mind off of Jeezy. She had so much faith that he would survive, but it wasn't looking good.

"Hey, Ma. What's going on?"

"Have you heard from Whit?"

I scoffed. "You know she not gonna reach out to me."

"I know. Sorry. I shouldn't have asked. But the kids keep asking about her. I can tell that Willow really misses her."

I cringed. My kids were taking Whit's absence bad, but Willow was taking it the worse. She had been super clingy and irritable, and she constantly asked for her mother.

"I'm sure she's hiding from you too because she figures you will tell me where she is eventually."

"Probably."

Ox and Megan had gotten rid of any evidence and discarded her body in the woods. Yet, before leaving Whit's house, we made it look like a break-in. We had flown to Miami on fake IDs, and Whit hadn't had any cameras outside or inside of her spot. So, there was no evidence of us ever being there. Whit didn't have any family, except some distant relatives. She never knew her father, and her mom wasn't shit. She had been raised by the streets and lost contact with her mother a long time ago. So, no one would look for her. But since I was her next of kin on most of her paperwork, I had filed a missing person's report.

"I'm worried about her," Ma said with a sigh.

"Don't be. She's probably somewhere just spending all of my money." Then I changed the subject. "Any word on Jeezy?"

She sighed heavily. "Nothing has changed. They keep telling me that I might have to make a decision soon. But fuck these people."

"You do whatever you need to do so that you won't have regrets," I said.

"I plan to. I love you, son."

My eyes closed as I relished in that. She called me son so genuinely. It rolled off the tongue with ease. I truly appreciated it.

A cherry red Porsche truck drove by as I told her, "I love you too, Ma."

I sat up as the truck pulled into Zuri's driveway. I hung up, grabbing the doorway, ready to hop out. But Bianca hopped out of the driver's seat instead. I froze, waiting to see if Zuri was with her. Just as Bianca rounded the truck, the passenger door opened. Bianca hurried to the opened door. Then a thick thigh eased out of the truck. Bianca assisted the other woman out. My breath hitched when I saw Zuri's wild afro as Bianca helped her out of the truck.

I licked my lips as I sat back, taking in the sight of her. She was beyond beautiful. She took my fucking breath away.

Just as I was ready to hop out, she placed her hand on her stomach, which caused her maxi dress to hug a pudge that was sticking out of her midsection.

I stopped breathing.

She walked slowly as if she was weak, but her hand lovingly rubbed her protruding belly.

She's pregnant.

She looked to be nearly five or six months.

I had never felt so sick. I had never had my heartbroken. I was the one that broke hearts. But I was sure that the pain in my chest that felt like death was heartbreak.

No wonder she never replied to my letter.

My stomach turned. I gritted, closing my eyes, unable to see that shit anymore.

I scoffed, looking away. I started the engine with a heavy heart. Yet, before I could even dwell on the shit, my phone rang.

Tapping my AirPods, I answered as I sped off, "What up?"

"What up, bro?" Ox replied.

"What's going on?"

"You good?" he asked.

"Yeah."

"You don't sound like it."

"I am. What's up?"

"We gotta go holla at Vaughn. This shit don' got out of hand quick. They at war over there, killing motherfuckers left and right. The police heavy over there, fucking up the money."

"I'm on my way."

I was quiet as fuck on the way to Vaughn's spot out West. I could feel Ox watching me curiously. I couldn't believe that a woman had me in my bag like this, but I was definitely feeling some type of way. Besides my feelings for her, I had never had an issue getting what was mine. However, every time a nigga bossed up to go get her, it was something in my way. I was starting to feel like maybe Zuri wasn't mine after all.

Vaughn was obviously surprised to see us when he opened the door. He was a nigga that Ox had started supplying to while I was locked up, so we weren't acquainted. I had only met him when we met up with the crew to let them know that I was back.

"What up?" he asked nervously as he let us in. "You want a drink or something, my nigga?"

"Nah, this ain't no social visit," I spat.

Immediately, his body stiffened as he led us into his spot. I looked around to ensure none of his hitters was inside with him.

"What up?" he asked as he plopped down on the couch.

"What's this I hear about all the shootings and shit over here?" I asked, standing over him.

He chuckled. "Man, you know how it is with these trigger-happy niggas, especially when they start getting money."

"But it's your crew, right?" I pressed.

He shrugged. "Yeah, they got beef with some niggas a few blocks up."

"Handle that shit."

He looked up at me, arching a brow. "Nigga, I sell drugs. I ain't in that."

Ox's guard went up as he sat next to me.

"You in it, bitch, if these niggas making money off your product," I told him.

His eyes blinked slowly. "Bitch?"

My jaw tightened. "Bat another eye, and I will beat the fuck outta you."

"Aye, my nigga—"

Before I knew it, I was caving that niggas jaw in. My fist dove into the side of his face. His head whipped to the side as his body flew backward, causing the couch to crash onto the floor. Before I knew it, I was stomping that nigga's chest into the ground.

"Yo', yo', yo', yo', yo'," Ox chanted, holding me back. "You proved your point. You gon' kill the nigga."

Vaughn was fighting for air and scowling in pain. His nose was *leaking*.

Glaring down on him, I warned him, "Motherfucka, handle your business before you have to find another connect. Handle whoever the issue is before I handle you." Then I made an about-face and stalked out of the trap.

I could feel Ox on my heels as I jogged down the steps.

"I'mma ask you one more time, are you good, bro," I heard him say.

I could only grimace, nostrils flaring as I took large, heavy steps towards my trap car that was parked at the curb.

I wasn't okay, but I couldn't tell Ox that shit. I didn't know how to say that a woman that I barely knew had broken a nigga's heart.

I'd been on edge the rest of the day. I was restless, anger brewing. I drove around the city; visions of Zuri's baby bump twerking in my fucking head. I needed to take my frustrations out on somebody.

Hours later, I found myself creeping through Vaughn's backdoor. I had learned to masterfully pick locks when I was hitting cribs at eleven and twelve years old. My hammer was in my hand, trigger finger ready, as I crept through the dark trap house.

I could hear Vaughn's gloating in the living room where I had just stomped his ass out in a few hours before.

"Swear to God, my nigga, I'm killin' that motherfucka. Coming in here like he run shit."

His call was on speaker. As I crept up the hallway, I could hear the person on the phone saying, "Well, the nigga *do* run shit," with a chuckle.

"Fuck you, dawg!"

"The nigga got a point. Your crew outta hand. You gotta teach them lil' niggas how to get money in silence. All that trigger happy shit they on is stopping the money. The police steady in the hood. I had to pull my corner boys off the street."

Once up the hall, I leaned against the entryway, watching Vaughn pace the floor, smoking a blunt. His face was swollen and black and blue. The nigga was so goofy that his guard was down in his own trap house.

"I feel all that shit. But ain't no nigga comin' in my shit telling me what the fuck to do with my —" His words lodged in his throat as he finally noticed me in the entryway.

An evil smile slowly crept through my beard as I aimed at his head. Instantly, panic covered his face. I was pulling the trigger just as he started to plead. "Bro, I—" The bullet split his forehead open. His eyes widened with fear on impact as his head flew back, and his body slumped to the floor with a hard thud.

"Bro, what the fuck?!" the person on the other line was calling for him. Vaughn's hand was still gripping the phone. "Bro? Vaughn?"

I sighed, finally feeling some relief. My footsteps were heavy, accompanied by the gurgling sounds of Vaughn fighting for air. I looked back, peering up the hall towards his body. His eyes ballooned towards the ceiling as blood suffocated him. I waited until he finally succumbed to death and then continued to creep out of the house. Yet, as I stepped into the night, the relief was short-lived. I still felt the irritable stinging pain in my heart that I was so unfamiliar with.

CHAPTER 10
ZURI TURNER

Dom's funeral was devastating. It was already so heart-wrenching that he had lost his life at such a young age, but to lose it so violently at the hands of someone else was crushing for everyone in attendance.

Bianca had come with me to ensure that I remained as calm as possible. She was so scared that I would cry myself back into the emergency room. However, I had been able to hold it together. Once at the funeral, I saw the pain of those related to him, his close friends, and more loved ones who had known him for much longer than I had. I felt unworthy of the sadness that I felt. I had only known him for a few months, when they had known him for a lifetime. I wasn't even valid enough in his life to be listed as a "special friend" in the obituary.

By the end of the ceremony, I was able to have an appreciation of ever knowing him and for God giving me him for the short time that He had. I was able to say goodbye to him with happiness in my heart during the last viewing and thank him for putting a smile on my face during the most trying time of my life.

"Do you want to go to the burial?" Bianca asked, holding my hand as we walked out of the church.

It was nearing the end of September, but it was still beautiful outside. Global warming had Chicago staying warmer later in the year. The sun was beaming, making the atmosphere beautiful on such a dreadful day.

"No, I don't think so," I said with a long sigh. "I don't want to see him being put in the ground."

I would have preferred remembering how I had seen him last, kissing me and smiling into my eyes, except for in a casket. But I forced myself to. He was so handsome as he lay there on the white satin pillow. He was impeccably dressed in a fitted suit. His expensive jewelry adorned his neck and wrists. His skin was still as smooth and chocolate as it had always been. Someone had ensured that his locs were styled regally in a high bun, and he was lined up to a crisp. He was so beautiful in that casket that it looked as if he were sleeping.

"Okay," Bianca said with a small smile.

We then started to make our way to my truck.

"I'm so hungry," I groaned.

"Your fat ass is always hungry."

I chuckled softly. I would have laughed louder, but the doom over the day weighed on it. Yet, I had no argument for her. I was now six months pregnant. Being pregnant at this age was much different than being pregnant as a teenager. Back then, I barely felt any symptoms and had all the energy in the world. Now, I could barely walk for too long without back pain and becoming winded. And I was *always* hungry.

"Excuse me..."

Me and Bianca turned towards the voice that was behind us that sounded as if they were trying to get our attention.

There was a brown-skinned woman approaching us hastily. She was beautiful, even with the tears in her eyes and a stern look on her face.

"Are you Zuri?"

"Yes," I answered curiously.

"I thought it was you." Then her stern look became menacing.

"You were the only person in there that I had never seen before but had the nerve to be just as sad as the people that actually knew him."

"Aye!" Bianca instantly stepped in between us, causing me to hold my stomach, shielding it from the impact of her pushing me aside.

The woman looked down at my stomach and gasped. "Is that why he put your name on the insurance policy?" she spit with narrowed eyes.

"Wh-what are you talking about?" I stuttered as Bianca's eyes bucked and looked back at me.

"My brother made you the beneficiary of his insurance policy, and after asking his friends, I found out that you are some chick—"

"Watch your fucking mouth," Bianca gritted.

"I'm just trying to understand why my brother left his insurance policy to a woman that he doesn't even fucking know!"

"Well, clearly, he knew me well enough to make sure that I was taken care of." I was trying to gloat and stand my ground, but the fluttering in my heart was making my words breathy.

"He didn't even know you well enough to tell his family about you. Hell, I couldn't even get in touch with you to tell you about the policy. So, me and our parents had to pay for the fucking services out of our own pockets. We already struggling."

"I didn't know that he had done that, and maybe he hadn't told me because he didn't plan to be murdered, so excuse him for not being more organized."

His sister's eyes narrowed. As she took a step towards me, I prepared myself to drill this hoe, pregnant or not. Yet, Bianca was already pushing her back.

"Is that even his baby, bitch?" the sister spit.

Funeral attendees walked by us on the way to their vehicles, gawking at us and my belly.

"I'm really trying to spare you because this is your brother's funeral," Bianca warned as she stood toe-to-toe with this bitch. "But I strongly suggest that you back the fuck up before you get dragged out here."

Gnawing on her bottom lip, the woman glared at me. "I'll be in touch. I'm not letting you get that money. My parents deserve it, not you."

She then spun on her heels, stomping back towards the church.

I sighed with relief, but wonder and disbelief had my breathes short.

"Let's get the fuck up outta here," Bianca said with a slick smile on her face as she looped her arm with mine. We then hurried towards my truck, which was a few feet away. I popped the locks and rushed to the driver's side. Me and Bianca climbed in at the same time, and as soon as we slammed our doors, we started to freak out.

"*Biiiiitch!*" Bianca screamed.

"Oh. My. God!!!!" I shouted with tears of joy in my eyes.

"Damn, what kind of pussy was you putting on that nigga?" Bianca asked.

I shrugged as I started the engine. "I don't know."

"How much do you think it is?"

"I have no idea. We never talked about it," I said, blinking slowly as I pulled off.

I gripped the steering wheel tightly, excitement causing my body to become rigid as I drove.

It wasn't the money that I was happy about. It was the fact that Dom thought of me *that* much.

Dom *truly* loved me, and I would cherish that love for the rest of my life.

ANNAN "LAW" WOODS

♫ *We pop out with them Glocks out, now everybody got switches*
I don't talk about what we talk about, I don't want everybody in my business
I done told the truth about bro'nem, now everybody in they feelings
She done set the standards for the bad bitches, now everybody got titties ♫

I wasn't in any better of a mood the next week, but I forced myself to realize that I had lost Zuri. I put all of my attention on now being a full-time dad, getting money, and Persia.

That day, I was taking her downtown. She wanted to get dressed up and go to a fancy steakhouse because her birthday was coming up. She wanted to start celebrating early. She had always been one of those people that celebrated their birthday all month. So, we made reservations at Steak 48. I threw on a pair of fitted black jeans, Givenchy black leather loafers, and an all-black Givenchy short-sleeved tee. Normally, I kept the jewelry to a minimum because these lil' young hittas weren't to be trusted in the streets. But since we were going out of the city limits, I draped my neck and wrists with a diamond cut Cuban link and bracelet and iced out Rolex.

As I road through the city with "No Interviews" blasting in the Bentley, I spotted a detective car and sat straight up.

Peering at it as the driver's door swung open, I grinned devilishly. "This motherfucka."

I slowed my ride to a slow crawl as I approached the car on my passenger side. I rolled the window down and honked the horn, which got Detective Payne's attention. He peered into the passenger side window as I inched the car passed him. As we made eye contact, I winked and kept riding.

Looking in my rear-view mirror, I saw him standing next to the detective car, glaring at my ride as I sailed through a green light. I thought he would hop into his car and chase me, but his fat ass just continued across the street to Marlon's Chicken.

Whit and Vaughn had taken precedent over taking care of that bitch ass nigga. But he was next.

"You look nice."

Persia smiled up at me, batting her mink lashes. "Thank you."

I wasn't just blowing smoke. She did, indeed, look beautiful in the floral tube top and matching flowing maxi skirt that swept the floor. I usually only saw her in skimpy clothes that she walked around the house in or loungewear because we were usually kicking it in bars or casual restaurants. That night she looked nearly angelic. But those curves had the flowers on the chiffon dancing uncontrollably as she tipped around the house in her five-inch heels, gathering her purse and keys.

I stood in her large living room, admiring how the skirt sat up on all that ass. Persia's hustles had afforded her a nice crib in the Kenwood neighborhood.

"You ready?" she asked, blushing under my eyesight. I was still admiring how pretty she looked.

"Don't start," she warned with a grin.

Since finding out that Zuri was pregnant, I had been taking my frustrations out on that pussy. Every time I was around Persia, I had been drillin' her ass.

Chuckling, I mentally told my dick to chill and then told her, "Let's ride."

I guided her out of the door of her crib by the small of her back. The weather was starting to cool, so it was a brisk sixty degrees.

"You think you gon' need a jacket?" I asked her.

"It feels okay out."

"But we're going downtown," I reminded her. "You know it's cooler there since it's by the water."

We both stopped on the steps as she contemplated. As she turned to go back into the house, the flashing of many red and blue lights caught our attention,

My head whipped around as my heart instantly beat uncontrollably. Since Detective Payne's obsession started years ago, I had been hounded with those fucking lights. The last time I had, I had been arrested.

PTSD ran rampant. Alarm shot through me, especially since I had my hammer on me. Persia looked towards me, chest caving as the squad cars stopped in front of her house. I thought back at how I had just taunted Detective Payne not even an hour ago.

Two officers jumped out of each of the three squad cars and rushed towards Persia's crib. I stopped breathing, wondering what the fuck Detective Payne had pinned on me now.

The possibilities were endless.

I swallowed hard, refusing to cower in front of them or Persia. Whatever it was this time, I would beat it like I had every other charge that I had been both guilty and not guilty of.

"Persia Mitchell?"

My head whipped towards her as the arresting officer questioned Persia with his cuffs in hand.

She sucked her teeth, rolling her eyes. My head tilted as I saw no surprise in her eyes that they knew her name.

"Yeah?" she spit.

"You're under arrest. You have the right to remain silent—"

She groaned, turning around, giving the arresting officer her wrists. My brows rose at how she had so easily let them arrest her.

"What is she being arrested for?" I asked calmly to keep from drawing their attention to me.

I watched as Persia coolly allowed the arresting officer to walk her down the stairs. The many officers followed, all except one, who I recognized from patrolling my hood often.

"She has a warrant for her arrest," she told me.

My head jerked back with surprise. "For what?"

"Credit card fraud. It's been a warrant out for her arrest for a year. She's facing a lot of time. She had a whole fraud operation that she headed for a while." The officer gave me a sympathetic look as she stared up at me. "Get her a good lawyer."

ZOEY TURNER

Taking a deep breath, I inched into my aunt's small room.

Since moving in with her, I felt as if I was finally at the lowest point in my life. I had gone from five-star steak houses to sharing a frozen Home Run Inn pizza with my cousins. I was no longer sleeping on signature, expensive sheets in a king bed. I was now on a pullout couch in Zina's dusty ass basement.

"Auntie, let me get a few dollars?"

It burned me to even have to ask, but I was now broke. I didn't have a dollar to my name.

"What's a few?" she asked with a raised brow.

I shrugged. "Like a hundred."

Zina started to cackle. My eyes rolled as I toyed with the many perfume bottles on her dresser.

"Girl, a hundred dollars!?" she laughed. "What the fuck makes you think that I got it like that?"

I smacked my lips, unable to take her seriously. My aunt had four kids and hadn't been working since she was about six months pregnant. Though she was staying in Englewood in a single-family home that badly needed to be renovated and redecorated, she was able to somehow pay her rent and bills. So, I was sick of her always acting broke.

"I'm sorry, auntie," I sighed. "I'm just hungry."

"And I'm sure your bougie pallet is used to fried lobster tails and Tomahawk steaks."

The sound of that had my mouth watering.

"But I got some lobster tails in the freezer and some fish fry in the cabinet. Take your saditty ass on in there and make you something to eat," Zina laughed.

I glared at her as she bounced her baby while she breastfed, sitting cross-legged on the bed.

"I'm going out with my friends," I lied.

In actuality, I was feening for a night out. I wanted to hit up a club and try to bump into a few rich niggas so that I could get the fuck up outta here. I had to start thinking like the rest of these thirsty hoes out here. I needed a nigga to finance me pronto.

"Ain't your friends at college, where you should be?" Zina taunted me.

"I'm going out with my friends that didn't go to college, auntie," I mumbled.

She stared at me with a smirk.

"Please?" I begged.

"I ain't got a hundred dollars."

"Anything?" I pressed.

Smacking her lips, she replied, "Fine. I'll send you forty dollars..."

That pitiful amount made my stomach turn.

"I'll Cash App you," she continued while I tried to look appreciative. "But you need to get a job. I told you when you moved in that you would have to pitch in. What you plan on doing with yourself since you ain't going to school?"

"I told you I want to be an influencer—"

"Girl!" she bellowed. "You got a thousand followers. Fuck outta here. Get a fucking job!"

I clung to my composure. I wanted to smack the shit out of her broke ass. But instead, I laughed along with her, grimacing on the inside.

TWO MONTHS LATER

CHAPTER 11
ZURI TURNER

"**B**riana, get your sister!" Zadah shouted.

I groaned, irritated already by Zadah's presence. She could have coughed, and it would have gotten on my nerves just the same. She and I had barely been talking since her outburst about my business a few months ago. She was a messy bitch, and I couldn't believe that I was related to her.

"*Whyyyy?*" my niece whined. "I'm doing something."

I scoffed lowly, seeing a spitting image of Zadah's attitude in her oldest daughter.

"On the fucking phone that I pay for, right? So, get your ass up!" Zadah snapped from the dining room table.

Briana groaned, but she stood and did as her mother told her to, stopping her little sister, Chanel, from destroying my father's photo albums under the coffee table.

"Come on, Zuri! We're ready!"

Hearing Zina in the kitchen, I smiled nervously. I stood, feeling the weight of my expanding belly on my back. I was now eight months. Every day, it amazed me how big my stomach was getting. I had a beautiful baby shower a couple of weeks ago. I had preferred a small, private shower because everyone was under the impression that I was having a baby by my ex-husband, who was still in hiding from the FBI. Trying to reduce the stress of dealing with that and mourning Dom was difficult enough, and my OB/GYN was still concerned about my constant high blood pressure. So, I wasn't about to be stressed out at my own shower because I was answering questions about my "baby's daddy". Zadah wasn't invited, of course. Nor was Zoey, which made the day still very stressful.

Dom's sister, Robyn, also had the nerve to be trying to sue me for the insurance money. I had been planning on giving her parents the three-hundred thousand dollars as soon as the payment was released. But when Robyn sued me, I didn't, just to be ornery. She was accusing me of forging the documents somehow or scamming her brother into making the policy with a false claim that I was having his child. Of course, none of that could be proven until I had my baby, which would only prove her point that my baby wasn't his. So, I was struggling with fighting the case out of stubbornness or doing the nice thing that I had planned by giving it to his parents.

Since things had been so crazy, I had been waiting until only my family was around to have the gender reveal. I had allowed Zina to construct the reveal, so I waddled as fast as I could out of the living room. The kids had heard Zina, so all of them hurried out of the various rooms that they were in, in my father's house, and followed me. Along the way, my mouth watered at the smell of yams, collard greens, and a fried turkey. My father had cooked it all, amongst other things. But we weren't going to start eating Thanksgiving dinner until after the reveal.

"What do you want to have, Auntie Zuri?" Justice asked as she held her brother, Tremere.

I smiled bashfully as we all left out the opened sliding patio door. "I'm hoping it's a boy, but I'll be happy either way."

"I want it to be a boy so Tremere will have a cousin close to his age," Zina gushed as she stood on the deck.

I blushed. "Yeah, that would be nice."

Looking behind me, I saw Treyvon and Zadah standing behind, near the patio door.

Good. I want that bitch as far away from my happiness as possible.

I didn't want anything to do with Treyvon and Zina's scandal. So, I asked very few questions. But I was the only one who knew, so sometimes Zina confided in me. She had told me that Treyvon spent a lot of time at her house with the baby. He wanted to spend so much time with him that it was becoming hard to keep him away while the kids and Zoey were home. He had kept his promise by taking care of her as long as she kept the secret.

"Okay, so Daddy is going to throw you a baseball. When you hit it, it will explode and show pink or blue." As Zina explained it to me, she handed me a wooden bat. "And hurry up because we hungry."

Everyone laughed and agreed as I took the bat. "Ain't nobody hungrier than me, trust."

I followed Daddy down the steps and into the backyard. I got teary-eyed as Daddy and I positioned ourselves in the grass. This should have been Dom throwing the ball or whoever the father of this child was. I had already had one child under scrutiny and judgment, and now I was having another under the same shame.

I swallowed my disgrace and fought the tears.

"Batter up!" my dad shouted.

I positioned myself in a batter's stance. "Daddy, don't throw the ball too hard."

"I got you, sweetie," he smiled.

"It's a *boooooy*!" Zina sung.

"It's a girl," I heard Justice respond.

Then all of my nieces and nephews started to shout what they wanted the baby to be as Daddy threw the ball.

Swinging, I missed.

We all laughed as Jerell ran to get the ball and then threw it back to Daddy.

"A'ight, now. C'mon, Zuri. We're hungry," Daddy said.

"Okay, okay," I chanted, taking a deep breath.

This time, Daddy threw it straight to me, and I was able to swing and hit it. On impact, it exploded with blue dust.

The backyard went up in cheers as I threw my hands over my face and began sobbing. There were so many different emotions mixed with those tears. This baby was the light in a very dark time in my life, but I wished that I was giving him a father that would be there for him. Yet, I quickly recalled that yearning to do that had led Zoey down a dark path. I had to be prepared to love this child enough for me and its father. That would have to be enough.

If Rashaad was his father, he would basically be fatherless.

Even though I now knew that Law was out of jail, I still didn't trust my heart to reach out to him. I had fallen in love with him, but I had no idea who he was outside of that small room we had spent so much time in. He was very much a dangerous man that was deep in the streets. After ruining Zoey, I wanted to be even more careful with the decisions I made regarding this child. I could no longer think with my heart; I had to think with my head.

"Oh!" I exclaimed, feeling a popping sensation in my cervix, followed by a gush of liquid that ran down my legs.

My father hurried toward me. "Zuri, you okay?"

"I-I-I," I stammered as I tried to look between my legs. Yet, my stomach was way too big.

"*Eeew*, Auntie Zuri peed on herself," Chanel said.

"No, she didn't," Zina hushed him. "Her water broke."

My Daddy rushed towards me, and my eyes darted at him, panicking.

"It's okay," he quickly assured me.

"It's early, Daddy," I began to cry.

"That's all right," he softly convinced me.

I was fighting to catch my breath, to calm down. "Is it water or blood?"

He looked down, and relief came over him. "It's not blood."

"Okay," I sighed with relief. But, still, I was going into labor a few weeks early, so I was still in disarray. Considering the stress that I had been in for my entire pregnancy, I prayed that my baby would be okay.

AANAN "LAW" WOODS

I had hoped to spend that Thanksgiving eating a spread at Ma's dinner table. Yet, unfortunately, my family was spending it saying our good-byes to Jeezy.

Time had run out. There was nothing else that the doctors could do for him. He was now in septic shock, and it was time to pull the plug.

I was sitting next to Ma, holding her hand as she held Jeezy's with the other. Shay was behind me with her arm around Reese. We had left the kids with a sitter.

As I heard tears being shed around me, I wished that I was as sorrowful of his death so that I wouldn't look so cold. However, I had no tears for Jeezy. He had been an asshole his whole life and wreaked havoc in Ma's life. He'd caused her more headaches than pride. So, as I sat there comforting her, I felt relief for her that she could finally stop worrying about what he would do next to stress her out. She no longer had to worry if he would die in the streets or be locked away for the rest of his life. She could have comfort in knowing that he would die peacefully with his loved ones.

"I love you, Jeezy," she whimpered. "I love you so much."

I flinched, hearing the heartbreak in her words. I switched hands that held hers so that I could put my arm around her.

Heavy footsteps entered the room, making us all cringe. We peered up at the doctor with hesitation.

Pressing his lips together in a thin regretful line, he said, "It's time. Are you ready?"

My mother began to sob, weeping out loud, her body doubling over.

Reese's sighing could be heard behind me.

So, I spoke up. "We're ready."

Ma clung to my hand so tightly as the doctor inched towards the machines that were keeping him alive.

"First, I'm going to disconnect the supportive medication. But I will continue the meds that keep him comfortable. Then I'm going to disconnect the vent, and he will be gone." The doctor then began to slowly move about the room, turning off the machines that were helping Jeezy live.

Ma's body was trembling as she rocked back and forth. I cringed every time she wept and felt useless. I had always protected her from everything. But this I couldn't shield her from. Only time could heal her, and even then, she would never be the same.

❦

Though my family was suffering, I was at peace. Jeezy and I had never had a relationship, and he had caused me more stress than brotherly love. Whit nor Vaughn's murder had made headlines, and DC had told me that there were no leads on their murder cases. There were only two things still weighing over my head, and as I sat on Detective Payne's couch, I was ready to rid my stress of one.

I groaned as my cell started to ring again. It was another unknown number. I knew that it was Persia calling from lockup since the unknown numbers had only started an hour after she was arrested. I wanted nothing else to do with her. She knew that because of my hustle, I couldn't be around any additional illegal shit, especially without knowing. She had put me at risk of getting locked up again, so she was dead to me.

Just then, I heard the front door notification on Detective Payne's alarm. Yet, I remained cool, watching the front door in the darkness.

He was clueless as he walked into his house. He stepped out of the foyer into the living room, flipping on the light.

He gasped, seeing the large figure on his couch. He then instantly reached for his gun in his back.

"Don't do it," I warned him, pointing my hammer at him.

He froze, abandoning his pursuit for his pistol. "Kill me, motherfucka."

"You deserve that, don't you?" I smiled wickedly. "You've been causing chaos in my family for years, arresting me over bullshit, planting evidence on me. You deserve for me to kill you. I should have years ago. It would have saved me a lot of headaches."

The biggest headache was meeting Zuri. Had I never gone to prison, I wouldn't have this ache in my heart for her. For that alone, this motherfucker deserved to die the most heinous death.

"Then do it then, nigga," he gritted.

I stood slowly. His eyes enlarged, but he tried to play it cool.

I chuckled, walking towards him, still aiming my hammer at his head. "Nah. You've been playing with me all this time. It's your turn to look around every corner for me. You won't see this shit coming."

I then brushed by him. I kept my eyes on him to ensure that he wasn't going for his gun. Walking backward, I left out of the house. I watched as he slowly turned around, but he never went for his gun as I slammed the door.

I trotted down the stairs with a smile on my face. I had parked two blocks away so that he wouldn't see my ride. Therefore, I strolled down the block, looking at the time descend on the timer I had set on my phone.

I watched it as it counted down with each step that I took. And since I knew what was coming, I didn't flinch when there was an explosion behind me. But I did turn to watch Detective Payne's house explode and go up in violent flames.

RASHAAD TURNER

"Que quieres, papi?" ("What do you want, Daddy?")

Luckily, I was fluent in Spanish, so I knew what she was saying and was able to respond. "Quiero que te sientes en esta polla mientras te come el coño." (I want you to sit on this dick while she eats your pussy.)

Her eyes widened with delight as she looked back at the other woman that was in the room with us. They giggled like schoolgirls while inching towards the bed.

I licked my lips, dick hardening at how eager they were to please me.

Being in Colombia for the last few months had been the best time of my fucking life. I had always heard that Colombia was full of beautiful women that fought for the attention of American men. That shit was true as fuck. I had been buying pussy for the price of a full gas tank back at home. I couldn't believe that I had been spending so much money on those ungrateful hoes back at home when these women were so cheap, beautiful, willing, and submissive.

"*Sssss*," I moaned as the one who took the instruction sat on my dick. Her pussy was so tight that I feared that she would slide the condom off as she bounced on it.

The other tanned, voluptuous beauty climbed into the bed and stuck her face between the other's legs. The one riding me opened her legs wider as she bounced on my dick, giving her friend access. The other eagerly started to suck her friend's pussy. The sight of their natural, radiant, modelesque beauty had my dick oozing with precum.

This was one of many sexual escapades I had had since running to Colombia. I had been able to afford any fantasy I had ever dreamed of; foursomes, orgies, and bitches worshipping my dick. They did anything that I paid them to do without any defiance.

I had been able to run away with the cash that I had stashed away. Two hundred thousand dollars had purchased me a home in Bucaramanga, where I had intended on hiding out for the rest of my life if I could.

With so much focus on hiding from the Feds, I had had little time to think of Zuri or Zoey. And now that I had been immersed with so much beauty, I wondered what the fuck I had been doing buying their affection. Most of the reason that I had stolen all of that money was to ensure their dedication like a fucking idiot. But looking at the women in my bed made Zuri and Zoey look like mortals, peons, average women that caused me nothing but headaches.

A MONTH LATER

CHAPTER 12
ZOEY TURNER

I was lying in the basement, staring at the walls. Zina's kids were running so rampant upstairs that they sounded like they were about to come through the fucking floor.

"*Arrrrgh*," I groaned, throwing the covers over my head.

Over the last month, I hadn't come up with a plan at all. I had been trying to up my followers by posting more risqué pictures on my profiles, but they had only awarded me creepy niggas in my inbox.

Looking for a job was not an option. There were too many people in this city that knew me. I wasn't about to work some fast-food job or in the mall so that someone could see me and tell everyone that I had fallen off.

The more I struggled, the more I felt that I wanted to call my mother and grovel. But it was apparent that that wasn't an option either. I had thought when she had the baby, she would reach out to me since I had a new sibling. She hadn't sent as much as a text message, however.

When my phone rang, I peered from under the covers. I reached for it and answered without looking at the screen to see who was calling.

"Hello?"

"Hey, Zuri!"

I grimaced quietly. "What's up, Ashley?"

"You comin' out tonight?"

Ashley and Brit had been trying to get me out ever since she, Brit, and Dior had come home for winter break. I couldn't let them see me like this, though. My hair wasn't done. I had sold a lot of my expensive clothes and accessories on apps like Poshmark and Offer Up to have some money in my pocket. My high-end labels had now been replaced with outfits from Marshalls and Discovery. I made that shit look good as fuck, but Ashley and Brit would sniff out the poverty in the cheap material as soon as they saw me.

"I don't know. I'll see. My guy is supposed to be flying me out to Cancun tonight as a Christmas present."

"Oh okay! That's *niiiice*," Ashley gushed. "No wonder you ain't in school. You got niggas taking care of you."

"Girl, fuck these niggas. I'm on my entrepreneur shit."

"Well, we miss you. Dior is coming out too. You should come."

I snarled. I hadn't been fucking with Dior since I moved out the night of the home invasion. I hadn't forgotten how she had started to act funky with me. I knew that once you live with someone, tensions increase because you're in each other's space. But I felt as if she were treating me like I was beneath her because I was relying on her.

"That's what's up. I'll let you know if I'm free to come out. I'll call you back, though. I'm walking into the Louie store."

"Okay, girl."

I hung up, groaning. Fronting like I was still a rich bitch to my friends and on social media had been exhausting. But telling my truth would be more painful, so I kept up the charade.

Laying there in the quiet, I could hear the lively sounds of Friday night outside of the window. It was December, but the weather was still cooperating. It was only about fifty degrees at night, which felt like summer to Chicago, considering it was December. Plus, it was the Friday before Christmas Eve, so the streets were busy.

"Fuck this shit."

I was so sick of being a loser. I threw the covers off of my head and my body off of that fucking couch.

I then threw on a hoodie, leggings, and gym shoes. I was very tight with the money that I had made from selling my clothes and accessories. I had hoped to turn it into more money somehow.

I climbed the stairs and entered the kitchen where Zina was cooking dinner while Tremere was strapped to the front of her. I was met with the chaotic, deafening sounds of Justice, Jerrell, and Jasmine playing tag or some shit in the living room like they lived in a circus ring.

I despised those kids.

They had no home training.

"Where you goin'?" Zina quipped with a smirk, looking me up and down.

"About to walk to the store. You need anything?"

"Yeah, some money on these bills that you're making go up. When are you going to get a job, Zoey?"

"I've been applying for jobs. Won't nobody call me back for an interview."

"Girl, please," she said, smacking her lips. "Who you think you talking to? It's the holidays. Every fucking company is hiring for temp work. You can work anywhere; Amazon, UPS, Walgreens, pick one."

Each suggestion that she threw out made me sick to my stomach. Every person that I'd gone to school with that hadn't gone to college worked at those same places.

Yet, I held back my griping and said, "I'll keep looking, Auntie."

She scoffed and continued stirring the red beans that she was boiling. I threw my hoodie on and left out of the kitchen door.

The quiet was so beautiful. I briefly closed my eyes and enjoyed it. Even with the sounds of motors, loud stereo systems, and voices on the busy block in Englewood, being outside was much calmer than being in that house with all those gawd damn kids.

I started to walk up the gangway towards the block. I really didn't need anything from the store. I just needed to see and hear something other than that house and those kids. I had been locked in there for months, unable to come up with a plan to get myself out of this shit. So many people were getting money. Most girls my age were either scamming or selling pussy. I had yet to find ways to do either. There was no way that I was going to show my face on some app like Only-Fans. I imagined that every nigga that I'd gone to school with was on that site jagging off like perverts. They were in the strip clubs doing the same, so that wasn't an option either.

My only real plan was to come up with enough money for a flight to a hotel in a big city that was poppin' so that I could use my money to be a bottle girl in one of the clubs. Those bitches were making thousands of dollars a night, and with my looks, I could do the same. I couldn't do it in Chicago without someone I knew seeing me. But saving up enough money to take care of myself for a while in a city like Miami, Dallas or Houston was taking some time.

"What up, shorty?"

I instantly sneered. Every time I was walking in the hood, niggas were trying to holla. But they were usually walking like I was, dirty, young, or all of the above.

"You can't say hello?"

My eyes darted towards the voice and softened when I saw that it was coming from an Audi truck. By looking at it, I knew that it was an older truck, but at least it was a foreign.

"Hi," I spoke, now soft and inviting.

"Can I get out and talk to you?"

"Yeah."

He put on his hazards and hopped out. It turned me on that he didn't give a fuck about stopping any traffic that would come.

Then he rounded the trunk, and the headlights shined on his face.

He was about six feet, dreaded, bearded, and chocolate with a cocky stance that showed through the MCM hoodie that he was wearing, so he obviously worked out.

I took my hoodie off to show him that I was pretty. Even with my hair slicked back in a ponytail, I was naturally beautiful like my mother.

"What's up? What's your name?" he asked with a cocky smirk.

"Zoey."

"Zoey," he mocked my tone. "You don't sound like you're from around here."

"I'm not."

"Then what are you doing out here walking on a Friday night?"

"I've been staying with my aunt for a while. She lives down the street."

"Well, you want to walk, or you want a ride?"

"I don't know you to be riding in your car."

He reached in his pocket. I watched as he fished out something. He handed it to me. It was his driver's license.

"Take a picture of it and send it to somebody. That way, you'll feel safe that I won't do anything to you."

I blushed. "Okay."

ZURI TURNER

Though I had gone into labor a few weeks early, my baby boy, Kingston, was born perfectly healthy. I'd had a C-section because he was breach. Therefore, he and I stayed in the hospital for observation for about a week until we were released.

"*Heeeeey*, Kingston. Hey, baby, with your cute self."

I smiled as Bianca cooed and fed Kingston on the couch. She had been such a great friend since all of this bullshit had happened in my life. She had been at my house every other day, spending time with Kingston.

Zina was too busy with her own tribe of kids to be of any assistance. My father tried, but he was out of practice. My helpmate was my postpartum doula. She was a wonderful older woman that took great care of me and Kingston. She had been in my household since I'd given birth. I didn't see how I could have made it without her.

A doula's role is rooted in a philosophy of women supporting other women during childbirth and parenting. A postpartum doula gives the mother physical and emotional support after the birth of the baby. She provides non-medical support in the weeks following delivery. And while the doula does help with infant care, her primary focus is on the mother. So, my doula, Marlene, would come over and cook, clean, and tend to Kingston to give me time to rest, run errands, or do some self-care. She had a morning shift and usually stayed for about twelve hours.

Having Kingston only made me miss Zoey even more. I never thought I would have another child. Since I did, I wanted Zoey to be a part of his life. But Zina often told me how Zoey was rotting away doing nothing with her life. That was a disappointment because I had risked all of this and endured this heartache for nothing. Every time I thought of that, I had nothing to say to her ungrateful ass.

"Who do you think he looks like?" Bianca asked as she smiled into his face.

I clicked my tongue. "You gon' ask me this every time you see him?"

"I'm just sayin'. I think he looks like Law."

I chuckled. "Girl, he don't look like nothing but skin, eyes, a nose, and a mouth. He's only a month old."

I had been trying to see who he might look like. I had even compared him to newborn pictures of Rashaad that I still had. But Kingston had no real features yet, so there was no telling. It would have been easier to call Rashaad and just do a blood test. But he was still on the run as if he was the damn cartel.

"You can fix all of this by calling Law," Bianca said for the umpteenth time.

Just thinking of calling him made my heart flutter. Since learning that he was out, I was torn with reaching out to him. I was still mourning so much; Rashaad, Zoey, and Dom, most importantly. I didn't want to rebound and end up in another fucked up situation. I loved Law. I felt more for him than I ever had for Dom. But he was in the streets. He had told me so many stories in our counseling sessions that I knew exactly what he was doing now that he was out. I knew that he would protect me and my child from that. But I couldn't take mourning the loss of another love.

AANAN "LAW" WOODS

Jeezy's death had brought the family closer. My kids were often at Ma or Reese's crib because Ma and Shay wanted them to have a mother figure. Yet, I spent a lot of time with them. Though Ox had given me the crew back, he and Megan enjoyed running shit so much that they handled most of the crew. I just met with the connect and showed my face when matters needed to be dealt with or when we needed to meet with our crew of hustlas that bought weight from us. So, I spent most of my time with the kids, taking them to school, picking them up, and going to August's games and practices. I had even gotten Willow into gymnastics.

"August, you 'bout dressed?" I asked, sticking my head into his room.

Since the next day was Christmas Eve, I was taking the kids to my mom's house. She had a game night planned for them.

"Yeah." I watched him as he walked about his room, gathering his bookbag.

I noticed the pout on his face. So, I asked him, "What's wrong?"

"Nothing's wrong. I was just wondering something."

"What?" I came into his room and plopped down on his bed.

He looked hesitant, standing in the middle of the floor, looking down at his feet.

"What?" I pressed.

"Is Mommy with Jeezy?"

I blinked rapidly. "What you mean? Why would she be with Jeezy?"

My heart started to pound. August knew that Jeezy was in heaven. So, I wondered how he knew that his mother was dead too.

"I don't want to get in trouble," he mumbled while fidgeting with his fingers.

"Come here," I told him softly.

He inched towards me, fear covering his face.

Once in arm's reach, I sat him down next to me. "Why would you get in trouble for asking a question?"

"Because the last time I said something about it, I got in trouble."

My brows furrowed. "Said something about what?"

"About Jeezy being Mama's boyfriend."

I tried to hide my confusion and anger. I didn't want to scare him into not saying anything more. But I could already feel the rage beginning to boil over. "What you mean?"

"Mama and Jeezy were boyfriend and girlfriend when you were in jail. But she made me promise not to tell you. I was the only person that knew. Willow and Serenity never saw him. Only me. I told grandma that she had a boyfriend—"

"Your grandmother knew that she was with Jeezy?"

His eyes darted towards me. "No. I never told her who he was. I only told her that Mama was with her boyfriend one night."

"Why would you think your Uncle Jeezy was her boyfriend?"

His eyes shied away, fearful.

"You can tell me. I won't get mad."

"I-Uh-I saw them kissing. And when Uncle Jeezy got hurt, she cried a lot. So, I was wondering if she was gone because she wanted to be in heaven with Jeezy."

Gritting, I swallowed back my rage. "No, she's not in heaven with Jeezy."

"Am I going to get in trouble?" he asked with a trembling voice.

I palmed the back of his head and brought it into my chest. I kissed the top of it, saying, "No. Now go to the front so we can get out of here."

He jumped up, relieved that he wasn't in trouble.

Once he was out of the room, my face fell into my hands as I started to recall everything that had happened. It all made sense now. Jeezy had to have been the man that showed the fake ID to sign my properties over. Only he hated me this much to help Whit do that shit. I wouldn't have been surprised if he had been able to talk her goofy ass into it.

My rage quickly subsided, though, because the people that I wanted to wreak havoc on were already dead. Whit had felt my wrath, and Jeezy, though dead, was a lucky motherfucker.

⚜

"Hey, Law." Stacy was mumbling as she barely looked up at me.

This was my first time visiting since her father's death.

Detective Payne had been found in the explosion, dead in the very spot that I had left him standing in.

As I inched into the living room, Stacy kept her head down. Once in front of her, I held her chin and lifted her head up. I knew once she looked into my eyes that she wouldn't be able to resist me.

When her eyes met mine, her body loosened.

I waited until Gabriella had disappeared down the hall before saying, "I'm sorry."

I knew that she knew that I had killed her father. If she didn't, I cared about her too much to lie to her face.

Her eyes squeezed together tightly. A tear streamed down her cheek from her right eye.

"I never wanted to hurt you," I told her, sitting next to her chair on the couch.

"I know," she said lowly.

"He kept fucking with me," I reminded her.

"I know."

"He was never gon' stop."

"I know," she cringed.

I lay a soothing hand on top of hers. She peered at me, seemingly hating the soft spot in her heart for me. I then leaned over and kissed her cheek, wiping a tear away with my thumb. She was paralyzed below the waist, but I'd felt her upper body shiver under my touch.

"I'm so sorry," I said, sitting back.

"I forgive you," she said, nearly blushing. "He had sizeable life insurance policies, so me and the kids will be well taken care of."

"I figured," I smiled. "I still got your back, though."

"I know you do." Then she sighed, smiling. "Anyway, how are you?"

"I'm a'ight. Been dealing with my kids and helping my mom get through losing Jeezy."

Saying his name left an enraged taste in my mouth. I wasn't surprised that his bitch ass had waited until I was locked up to try to fuck me. I just hated that I wasn't the one to kill his ass.

"I heard about that. I'm sorry."

I grimaced inwardly. "Be sorry for my mother and brother. Not me."

Then Stacy's eyes lit up. "Did you go get your girl yet?"

"Nah." Finally, I couldn't hold back my emotions. The green-eyed monster was controlling my expressions. "She should be a new mother by now."

Stacy frowned. "Huh?"

"I went by her crib one day, and she was pregnant."

"Okay?" She then tilted her head, smirking at me. "You don't take me as a man that would care that she was pregnant by somebody else."

"How so?"

"You take care of me and mine just fine."

"I *owe* you."

She tilted her head with a small smile. "After all this time, you do it because you love us."

I smiled genuinely. "I do."

"You love her as well, so you owe her too."

"I never told you that I love her."

She teased me with a smirk. "I can tell."

I fought not to give myself away with a grin. "How?"

"I can see your heart racing from here just because you're talking about her."

I pulled my eyes away from hers to hide the truth because I felt like a punk for still loving Zuri.

"I may be paralyzed from the waist down, but I'm still a woman. Trust me, if the feelings are mutual, that baby won't stop her either," Stacy told me.

"What if the feelings aren't mutual?"

She smiled, batting her eyes. "I don't see how they couldn't have been with a man like you, Law."

For the next hour, Stacy convinced me that I had been a coward.

"So, you're gonna go over there?" she asked as I finally stood to leave.

I sighed, frustrated with these gnawing thoughts and feelings for Zuri. She was the bane of my existence. Meeting her had been nothing but suffering because it had only left me in a painful need that was never fulfilled.

"Yeah," I sighed. "I'm going."

"Tonight?" Stacy pressed with a raised brow.

"Yes. Right now."

"And no matter what you see, you won't walk away?"

I laughed at her persistence. "No."

"You promise?"

"I promise, Stacy."

CHAPTER 13
ZURI TURNER

♫ You can see in my eyes (in my eyes)
That I'm too hypnotized (hypnotized)
Temperatures too high
I smile but then I cry
So stupid fucking high
That I forget about the lows ♫

A few hours later, I was sitting in the middle of the floor in my living room, wrapping presents. Bianca had stayed to keep an eye on Kingston while I did. However, he was sleeping in his bassinet now, so she and I had started to drink while I wrapped the seemingly hundreds of presents that I had for my nieces and nephews.

Kingston had put a genuine smile on my face since his birth. However, I was forcing myself to smile bigger because every time I thought of him, I also thought of Zoey, Law, and my failed marriage. Since the holiday season had begun, it had been very difficult emotionally for me. But Christmas was making it even more difficult to get my mind off of whom I had lost that year. So, as I wrapped presents, me and Bianca drank Casamigos, while letting Siri provide our soundtrack for the night.

"*Stop hallucinating over lame ass niggas!*" Bianca and I suddenly burst out singing in unison along with Alex Vaughn to our favorite part of "Mirage". "*Lame ass niggaaaas!*"

I laughed, watching Bianca stand and begin to sing into the Casamigos bottle like it was a microphone. "*I'll snap out of it in tiiiiime! Damn, damn! Damn near perfeeeeect. Beautiful you aaaare, yeeeeeeah! Or is it just a miraaaage?*"

Just then, my doorbell rang, causing her to frown at it interrupting her one-man concert. "You expecting somebody?"

I shook my head as I stood from the floor. "It's probably Amazon with another gift. That damn doorbell been ringing all week."

I looked around for my phone to look at the Ring app to see who it was, but I couldn't find it just as the bell had rung again. This time the person laid on it, so I abandoned my search and ran for the door.

Bianca was close behind, still holding her cup.

I snapped, swinging the door open, "Who the fuck—"

Anger covered my face as Bianca spewed, "Aw, hell nah!"

"Why the fuck are you laying on my doorbell?" I snapped, glaring at Robyn.

Since Kingston was born, I hadn't thought of Robyn or the lawsuit. I had chosen to focus on as less bullshit as possible, and Robyn was the least of my worries. I had planned to handle that shit whenever we were given a court date.

"Give my parents that fucking money," she slurred, swaying and obviously drunk. "They need it. They are old and need a lot of care. I can't keep taking care of them. You don't deserve it."

"See? This where you keep fucking up at. I would have given it to them because, as you see, I clearly don't need it," I said, waving my hands at my house. "But you keep throwing these jabs, so I can't give them shit. So, tell your mommy and daddy that their daughter can't keep her fucking mouth shut long enough to get a blessing."

She lunged at me, spitting, "Bitch—"

Yet, before I could even swing on her, Bianca had pushed me out of the way, threw her drink in Robyn's face, and started drilling this bitch.

"Bianca!" I called out in a warning laugh.

They were tussling on the porch, screaming obscenities at one another as they clawed, punched, and pulled hair. Robyn was hardly doing any damage because her eyes were burning and sticky from the Casamigos bath they had been given. So, Bianca was dragging that ass. I cringed at how loud they were. I was surrounded by white neighbors, so I knew they would call the police soon. I took a step forward to pull Bianca off of Robyn, but then a large figure hurling towards us caught my attention. I gasped, jumping back, staring at the figure as it jogged towards us through the yard. I initially thought it was someone that had come with Robyn that was coming to help her. So, I prepared myself to drag them too. But then, as the figure came closer and closer to the porch, its face was lit up by the porch light.

"Law?!" I gasped.

I was baffled... really.

For many reasons.

I had never seen him outside of the prison scrubs. He wasn't wearing a coat, as if he had rushed out of the car. He was coming towards me looking like a dope boy snack, dripped in diamonds, Givenchy from head to toe, locs wrapped regally atop his head, but a few had fallen out of the style.

I was fucking drooling... while Bianca was whooping Robyn's ass.

I was staring at his perfection, blinking slowly, bare feet frozen to the cold concrete. Yet, he didn't even look at me. He immediately softly pushed Bianca. It was soft to him, but it was rough to Bianca because he was three times her size. She stumbled, causing her to let go of Robyn. Then Law scooped Robyn up like she was a baby and tossed her ass in the yard.

She scrambled wildly to get to her feet like a little angry Chihuahua. Her nose was leaking. Her lips were already swelling.

Tracks were falling out of her head. She was breathing wildly, and she was ready to charge back onto the porch until Law pulled his gun out.

"Get the fuck on," he ordered so calmly that his confidence made a bitch pussy wet.

"Well, *shit*," Bianca said softly.

I looked over at her, and she was giving Law the same lust-filled eyes that I was.

Robyn hesitated for only a few seconds before she started to walk away. Her eyes narrowed as her lips parted to, what I assumed was, spit some more threats before leaving, but Law cocked his gun and aimed it at her, saying, "Pull it. I dare you. I shoot bitches too... With no problem."

"*Fuuuuuck*," Bianca swooned in a whisper.

This bitch, I laughed inside my head.

Finally, Robyn scurried away towards her car, which was parked in front of the house in front of a Bentley Bacalar.

With Robyn gone, Law and I were forced to acknowledge one another. Suddenly, the cold, December air was thick with tension. I was lost in the sight of him, not knowing what to say or feel. I was hypnotized by his presence. I watched the light of the porch play hide and seek in his diamonds, amazed at how dull they looked in comparison to him.

Bianca dramatically cleared her throat. "I'll go inside."

"We'll go inside too. It's cold out here," Law said. Then he grabbed my hand, causing my eyes to bulge and my body to tense up. He looked down at my hesitance and leaned his head towards the front door. "C'mon."

It was a simple word, but it sounded like fucking poetry being said by a goon in that deep, sultry voice.

I followed like an obedient little girl, timid and nervous.

Then my fucking baby started to cry, bringing me out of my complete dismay.

"I got him!" Bianca spat as she ran through the foyer towards the living room.

I felt Law looking at me. So, I forced my nervousness to look up at him. Yet, he wasn't looking in my eyes; he was staring at me... my body.

"You had your baby, huh?"

Your baby...

Even more shocked, my eyes narrowed. "You knew I was pregnant?" I was inwardly cringing from embarrassment. He didn't even know the whole situation yet, and I was already ashamed.

That's when he then appeared a little embarrassed. "I came by twice to say something to you, but I saw you."

"Why didn't you say something?"

He shrugged a shoulder. A hint of disturbance covered his face. "You were with your guy."

Your guy...

In that very second, I realized that Dom was indeed a rebound. Though he had been perfect in all ways and would forever have a special place in my heart, looking up into Law's eyes, I knew that my feelings for Dom would have never equated to how I felt for Law.

My feelings for anyone before or after him never could.

"The other time I peeped that you were pregnant."

Cringing, I asked, "You want to talk?"

"Please?"

Fuck.

The way that he was looking at me, the way that he was masculinely glowing under the light of the chandelier, had me in millions of pieces.

I swallowed hard, trying to smother the lust that was boiling over in my core.

On shaky legs, I led him to the den. "I'll be back, Bianca. We're gonna talk in the den."

"Take your *tiiiime*," she sang.

Me and Law chuckled as we made our way to the den.

So many thoughts were flooding my mind. But they were suffocated by the feelings that I had now that I was finally in Law's presence. I was reminded of the peace and security that he gave me. He was more than good dick. Being with him felt like I was with my partner, my peace, and the other half of my heart.

AANAN "LAW" WOODS

Once in the den, we stood in front of the couch, staring at one another.

I felt like a little boy again, twelve years old, staring at the pussy and a beautiful girl up close for the first time and not knowing what the fuck to do with it or her.

But this wasn't us. Despite the distance and her running from me, she knew me. I could tell by the way that she couldn't breathe that she still wanted me.

There wasn't a need for us to be timid or shy with each other.

So, I closed the space between us suddenly. She looked up at me, eyes large like an owl. I gently put my hand around her neck, biting down on my lip. I could sense that the smile on my face didn't put her in fear.

"Why the fuck didn't you reply to my letter?"

She tried to pull my hand away, but even only holding it with a slight grip, she couldn't. So, she started to swing on me, which felt like small pinches.

"Why would you make that dumb ass bet with that ignorant ass nigga?!"

"He thought I was feeling you. That was before we started doing us, and even before that, I didn't plan on going through with that shit. I was fucking locked up. You know how that shit goes in there with them niggas. I couldn't let him think I was feeling you. You wanted me to look like a pussy or draw even more attention to us?"

She batted her eyes, her fight slowly leaving with each word.

I let her neck go, still staring down at her. "Had you given me the opportunity, I would have told you that shit then. But, nah, you want to make a nigga chase yo' ass. I've been trying to get in touch with you. I been worried about yo' ass. You think just because you ignore me that I won't still worry, still need to know how you doin'? Got me driving by here like a creep and shit —"

Her eyes bucked wider.

I gritted. "I had to see you with that lame-ass, pretty boy ass, wanna-be-me-ass nigga." Then I bent down, placing my hands on my knees so that I could look her right in those cat-like eyes. "You can't replace me, baby. You can't replace what we had with the next nigga. You know that shit. That's why you standing there looking at me like that. He ain't me. Not even if you have his—"

She took my power, taking my beard into her hands and kissing me. My knees buckled.

I was a beast. My body was so large in stature that I was immediately menacing to others. My presence as a man was intimidating. But that was nothing in comparison to the power that she had over me. I was then weak. All my swag was *gone*.

I think I moaned in that bitch mouth.

Trying to take my power back, I tore my mouth away and spun around. I then tore down the shorts she had been lounging in. I lifted one of her legs onto the couch. She was already moaning and panting as I crouched down. I looped both of my arms around and up under her and brought the pussy to my lips.

"Ahh! Law... Oh my God." Her voice quivered as I began to suck on her bud.

My tongue performed a delicate dance with her clit, between me sucking it with torturous finesse.

She tasted like memories, possession, *mine*.

She was quivering inside of my mouth as I tongue-kissed her clit long and slow.

"Oh God," she panted.

She was shaking, causing that ass to bounce on my face, which only made my dick harden into steel.

"Please fuck me, Law," I heard her beg. *"Please?"*

My tongue wasn't finished feasting, but the way that she was begging made me eager to oblige, so I stood.

She was ready, back arched, pussy in the air, but I softly smacked her ass. "Unt uh," I said, softly pushing her away. "I finally get to see you fully naked. Take all that shit off. *Everything.*"

She turned around, nipples so hard that they reached out to me through the t-shirt she had on. She tore off her shirt and bandeau top. She then kicked her shorts off of her ankles, where I'd had left them.

"You too," she breathed.

Smiling slowly, I started to strip. With each article of clothing that I removed, her eyes danced more and more. Those bitches were twerking by the time that she had got to my pants. She seemed to be staring mostly at my tattoos. She had never been able to see them so vividly before because they were always covered by my prison garb.

I wrapped my arm around her waist and brought her to me. I bent down, kissing her, making her taste herself. This time, she moaned into my mouth. With such a significant height difference between us, she had to stand on her tiptoes to keep up with me. I bent forward, helping her as my fingers found her wetness. I played in it, anticipating the moment that my dick was able to wade in that water. I softly plunged two fingers inside of her. She clung to me, throwing her arms around my neck.

I picked her up, still finger fucking that pussy. Throws of passion forced her to ride my fingers as I brought her to the nearest wall and pressed her against it.

I removed my fingers and brought my dick to her center.

I then dove in and went to work.

☙❧

"*Fuuccck*," I lowly moaned into Zuri's neck.

She was crippling me. An hour later, I was about to buss for the third time.

"Argh!" I howled, lifting up.

But she pushed me out of her. She then stood on her knees from the missionary position and threw my dick into her mouth.

"Argh!!!" I growled as she started to suck and jag it at the same time as I bussed down her throat. "Fuck!"

She had the nerve to moan while she killed me sexually.

I wanted to *punch* her ass.

But instead, I softly pushed her off by the shoulders. "Gawd damn," I breathed hard, trying to catch my breath and fighting the urge to ask to marry her right then.

I had missed that pussy and was reminded that it was the best as soon as I was back inside of it.

We had both cum multiple times, so we collapsed on the carpeted floor. She reached for the couch that was only inches away, weakly pulled down the black throw, and pulled it over us.

For a few moments, we lay there in silence. Only the sounds of our heavy breathing were in the room, along with snoring that was coming into the den from a few feet away.

"Is that...?"

"Bianca's ass," Zuri laughed.

"Well, damn," I chuckled.

"That's that damn Casamigos."

"Oh, y'all was in here getting lit, huh?"

"Yeah."

"So, you were drunk?" I looked at her, hating that she made me so weak that I actually felt a bit of disappointment.

"I was tipsy, but I knew exactly what I was just doing."

"Good."

"*Sooooo...*" She started to bite her bottom lip nervously as her words trailed off.

To ease her nerves, I brought her towards me and put her under me. "So?"

"What did your letter say?"

My eyes whipped towards her. "You didn't even read the motherfucka?"

She giggled. "No."

"Bitch."

She started cracking up. "What did it say?"

"This dick just said everything that the letter said."

Her smile slowly faded into lust and admiration. "Okay." Then her smile faded into sympathy. "I'm sorry."

"For what?"

"For not reading the letter, for running, for not giving you a chance to explain."

I nodded. "I appreciate that."

Her eyes bucked as we stared at each other.

"What?" I questioned her expression.

"Say you're sorry too!" she spat.

I shrugged. "What I'm sorry for? I didn't do shit."

She threw her head back, laughing. "*Wow.*"

"I didn't do shit but give you good dick and love you."

Her smile faded, and a look of admiration replaced it. "You.... You love me?"

"Of course, I do," I said, kissing her forehead. "And I'm taking you from that pretty nigga."

She laughed lightly, but her words were sad as she said, "You don't have to."

"Oh, y'all done?" I started to get angry, realizing that this nigga had left her and with a baby.

"He's...." Then she sighed deeply. "He's dead."

I swallowed hard, feeling stupid. "Oh... Damn. I'm sorry."

"He was murdered."

"I'm sorry to hear that. You okay?"

She blew a heavy breath. "I mean.... I'm dealing. We had only known one another for a few months. I met him after I quit the County. He came into my life at a horrible time. Me and Rashaad were divorcing, and some other shit was going on. I had found out that I was pregnant so..." Her words paused as confusion caused my expression to change.

"So, he wasn't the father," I realized.

Her eyes pulled away from mine. "No," she answered softly.

My eyes narrowed as I sat up on my elbows. "Rashaad?"

But my heart started to beat against my chest wall like a sledgehammer because I knew that bitch ass nigga wasn't the only option.

Biting down on her lip, she shrugged. "It can be his... or yours."

I sat up slowly.

"I'm *so* sorry," she insisted, reluctance and sorrow painting her beautiful face. "I didn't tell you because it was so much going on. And, despite how I felt about you, with that whole bet situation," she said, sitting up. "I was scared that you were another terrible decision that I had made, even though in my heart, I knew you weren't. But I didn't trust my heart," she rambled. "It's failed me so many times, with Rashaad, with Zoey."

My head whipped towards her. "Zoey?"

"She..." Her shoulders sank. "Rashaad was cheating on me with her."

"The fuck?!" I barked.

"See?! My life was in shambles," she whined and pouted. "I had so much going on. Everyone around me was deceiving me. I didn't know who was being real with me anymore."

I put my arm around her shoulders, pulling her into me. I had so many questions, especially about Rashaad cheating on her with her daughter. Yet, it was obvious that she had been dealing with so much hurt that I didn't want to deepen it by making her talk about it. I knew that I would get the details when she was ready.

So, I just held her and assured her. "I'm as real as it gets, baby. I'm here to protect you from everything, so I can't inflict pain on you when I'm willing to kill the next motherfucker for hurting you. *I got you*, in every aspect that those words mean. You ain't never gotta worry about me."

CHAPTER 14
ZURI TURNER

The next morning was Christmas Eve. I was awakened by the smell of biscuits and gravy.

When my eyes fluttered open, I had forgotten for a brief moment why I was in the den. I then swiftly remembered how quickly things had turned around. It's amazing how fast life can transform from bad to good. Law had come out of nowhere so suddenly that it was quite unbelievable. I would have almost thought that him being there the night before had been a wild dream had he not been–

"What the fuck?" I muttered, looking next to me.

I sat up, looking around the room.

Law was gone.

The only thing still in the room that confirmed that he had not been a dream was his smell on the throw pillow that he had fallen asleep on as we talked until the sun came up.

I told him everything about Rashaad, Zoey, and Dom. He then told me about Jeezy's passing, and that Jeezy and Whit had stolen from him. When he said that he was now a single father because of it, I understood without him going any further.

Seeing that even his Givenchy sneakers were gone, I looked around for my phone. It was still on the couch, so I reached for it.

I didn't even realize that I was holding my breath in anticipation until I felt my heart ease, and I started to breathe again when I saw that he had sent me a text message.

Law: *I'll be right back.*

Smiling, I stood, groaning because I could feel the effects of the intense workout Law and I had had. It was a good pain, though, since I hadn't been worked out like that in months. I was so glad that I had healed from delivering Kingston so that I could get and enjoy that unexpected dick.

I searched the den for my shirt and shorts and slipped them back on. I then padded out of the den and through the foyer, listening for sounds of Kingston. Peeking inside the living room, I saw that he was lying on Bianca's chest, asleep along with her.

I followed the smell into the kitchen, where I saw Marlene with her back to me, cooking at the stove. Since she would come over so early in the mornings, I had given her a key.

Hearing me come into the kitchen, she turned around. When I saw the peculiar look on her face, I asked, "What?"

"You had a good night."

I giggled. "Yeah. Me and Bianca were drinking while I wrapped gifts."

She clicked her tongue. "Girl, ain't nobody talkin' about you and Bianca. I'm talking about that fine ass man that walked up outta here this morning."

"Huh?"

"If you can huh, you can hear!"

I laughed, plopping down on a stool at the island. "You saw him?"

"Yeah. I think I woke him up when I came into the house. You know most men don't sleep through that type of shit, especially ones that gotta watch their backs."

"Oh."

"Don't 'oh' me. Who is he?"

"That was Law."

Marlene completely abandoned the stove, dropping the tongs on it, and spun around with her mouth dropped to the floor.

She was the only other person, besides Bianca, who knew that Kingston could have possibly been Law's. After giving birth to him, I had been so bombarded with depressing and needing thoughts of Law that I confessed to her everything that had been happening to me in my life since I met Law.

"Shut up," she said, inching towards me with nosiness. "Where did he come from?"

"He just showed up last night."

"And how do you feel about that?"

"Better. Honestly. Much better. I didn't realize how much I needed him until he came back. I feel like I'm breathing better than I was before."

"That's so sweet."

Just then, the doorbell rang.

"I guess I'll cook a little bit more. He's coming back, right?"

"Yeah. That might be him."

I climbed off of the stool and rushed to the front door to keep it from ringing again and waking Kingston. Surprisingly, he slept way more than Zoey had when she was a newborn. As long as he was fed and changed, he was always nodding off, and I took full advantage of that.

Peering through the peephole, I saw Law standing on the porch. Even through that tiny hole, laying eyes on him lit a desire in my heart that I had only felt one time before, and it was with him. Once he had broken the ice last night, it blew my mind how we had fallen right back into the perfect bond and chemistry that we had had before. But that only proved to me that he was indeed mine, and I was his.

We had simply found each other again.

"Where'd you go?" I asked, opening the door.

He lifted a Walgreens bag to answer his question and walked through the threshold.

"What's this?" I asked as he handed it to me.

"Look."

I peered inside and instantly pouted. "Law..."

"I want to know."

I cringed as I shut the door. The DNA test suddenly felt so heavy in my hands. Prior to last night, I was comfortable not knowing who Kingston's father was because I was too afraid that he was Rashaad's. I did not want my son to belong to him.

Seeing my sudden change in mood, Law came to me and brought me to him. I buried my face in his chest and held him tight around his waist.

"You know it don't matter to me whose he is, right?" he pressed. "I'm still gonna be here."

"I want you to be his father," I was finally able to admit.

I faulted myself for not trusting my feelings for Law before this. If I had, I would have been able to fill a void in both me and Kingston's lives. Law was a real nigga. He would have been there for me and Kingston, no matter who his father is. I knew that I was just allowing Rashaad and Zoey's disloyalty to make me second guess what I knew in my heart. And because of that, I wanted him to be Law's in blood as well.

⚜️

ONCE MARLENE WAS FINISHED COOKING, I WOKE BIANCA'S DRUNK ass up, and we all ate breakfast at the dining room table. It was the first time that I had had a group of people at that table since Zoey and Rashaad had left.

As I ate the salmon croquettes, grits, and biscuits and gravy, a surreal feeling came over me. I felt like these people were my new family.

"I'm excited."

Watching Law as he held Kingston, I smiled. Law looked so handsome while holding my baby with such a protective stance. He was already a father to him without knowing if he truly was.

After eating, Bianca left. Marlene went upstairs to start doing laundry. Me and Law were in the living room talking. He had asked to hold Kingston and had never let him go. Looking over at Law, I saw that he was beaming into Kingston's face, who was finally awake. Kingston looked so tiny in Law's large hands and arms.

"Why?" I asked.

"I want my son to experience the things I never did as a child. When my kids were younger, I was heavy in the streets. I didn't have the time or maturity to do that. But before I got locked up, I started making sure they had certain experiences that I couldn't."

I was growing jealous of the children that he spoke of as if one of them weren't potentially one of mine. "I see."

"It's small shit that I can't believe I never did because I was taking care of myself at a young age," Law said. "I've never even been to a Chicago beach."

My brow rose. "Really?"

"I know. That's sad, right?"

A lot of people that grew up in the hood never left it because they didn't have the knowledge of what was outside of it or the means to get to it. And that was passed on to their children.

"No," I told him. "How about I've never been to a carnival."

"Really?"

"Yeah. It's certain things that I never experienced as a child, either because I was in the streets too or raising Zoey. Then when I got older, I didn't have a desire to because it felt childish. But I always wanted to go to a carnival and have a guy win me one of those big bears." I then started to grin, feeling as if my chocolate skin was turning red.

He smirked playfully. "Corny ass."

And I blushed. "Whatever."

Then, he suddenly got serious as he watched. His chiseled jaws tightened.

"What?" I asked, getting nervous.

"What I told you about Whit... It doesn't scare you away from me, does it?"

I answered quickly with confidence, "No." I then put a hand on his massive thigh to assure him. "She stole millions from a street nigga. She thought that because she was your children's mother, it would save her. But it only made her deceit even worse. And I don't have to worry about you doing anything like that to me because I will never be disloyal to you."

He grabbed the back of my head, bringing it to his lips. "I love you."

My heart turned into mush at the sight of this astounding man telling me those words with such confidence. "I—"

"You don't have to say it back," he cut me off. I looked up at him, wondering why. He told me, "For a nigga like me, for the hard life I've lived, the words you just said were better than any 'I love you'."

❧

THE NEXT DAY BEING CHRISTMAS, I JUST KNEW THAT I WOULDN'T see Law. The night before, he had left to be with his kids at midnight. Yet, we still were on FaceTime after his kids had gone to bed at two in the morning.

I had been feeling so overwhelmed. Law had told me that he loved me, but that didn't intimidate me because people said things all of the time. But as soon as Law had come over and then told me those words, he was showing it. Things felt so real and serious so fast. I had never felt this owned in my life, not even with Rashaad.

When my Ring notification went off, I knew that it had to be Law. It was eight o'clock at night on Christmas day. I had taken my nieces, nephews, and dad their gifts earlier that day. I had given Zina a monetary gift, and I was still pissed at Zadah, so she wasn't getting shit from me. Bianca and I had exchanged presents before she left the day before.

Standing up from the couch, I peered over into Kingston's bassinet. He was sleeping as always. I was really blessed to have such a mild-mannered infant and prayed that he would stay that way.

But I knew better.

On my way to the front door, I fluffed out my curls with my fingers. I had thrown on a Skims boxer and tank set in case Law did come back.

Opening the door, I started to giggle uncontrollably. "Oh my God."

I had never seen that many roses in my life. Law was struggling to carry what looked like over one hundred roses and tons of shopping bags through the threshold. I moved out of his way, feeling my eyes water with appreciation.

"*Awwww*, Law," I cooed as I locked the door.

"Merry Christmas, baby," he told me, handing me the enormous bouquet.

"Wow. I don't even have a vase big enough for these."

"Split them up."

I slid into the kitchen on my furry house shoes with Law close behind me. I batted my eyes rapidly, forcing myself not to cry.

"I told you that you didn't have to come over here," I told him. "Where are your kids? They aren't mad that you aren't with them?"

I went about the kitchen, placing the roses in every vase that I could, adding water to them.

"They are with their cousins playing with all of the shit that they got. They ain't thinking about my ass."

When I was done, Law was standing at the island next to the shopping bags he had placed on it.

"I got you something," he was so proud to tell me.

I smiled bashfully as I went towards the island. "When did you even have time to get me a present? And what store was open?"

"Don't worry about that," he said with a playful smirk.

I was smiling so hard that my cheeks were hurting. Law had appeared out of nowhere, completely unexpected. Yet, he had taken the time to turn this holiday season into the best I'd ever had. Rashaad had showered me with gifts, but I had never been given any of them with such unconditional love and passion.

I went through the bags, amazed at the lengths that Law had gone. He had gifted me a white iced-out diamond Cuban link with a matching bracelet. He had had on the same, but mine was thinner in width, so they were more feminine. He had also gotten me a Christian Dior book tote with matching gym shoes.

"You don't have that one, do you?" he asked as I gushed at the bag. "I saw you with so many of them that I couldn't remember."

"No, I don't have this one. I was actually looking at it the other day."

Since I was no longer married or working, I had had to slow down my spending. So, I had been doing a lot of window shopping online. Holding that purse in my hands felt like good memories of shopping sprees.

I smiled up into Law's heavy-lidded eyes. "Thank you so much, baby."

"There's more," he said with even more pride.

I shook my head, still blushing. But, as I went through the other bags, I started to cry. In them were gifts for Kingston, personalized chains and bracelets, a Moncler snowsuit, Versace, Balmain, and Burberry onesies and little outfits.

"Thank you so much," I cried.

He laughed softly at my tears, seemingly trying to keep his severe manhood from blushing. He put his arms around me, flushing our bodies against one another's. Feeling his lips on my forehead, I felt so unbelievably lucky.

Law was unreal.

ANNAN "LAW" WOODS

"Swoosh! That's game, nigga!" Reese boasted as the ball went through the net.

I clicked my tongue, waving away his gloating. "Whatever. You know you only won because I ain't been playing for a minute."

"You wasn't whooping ass on the court in the County?" he taunted me as we stalked towards me.

"Ain't no yard time in the County, lame ass nigga." I shook my head as we walked off the court in the Y. My brother was so fucking square that he had never even been arrested before.

Reese and I walked towards the bleachers and took a seat to watch our boys finish their game. Reese's son, Marshawn, was a year younger than August. He and August were playing a one-on-one game as well. I had already run drills with him while Marshawn and Reese watched before we started to just play some casual one-on-one games. I was intent on honing August's basketball skills the way that no one had mine.

"What you been on?" Reese asked as we caught our breaths. "I ain't heard from you in the last few days."

I didn't want to act like a schoolboy, but the slow beaming smile crept on my face anyway.

Reese's brow rose. "What?"

"I finally got up with Zuri."

"'Bout time, motherfucker!" Reese spat so loudly that his booming voice ricocheted off of the court's walls. "How that go?"

Since the morning after, I had been with Zuri ever since. I had been under her so much that my kids had been with Ma. Ma loved it, but I was starting to feel like a bad father. So, I had pulled myself from under Zuri that morning, but I was already ready to get back to my baby.

"It was cool." I tried to shrug like it was nonchalant, but the way that my tan skin felt like it was reddening was giving me away. "She... Uh... She had a baby."

Reese's eyes bucked dramatically as he took a sip of his water. "Word?"

"How you feel about that?"

"I feel cool with it because it could be mine."

Reese nearly choked on his water. Coughing, he forced out, "What?!"

I nodded slowly, staring at August. Since learning about Kingston, I wondered how my kids would adjust to me having a new woman and possibly a new baby. I was ready to stop bullshitting and make this shit happen with Zuri. We had wasted too much time. I wanted her to be mine, especially since she possibly had my son. But my kids were already trying to adjust to Whit being gone. I didn't want my shit affecting their lives any more than it already had by throwing another woman and a kid into that.

"Yeah," I nodded slowly. "I possibly got her pregnant while I was locked up."

"She was actually honest about it possibly being somebody else's?"

"Yeah. It was her husband, shit." I shrugged. "What could I say? I knew she was married."

"She still married?"

"Nah. They divorced, and that nigga on the run from the Feds."

Both of Reese's brows rose. "Damn."

"Yeah, so, if Kingston is his, he ain't gon' be in the picture."

Reese smiled. "Kingston? That's his name?"

My lips turned upward as I nodded slowly. "Yeah."

"You got a picture of him?"

I reached into my pocket, took out my phone, unlocked it, and went to my photo gallery. I had taken too many pictures of him while I had been at Zuri's crib for the last few days. I handed Reese the phone, and we looked at them together.

As Reese smiled, swiping through the pictures, I told him, "He's too young to tell if he looks like me. But we took a DNA test a few days ago. So, I'll know in like two weeks."

Handing the phone back, Reese looked at me like he was proud. "You look happy, bro."

"I am. She's it, man. She's the one."

Reese's eyes widened.

I smiled coolly. "What, man?"

"Shit, I knew she was it, but what made you finally figure it out?"

"You."

Reese's eyes narrowed, intrigued.

"The way you look at Shay, the way she makes you smile, the peace you've had for all these years; I knew that was what finding the one was supposed to feel like. That was what finding your soulmate was supposed to be. That's why I never married Whit. She never gave me that feeling. But Zuri does. Without even trying, she just does."

CHAPTER 15
ZOEY TURNER

"**Y**es, Lobo, fuck this pussy," I moaned, throwing my ass back on his dick.

The dick was okay. It was average size, but he was a monster on the head. I was putting on, though, because I needed whatever dollar I could trick out of this nigga.

"Damn, you know how to work this lil' motherfucka, huh?"

I giggled. "Shut up." Yet, I continued to throw my ass back.

Lobo was the guy I had met a few days ago on the block. We had been texting a little bit every day, but with the holidays, we hadn't been able to see each other.

As soon as he called me a few days after Christmas to hang out, I was game. His invite had been the most excitement that I had had since I moved out of Dior's house.

I was broke. Zina was riding my nerves every day about getting a job. Had I had another place to stay, I would have gone there because Zina was blowing me. She had acted as if she was so cool with me staying with her. She had been the one to offer as soon as she'd found out that I had left my mom's house. But I was now starting to think that she had only asked me to move in because she expected me to help her with her bills.

My mother had played the fuck out of me the last time that I had called her. So, I knew better than to ever try again. I knew that her anger hadn't subsided because I knew my mother. Prior to my disloyalty, she loved and spoiled me. She would never allow me to exist in this world without her taking care of me. If she was, I knew that to her, I no longer existed.

The pressure that Zina was putting on me to help out was so bad that I resorted to hiding out in the basement. I barely went upstairs to eat or show my face when Zina was at home because she would start getting on me about dumb shit.

Becoming a social media influencer was a dream in the past. The life that I needed to live to make that work was no longer accessible to me, and I didn't have enough money to fake it.

I was down so bad that I was fucking a nigga that I had only been texting for a few days since meeting him. Lobo was the third man that I had ever fucked, but the first that I had felt like a hoe with.

Making matters worse, I felt like a cheap hoe at that because the nigga had only rode me around the hood and gotten me something to eat at a gyro spot before he was asking to come back to my crib. When I suggested we go back to his, he said his was too far out the way, which was disappointing because I wanted to see if his place would be a good spot to escape to when Zina was tripping.

He had at least stopped and got us a fifth and some weed before coming back. Then I'd snuck him in through the back door because I didn't want Zina to see us.

"Mmm, yes, right there," I encouraged him as I felt his dick cement. He was actually hitting a spot, so I threw my ass back even more.

"Yeah, that's it," he barked lustfully.

I whipped my head back. "*Sshhh!*"

Then he smacked my ass.

"I know good in the fuck well!" Zina's voice interrupted our fucking, causing me to jump out of my skin. Her words were then accompanied by her heavy footsteps on the basement stairs.

"Shit!" I panicked, looking for my clothes. Lobo got in sync and started to do the same.

Yet, my limbs were trembling too much to successfully find anything, so just as Zina's angry mug rounded the wall, I slid under the covers.

As soon as she saw Lobo, she spazzed. "Unt uh! Get the fuck out now!" she spat at Lobo as he buckled his pants.

"Zina, really?!" I whined, embarrassed.

"I don't give a fuck if you grown! If you grown, pay a fucking bill, or is he?" She then actually looked at Lobo as if to wait for him to offer. He scoffed, shaking his head as he slipped his feet into his Timbs. I cringed with embarrassment.

"That's what the fuck I thought," she sneered, pulling her eyes away from him. "This nigga couldn't have gotten you a room at least? Nah, he gotta ride." She rolled her eyes at my humiliation and glared at him. "You still here, nigga?"

Lobo jeered, grabbing his bottle and weed off of the floor. He then stalked to the backdoor. I threw my face into my hands, feeling as if my potential was walking out and would never come back.

As soon as the backdoor slammed, Zina went in. "Really, Zoey? You are really trippin'. You got random niggas in here where my fucking kids lay their heads at. You don't even know him! He ain't a good dude. He been in a lot of shit and got beef with a lot of people. I know him from around the hood. Do a background on these niggas before you give them some pussy."

I kept my face in my hands to keep me from saying anything that would get me kicked out.

"And I don't want no random niggas in my house where my kids are. Make these niggas get you a fucking room if you wanna give that pussy up. I'm not playing that shit." Luckily, I began to hear her house shoes slide against the basement floor away from me. "No job having ass. The fuck."

RASHAAD TURNER

Life had been unbelievably great since getting to Colombia. I was now a regular in the clubs, shops, and restaurants that I frequented. The weather had been impeccable. There were so many new financial opportunities that I had planned to start taking advantage of in the new year. My money had much more growth potential there. The women adored me. I had been fucking the baddest women that I ever had in my life.

"What are you having today, Mr. Douglas?"

Even the woman waiting on me at Saluda's was impeccable. Her long, dark hair was thick and hit the back of her knees. Her natural body was toned, curvy, and void of any imperfections. Light eyes popped off of skin that had been kissed by the Colombian sun.

I ordered a few entrees and a bottle of their best tequila. I most likely wouldn't finish the bottle since I was dining alone. But I would drink most of it to ensure that I had enough stamina to handle my two hoes for the evening: Theresa and Maria.

As the waitress walked away, I admired her beauty. Every woman in Colombia was fucking stunning. I couldn't believe that I had been wasting my time and money on those basic hoes in America.

My phone began to buzz. I smiled devilishly, knowing that it was most likely Theresa or Maria confirming our plans for the evening. As I reached for my phone, I noticed a commotion at the receptionist's desk near the entrance. Four Colombian police had entered the restaurant and were speaking hastily with the receptionist.

I froze when the waitress pointed to my table. I looked around frantically for an exit. As my eyes darted around the room, I could hear the thuds of their combat boots as the officers stalked toward me.

"Rashaad Turner!" he barked in his Spanish accent.

I decided to play it cool. I looked around as if they weren't talking to me, as if they couldn't have been.

Yet, they stopped at my table, snatching me out of my chair by the arm.

"My name is Samuel Douglas. I have my passport. Check my pockets," I insisted.

He ignored me, though, dragging me away from the table. "Rashaad Turner, you're under arrest for—"

"My name is Samuel Douglas," I barked. "Check my passport!"

Some of the officers laughed as the one escorting me out started to read me my rights. They weren't listening to me, nor were they willing to even look at my passport. There was no due diligence overseas. I knew better. So, I stopped trying to plead my case. I lowered my head and allowed them to escort me out of the restaurant.

As they tossed me in the back of a filthy van, a death-like feeling of doom came over me. And I knew that was because my life was over. I would now be facing more time, and it was possible that I would never get out of prison.

ZURI TURNER

By New Year's Eve, it felt like Law and I were in a full-blown relationship.

"You okay?" I could feel Bianca's eyes on me as I adjusted my outfit in the full-length mirror in my bedroom. "I know you not trippin' about Rashaad being arrested," she spat with disgust.

I sucked my teeth, spitting, "Hell no."

That morning, I had gotten a call from the Feds that Rashaad had been apprehended in Colombia and extradited to the United States. I wasn't that all familiar with the law, but from working at the County briefly, I knew that Rashaad was now facing even more federal time because his dumb ass had run.

But I wasn't sad at all. After finding out about him and Zoey, nothing surprised me with that motherfucker.

I was just happy that he was no longer my problem.

"Then what's wrong?" Bianca asked.

"What makes you think something is wrong?"

"Because you don't look like a woman that finally got her nigga and is about to spend New Year's Eve with him."

"How does that woman look?"

"Happy, bitch!"

Chuckling, I looked at her through the mirror, still playing with the faux leather dress that I'd stuffed myself in.

"I am happy," I tried to insist.

"I can't tell," she said, sucking her teeth. "For real, though. What's wrong?"

I sighed, turning away from the mirror. I then moped towards the bed and plopped down on it. "I don't want to say. I feel stupid for even feeling this way."

Bianca sat up. "What is it?"

"I... I feel like things are moving so fast for Law and me. One minute, he wasn't here, and then... Bam! We're in a full-blown relationship."

It had only been a week since Law had come back into the picture. Ever since, it seemed as if we had spent every waking moment together. It had been surreal, but each day it was becoming unbearable. I didn't know if it was time for what we felt for one another. Regardless of if Kingston was his child or not, I felt as if I was suddenly in a very passionate relationship with a man that I barely knew.

"You all committed to one another?" Bianca asked with a raised brow.

"Not verbally. But you know how it is with street niggas. They call you their bitch one day, and then that's what it is."

Bianca smiled devilishly, liking all that shit. "Mmm humph." Then she sucked her teeth, noticing that my excitement didn't match hers. "Okay, and what's wrong with that?"

Shrugging, I pouted. "I guess he's just a bit much for me. He's always here, always calling, texting. It feels so permanent so quickly."

Bianca nodded in a matter-of-fact way. "You know what it is?"

"What?"

I desperately wanted to know. I did not want to feel this way. I knew that Law was the perfect guy, and I would be stupid to run from him. But his love was feeling so overwhelming.

"You aren't used to this type of treatment," Bianca said. "You were married for ten years, but Rashaad wasn't loving or affectionate. He dealt with you and threw you some money. You aren't used to the passion or a man even wanting to spend every day with you because he is only fucking you."

I chuckled dryly. "Facts." Then I told her, "But he's talking about moving in already."

He had only made mention of it while we were shopping for New Year's Eve the other day. He was wondering how his kids would feel once we moved in together. It still shocked me that he was even thinking in that direction so suddenly.

"He mentioned it casually, but the fact that he is considering it is crazy. We got to know each other for months, but we never dated. Now that we've reconnected, I feel like we skipped the dating part."

"Girl, that man fucks with you," Bianca said, waving off my anxiety. "That's how a real nigga is when he chooses you. He claims what he wants. Would you rather it be the latter? Some nigga you love barely calling you and you having to beg for his attention?"

"Hell nah. I've been there."

Bianca giggled. "Exactly. So, fix your fucking face. Just make him take his time to get to know you."

ANNAN "LAW" WOODS

♬ *Sexy motherfucker, you the baddest one (woah)*
Gave you all my love, that shit been addin' up (woah)
We should get away somewhere and run it up (woah)
You tryna fall in love ♬

"*Gaaaawd* damn," I muttered under my breath into my glass of Glenlivet.

I felt like a pervert watching Zuri as she walked across the room with Megan. She even had the nerve to be dancing as she walked to "Baddest". That leather dress was hugging her body like a glove. She was turning heads like a motherfucker as she followed Megan to the restroom.

Every time I looked at that woman, I was more and more convinced that she was it. I didn't need anyone else.

When I looked at Zuri, I felt like I was looking at "mine".

Zuri was *mine*.

She was beautiful, with flawless chocolate skin, big natural curls, and voluptuous curves. But under all of that beauty was a soul that belonged to only me.

I was convinced.

"You know you already fucking her, right?"

I tore my eyes away from Zuri and saw Ox giving me a taunting smirk.

"I'm just saying," he chuckled. "You're looking at her like you've never hit that before."

I grinned. "Because every time I hit that, it feels like the first time."

Ox barked a short laugh and then put his glass in the air to toast with mine.

As we threw our shots back, I was appreciative of the ending to this hectic year. That entire year had been full of so many uncertainties. I had never expected to end it on this high of a note.

Now that I finally had Zuri back, I wanted to spend this New Year's Eve with her, my right hand, and his wife. My brother's lame-ass always brought his New Year's Eve in with his wife and kids. Ma was happy to keep an eye on mine, and Marlene was babysitting Kingston. So, the four of us draped ourselves in our finest and headed downtown. We first had dinner at Prime and Provisions. We then hit up a party that one of the homies in the hood was throwing at Tunnel. We were tucked in a VIP section waiting on the clock to strike midnight.

"A'ight, a'ight, a'ight!" the deejay interrupted the music. "We got five minutes to midnight. Five minutes to midnight, y'all!"

Zuri and Megan were coming back just in time. My eyes drifted to Zuri as she and Megan parted the crowd as if they were drawn to her. Watching her, I knew that I was gone. She had me. I was obsessed with loving her just like I was with my own flesh and blood. She could have anything she wanted, anything she needed, as long as she blessed me with her presence in my life.

I had wasted ten years with a woman, never even experiencing what love was, what needing a woman was. And now that I had it, I didn't want to let go. I knew that I was possibly scaring her because I was ready and willing to move so fast. But if she was going to run, I was going to put on my Air Max's and chase her little ass.

She wasn't getting away from me again.

I stood as she stepped into the VIP section to give her room to return to her seat next to me.

"What are you staring at?" Zuri was flushed as she looked up into my eyes. She could hardly keep herself from smiling.

"You," I simply answered, looping my arm around her waist. I then brought her flush against my chest. "Just you."

Her lips pursed together as she gave me a gaze of disbelief. Her doubt was okay. Hell, I couldn't believe myself. She was bringing out devotion and energy from me that I didn't know I had.

"Okay, y'all! Here we go!" the deejay announced over the beat of "Dreams and Nightmares". "The new year is coming! Let's toast up to a new year of love, joy, and peace! May your troubles be less and your blessings be more! In the new year, may your right hand always be stretched out in friendship, but never in want! Here we go! Ten-nine-eight-seven-six-five-four-three-two-ONE! Happy New Year!"

Blowing horns accompanied our shouts and cheers. My grin had never been so fucking wide and hard. I was intent on making this new year and every one after perfect for her and for us.

Zuri wrapped her arms around my waist, looking into my eyes. "Happy New Year, baby."

"Happy New Year. I love you," I spoke into her ear.

She cupped my face, lacing her fingers in my beard as she stared dreamingly into my eyes. "I love you too."

"I got us. I'm going to make sure that we're always happy. I got you. I'm going to make sure that the best of your past is going to be the worst of your future. I promise."

CHAPTER 16
ANNAN "LAW" WOODS

A week later, I was sitting in front of August and Willow's school, waiting for the end of the school day. Serenity had turned five over the summer, so she was finally in kindergarten. I had already picked her up. She was in the backseat, knocked out as if she had worked a full eight-hour shift.

An unknown number called. Since it was on my personal line, which few people had the number for, I answered.

"Hello?"

"You have a collect call from a prisoner at Statesville Correctional Center. If you would like to accept this call from..." My eyes narrowed, wondering who the fuck could have been calling me from the joint. I didn't have any homies locked up. If it was Persia, she was about to get cussed out. But then I heard a familiar voice announce itself, "Unc."

I accepted the call quickly.

"Young Blood!" Unc greeted.

A wide grin pierced through my beard. I had thought of Unc since I was released. I owed my freedom to him. Yet, I didn't know much about him personally to find out what facility he had been sent to.

"Unc! What up?!"

"What up, kid?"

I was taken aback when he sounded as happy to hear from me as well.

"Man, how you get my number?" I asked.

"I got my ways too, young blood. You ain't the only one plugged," he boasted cockily. "How you been?"

"I can't complain, man. How 'bout you? How you holding up in there?"

Unc clicked his tongue. "Man, you know I got this shit, young blood. It's a walk in the park. These young niggas ain't fucking with an OG. I'm good. This time is a breeze."

Me and Unc wrapped for about fifteen minutes about what I had been up to. He rarely wanted to talk about himself. He just wanted to hear about my life outside of prison. I told him all about my kids and Zuri. He was proud that I had finally got my girl. The most he would say about himself personally was when I asked how his daughter was holding up. She was still a mess, feeling as if his incarceration was her fault, but each day, she was getting better.

Knowing that our call was soon coming to an end, we started to say goodbye.

"What's your info so I can take care of you while you're in there?" I asked him.

"Nah, young blood. I didn't call for all that."

"Still, man. I owe you."

I wanted to go into more detail. I wanted to show him way more gratitude verbally and in any other way that I could. If it had not been for him, I wouldn't be in my family and Zuri's life. He had given me a second chance, and for that, I would forever be grateful and in his debt.

"You don't owe me shit," he insisted. "I was facing this time regardless."

"But—"

"Pay me back by living life to the best of your ability," Unc interrupted. "Take care of those kids and marry whoever that woman is that has your nose open." As I chuckled, he added, "And answer the phone for me when I call."

ZURI TURNER

"Shit! Shit! Shit!" I chanted, throwing the mail down on the coffee table. "*Fuuuuuck!*"

Screaming, I scared the fuck out of my baby, who jumped out of his skin in my arms and started to cry.

"Mommy's sorry," I cooed as I started to bounce. "I'm so sorry, baby."

Soothing him while trying to soothe my own panicking was fucking failing.

"Oh my God," I whined as tears came to my eyes while staring at the envelope facing me on the cocktail table. "Shit!"

The DNA results had come back, and I just didn't want to know. Law couldn't wait to get the results because, for him, it didn't matter. He was ready to be a father to Kingston no matter what, as he would with any children I would have had when we got together. But I wanted nothing to do with Rashaad, especially not having his baby. I *needed* Law to be Kingston's father. I *deserved* for him to be. Kingston deserved it. He deserved a good father who was loving and attentive, whose love was unconditional, who was loyal. Not some narcissistic, cheating, hoe that was a complete fucking embarrassment.

"Fuck!" I whispered harshly, now pacing the floor.

I just wanted this to go away. I could have lived the rest of my life not knowing. Lying to everyone about Rashaad being the father was me keeping people out of my business. But he couldn't biologically be the father.

He just couldn't.

As I freaked out, my phone began to ring. I knew who it was. If we weren't together, not two hours would go by before he checked in again,.

I peaked at the phone as it lay next to that envelope that had ruined my day and would possibly ruin my life.

It was indeed Law. Cringing, I double tapped my AirPod and answered it. "Hello?"

"What's wrong?" Law was instantly alarmed by my tone.

"Umm..."

"What?" he urged.

My entire being recoiled as I replied, "The DNA test results came in."

He went silent. I gnawed on my bottom lip nervously. Hoping that he didn't-

"I'm on my way."

Say that.

Fuck.

⚜

Law got there in ten minutes. His eyes were the size of nervous golf balls as he entered the house.

"Hey," I mumbled.

He smiled down at my nervousness, grabbed the back of my head, and kissed my forehead. For a second, I closed my eyes and enjoyed the feeling of his full lips on my forehead.

I loved his forehead kisses. They were so loving and protective.

He then grabbed my hand. "C'mon."

He guided me to the living room as if I didn't know how to get there myself. I reluctantly followed, legs feeling heavy with anxiety and nervousness.

"Where's the baby?"

"Sleeping."

"That lil' nigga always sleep." He then chuckled, but I could hear his own nervousness. He didn't care whose child Kingston was, but I knew that it would have made him so happy if Kingston was his child.

Standing at the cocktail table, I pointed at the letter with a trembling finger.

He bent down, picked it up, and ripped it open. I held my breath the entire time. I squeezed my eyes together tightly as he pulled the paper out of the envelope. The seconds that went by were agonizing. They felt like hours of complete torturous silence.

Then suddenly, I felt Law taking me into his arms. He was holding me so tight around the waist against his chest that I could barely look up into his eyes. But I was able to through the curls that were falling in my face. The tears in his eyes didn't give me any indication of what the results had read.

"Law?" I asked, voice trembling nervously.

Finally, he answered, "He's mine."

I breathed. Relieved, I nearly dropped to my knees.

Law let me go. "Whew! Where my son at?!"

Giggling, I stood up, feeling tons of pressure leave my chest. "Don't wake him up."

"Fuck that," he said, looking over in his bassinet.

Luckily, Kingston was upstairs. But Law didn't care. He took long strides out of the living room.

"Law! Don't you wake him up!"

He took the stairs two at a time, making me chase after him on my short legs.

By the time that I got into my bedroom, Law had gotten Kingston out of my bed. He was wide-eyed as Law cooed in his face. I took a moment to lean against my dresser and just watch Law love on our son. He was so adorable, making baby noises and kissing all over Kingston's face.

"I want you to meet my kids."

I blinked owlishly, not saying anything. Luckily, Law's back was to me, so he couldn't see the peculiar look on my face.

"It's time," he continued.

"Y-you think so?"

"Yeah," he said, turning around to face me. "We're a family. They are a part of that."

"Of course they are." I finally entered the room, sitting at the foot of my bed. "I was just wondering, with their mother leaving just recently, how they would feel about me. She was all they had known."

"They're gonna have to get used to it," he said with a shrug. He was still smiling into Kingston's face, still oblivious to how uncomfortable I was suddenly feeling. "I mean, we're going to be living together soon—"

"Are we?"

"Why wouldn't we?"

"I mean, we've only been together for a month."

"It's been longer than that."

I tilted my head, looking at him. "Are you talking about when you were locked up?"

Finally, he looked at me, smiling. He was so happy that his joy was contagious. I smiled beyond my reluctance.

"Yeah," he answered, shrugging.

"We were fucking."

"That's not all we were doing. Just because I didn't physically take you anywhere, I emotionally took you places no man ever has."

I sucked my jaws in and folded my arms in response to his cockiness.

He gave me a sexy, half-smile. "Tell me I'm lying."

I shyly laughed, lowering my eyes, knowing that I couldn't. In jail, he had managed to court my mind and body more than any man ever had.

"That's what I thought," he said, now bouncing Kingston, who was staring up at him. "So, it's not too soon. And if it is, so what. It's not too soon for us, for how we feel about each other. And I want to be with all my kids. It's time, baby."

I let him go on, convincing me that we should move in together soon. Yet, I only felt myself suffocating. I wasn't used to this family dynamic with anyone but Rashaad and Zoey. For most of my life, they had been all the family that I knew. I had only been Zoey's mother and was now adjusting to being a mother to Kingston after eighteen years of the same routine with the same child. And even though I loved Law and appreciated him being back in me and Kingston's lives, I wasn't as ready to merge our families together as he was. I was filled with fear and doubt when he was so damn sure.

ZOEY TURNER

The aroma of delicacy hit my nostrils and caused me to float up the stairs. I peeked my head into the kitchen, and instantly Zina gave me a warning look.

"What you want?" she sneered playfully.

Zina was sitting at the table in front of a rack of lamb, a double stuffed baked potato, and macaroni and cheese.

"*Ooo*, Auntie, let me get one," I begged.

I had been eating like a fucking peasant for a long time, gyros, pizza puffs, and other bullshit that was breaking out my skin.

Looking at the stove, I saw that there weren't any leftovers.

"Where'd you get that from?" I asked her.

"My business," she taunted me, shoving one of the lamb chops into her mouth.

That motherfucker looked juicy as hell.

My mouth was watering.

"Give me one," I pouted.

"No! Damn!" she laughed.

"Please?"

"No. Get a fucking job, Zoey. I'm sicka you."

I pouted, even stomping my foot a bit. "C'mon, Auntie."

"No, girl. Gon' and move back in with your mom. She over there laid up with that rich nigga. She can afford your spoiled ass again."

My brows curled. "What rich nigga?"

"Some nigga named Law. I've never heard of him before. He got a Bentley, though, so he must be holding. And he ain't uppity like yo' step daddy... I mean, *yo' beau*."

I smacked my lips, giving her an icy glare, and she just laughed. I had only talked to Zina and her kids since everyone found out about Rashaad and me. I was still dodging my grandfather. So, I was able to dodge the questions. But Zina always had jokes.

Giving up on begging like a homeless person, I stepped into the basement doorway, standing at the stairs.

"I'm serious about you getting a job, Zoey. It's been months. I can't keep paying for you to be here."

"Mmm humph," I murmured as I closed the basement door. This was Zina's one time in her life that she could ever stunt on somebody. She was just as poor as I was. She got by on child support, government assistance, and whatever nigga that was hitting her pockets every now and then. She was no better than me; she had just found ways to get over. And she was using her pussy to get by, just like I was trying to.

⚜

I hadn't seen Lobo since Zina had embarrassingly put him out. Ever since, I had been shooting my shot via text. I was throwing the pussy, sending him sexy pictures and all. But he had barely responded to them. Finally, that night he came to scoop me.

"You know a nigga named Law?" I asked him as we rode down 63rd.

"Yeah." He then looked over at me curiously before putting his eyes back on the road. "Why?"

I shrugged. "Nothing major. Just heard my auntie talking about him."

"She fucking him?" he asked with a smile.

"What's that smile for?"

"That nigga got bread. If she is, your auntie don' hit a lick."

"Damn, he holdin' like that?"

"Hell yeah. He's the plug. If niggas ain't trying to work with him, they tryin' to rob his ass." Then I peeped how a devilish look entered Lobo's eyes. "It's hard to catch that nigga slippin', though."

"Humph," I muttered.

Just then, something caught Lobo's attention. He slowed his trap car down to a crawl as we approached 63rd and Indiana. There was a group of guys on a corner that had his attention. I watched as he went down an alley and then parked on Michigan. He left the car running but was getting out.

"Get in the driver's seat."

Before I could ask why, he hopped out. I jumped out of his car and ran over to the driver's side. By the time I was in the driver's seat and closing the door, he was gone. I looked around, wondering where he could have gone that fast. I assumed that he had gone into one of the houses on the block. So, I sat back and started to scroll my Instagram feed. I lived my fantasies through Instagram. The IG models and influencers that I followed were living the lives that I was supposed to be living.

Suddenly, gunshots rang out one after the other. I screamed, ducking down. But they sounded like they were on the next block, instead of the one that I was sitting on. I started to frantically look around for Lobo, but I didn't see him.

Finally, I spotted him running out of an alley.

"What the fuck?" I muttered.

He was sprinting towards the car wildly. I could see a gun in his hand.

Once at the passenger side door, he tore it open and hopped in. "Drive!"

I was trembling as I threw the car in drive and sped off.

CHAPTER 17
ZURI TURNER

"**D**rink up, bitch."

I forced myself to smile as Bianca handed me a margarita, which she had made herself at my bar. It was strong as hell. The amount of tequila in it was burning my lips as soon as I took a gulp of it.

Then my phone rang.

I cringed, knowing that it was Law calling again. I peered at it in my lap, and sure enough, it was him. He had been calling all day. I feared that he would show up at any moment.

Bianca gave me sympathetic eyes. "Answer the phone," she softly encouraged me.

I winced. "I can't."

It was the day after we'd found out that Kingston was his, since he'd scared the fuck out of me with talk of me meeting his kids and moving in together.

Bianca sat beside me on the couch. Of course, my little sidekick, Kingston, was right there with us. Surprisingly, he wasn't sleeping. He was in his swing, watching me with those eyes. Now that I knew who his father was, he suddenly looked like Law to me. But I knew that was just in my head. His features had still yet to start blossoming.

"You can't just dodge his calls."

I shrugged a shoulder. "I've been texting him back."

Bianca's head tilted dramatically as she looked at me as if I should know better.

I sighed and admitted, "I just need a minute to think."

He had stayed the night last night, but the moment he left to take his kids to school this morning, I had been forcing space between us.

"He's just excited, Zuri."

I pouted. "I know."

"He's clearly never been in love before."

"I know."

That was so obvious. Law was good at loving and taking care of me. But it was crystal clear that this was new to him. He had no reluctance when approaching this love. He had no fear. He was just eager and ready. Yet, I was full of anxiety.

"It's cute," Bianca said with a small smile.

"It is." I threw my forehead into my hands, wincing. "I just... This shit is scary as fuck. I've never been a mother to..." I paused to count, and when I got to the total, my eyes bucked. "Four kids. Four, Bianca. They don't know me. And he wants to move in together. I've never lived with anyone except Rashaad. I don't know how to. He won't give me a minute to get used to this shit."

"What are you scared of?"

"I'm not scared. When I'm with him, I fear nothing." And that feeling was so fucking amazing. It felt so good to be with someone who I didn't have to wonder if he truly loved me or had my back. Law protected me from everything.

"Then what is it?" Bianca pressed.

"I'm worried. What if this doesn't work? What if his kids hate me? What if I hate them? I can't go through any more heartbreak or bullshit."

"I don't see Law as the type of nigga who will let that happen."

"He's not," I admitted. "In my heart, I know that. But I don't trust my heart."

Bianca's sympathetic pout deepened.

"Anyway," I said, sighing heavily. "Guess what?"

Noticing that I had some tea, Bianca slightly sat up. "What?"

"The Feds called and told me that Rashaad took a plea deal."

Her eyes widened as she took a sip of her margarita. "For how long?"

"Twenty years. I thought they would give his dumb ass more time for running, but clearly, that first deal was just to scare him."

"Wow. So, it's finally over?"

"Yeah," I said with a heavy breath. "It's finally over."

"How do you feel about that?"

I shrugged. "I don't know. It all still feels so unreal; him and Zoey. They were completely different than who I thought they were. Rashaad sleeping with my daughter and stealing from the government. I still can't wrap my head around that shit."

She laid a hand on my leg, giving me a knowing stare. "You probably never will."

ANNAN "LAW" WOODS

I was pulling up on Zuri.

She had me fucked up.

I pulled into her driveway. I noticed Bianca's car but didn't give a fuck. I hopped out and slammed the door. Then I stalked through the cold towards the porch.

Though it was mid-January, it surprisingly wasn't as brutally cold as January in Chicago could be. I wasn't even feeling the cold under my hoodie, but that could have been because Zuri had me hot.

I knew that her distance that day had been because of the talk I had had with her the previous night about meeting my kids and moving in. I understood her reluctance. Her marriage had ended in a heartbreak that many women could never survive. And still, her life had been routine for so long. I was switching that routine up like a motherfucker, and it was too much for her.

Instead of ringing the doorbell, I beat on the door. I peered inside the foyer, seeing that the lights were on inside.

As soon as I started to beat on it again, she came scampering to the door, frantic and wide-eyed.

She tore the door open.

"Come out here," I demanded.

"Wh-what—"

"Come out here," I said with more force. "Let me holla at you."

"O-okay," she stammered, now nervous because she saw how angry I was. "Let me get a sweater."

She left the doorway, slightly closing it. I started to pace. Her fear had me pissed. She may not have known me for that long, but she knew me. By now, she knew that she had absolutely nothing to fear.

Soon, she was easing out of the front door wearing a long sweater that went along with one of those Fashion Nova sets that she often wore around the house to be warm.

"Really?" I barked. "You really gon' be this fucking immature and ignore me because you scared?"

"I—"

"You know what this shit is. You ain't no lil' girl, Zuri. You feel this shit between us," I fussed. "I ain't making shit up. Soon as I met you, we took each other's souls. When you were married to that bitch ass nigga, you were thinking about me. When you were under that pretty boy, you were thinking about me. And now you got me, and you gon' run?"

Her eyes were ballooned. She was taken aback by my anger. "I'm sorry."

"Nah, fuck that. That's how you do me?"

"I wasn't trying to—"

"If this how you gonna be, then I'm gon'."

Her mouth dropped.

"I'm not built for this shit. I can't take feeling this shit when I feel like I'm losing you. I was good before. I missed you, but I didn't feel this. This shit hurt. So, if this is what you want, cool."

"Law, wait!" I felt her pulling on my hoodie. "Wait! I'm sorry."

I gritted. Something was telling me to get the fuck up out of there. I didn't like this feeling of not being in control, of another person causing me this worry and pain.

"Yes, I was scared," she said into my back. "I don't know anything else but Rashaad and Zoey. I don't know how to be anyone else's wife or mother. I only know how to be theirs." Hearing the pain in her voice, I finally turned around, facing my biggest fears. All my life, I thought what I feared the most was dying at the hands of one of these haters or losing my life to prison. But, no, it was this. Giving my heart to a woman was so much scarier.

"And it's scary to know that I'm going to be someone else's," she said with pleading eyes. "To know that I'm being thrown into this place where I can be hurt again or fail again. But I was wrong for being scared because I should know that you would never—"

I grabbed her face and kissed her. Even though I was pissed at her, I didn't want to be the person that made her feel this worry or concern. So, I kissed her to let her know that it was okay, that she still had me. I pushed her back against the house, taking her. And she let go. Her body wilted and succumbed to me. That shit was so fucking sexy. My dick got rock hard.

I took her by the waist, guiding her over to the railing. I then bent her over.

She gasped, feeling the cold air against her ass as I pulled her leggings down.

"Law... Wait..." She tried to turn around, but I had pinned her in place as I pulled my dick out of my jogging pants.

Still, she tried to refuse. "We're on the—" She then gasped as I plunged into her juices. "Fuck!"

Holding her waist, I started delivering deep strokes. She held on to the railing, whimpering.

"Law... Baby... We're on the porch."

"I don't give a fuck," I moaned, succumbing to the pussy.

I started drilling her sweet center, not feeling the cold, only the warmth of what was mine. She tried to muffle her sounds, but my strokes were demanding that she praise me aloud. She started to whimper and call my name unapologetically.

"Yes, Law! *Yeeees*, baby."

Her pussy was gripping my dick. My own damn knees were weak. My dick was so happy to be where it belonged. A pleasure washed over me that I was feeble to. I couldn't fight that shit. Nor did I want to.

"Zuri," I groaned her name out loud. "Fuck, I love you."

Her body trembled under me. Her legs shook violently as waves of orgasms ignited. Feeling her juices flood my dick, I burst inside of her.

"Argh!" I barked. "Fuck!"

I held onto her tight as I caught my breath. She collapsed onto the railing, holding on to it for support.

Finally, I slipped out of her. I returned my dick to my pants. I then squatted and pulled her leggings up for her.

She slowly turned around, looking up at me.

"So, what's this?" I had got the pussy, but I wasn't about to play these games. "I'm not a punk, but I'm done playing with you."

Her head tilted as she crossed her arms. "I just fucked you on my porch. I'm in this." Then she slowly smiled up into my eyes and took my hand. "C'mon."

I allowed her to pull me into the house. She led me into the living room. As soon as we entered, Bianca was looking at us, sucking her jaws in with her lips pursed. "Y'all some *nasty* motherfuckas

ZURI TURNER

"Your daughter is about to get put the fuck out."

I rolled my eyes as I applied my lipstick. "What she do?"

Zina scoffed through the speakerphone. "She keeps sneaking that nigga into my house after I told her not to."

"How do you know?"

"I'm up all night with the baby. I hear shit."

"Then check her ass."

Zoey staying with Zina was starting to be a burden on me. Zina must have assumed, as I had for many years, that Zoey was responsible and would be on her shit when she moved in. However, I guessed that Zoey sleeping with Rashaad hadn't been the end of her self-destruction.

"I already did. So, if she keeps playing with me, she's getting put out. She's playing a dangerous game. That nigga ain't shit."

"What nigga is?" I smirked as I sprayed my face with setting spray.

Besides mine, I thought, playfully sticking my tongue out at my own reflection.

I was getting ready for a date with Law. Him popping up at my house and fucking the shit out of me on that porch a week ago had put me in check. I needed to stop acting like a punk and enjoy Law with open arms. Even if I ended up with another broken heart, it would be a privilege to have my heart broken again by him.

"Nah, this ain't the normal 'ain't shit'," Zina scoffed. "I know him from around the hood. He be into a lot of shit. His name is attached to a lot of murders and robberies. They saying he is the one that killed those three guys on 63rd and Indiana the other day."

Disgusted, I shook my head. My daughter's life had completely changed. I felt helpless every time Zina called me. Zoey was like a completely different person. I wondered who the fuck I had been raising. She was clearly a master manipulator because she had had me fooled. Even if she wasn't going to college, I expected her to do something with her life. I had raised her better than that, and she had much more potential. She should have been living her life's dreams and fulfilling her goals. Not living in Zina's basement, fucking some nothing ass, hood nigga that couldn't even give her a few dollars.

"She needs some help, Zuri," Zina told me.

"I know. But what can I say? She doesn't respect me. She hasn't even apologized."

I then got a text message notification. It was a text from Law saying that he was outside. "I have to go, Zina. Law is here."

"I guess. While you're over there living your best life with your new nigga, I'm over here dealing with your bullshit."

"You asked for it," I taunted her. "Bye, Zina."

"Bye," she groaned, hanging up.

Grabbing my phone, I ran to the closet to grab my Moncler. It wasn't freezing outside just yet, but Law had told me that I needed to dress warm. So, I was wearing some skinny jeans and a Gucci sweater with matching boots.

Once dressed, I hurried out of my bedroom and down the hall. I then trotted down the steps, shouting, "Marlene, I'm gone!"

"Okay," she shouted back from the living room.

Marlene had been a dream come true. She not only helped out

during her scheduled hours. Whenever I needed her, when Law wanted to take me out, she was there. She had grown a liking to me and Kingston, and she was slowly becoming like family to me. When Gloria, Law's mother, had come by to meet me and Kingston the other day, Marlene was here, and Gloria insisted that I could fire Marlene. Gloria felt like *she* could be the one spending all that time with Kingston instead, but there was no way I was firing Marlene. I needed her maternal presence with me.

Meeting Gloria had been a privilege, though. It made me feel like Law was really in this for good.

Once outside, I hurried towards Law's Bentley and hopped in.

"Hey, baby." I greeted him with a quick peck on the lips.

I inhaled his signature scent, Baccarat Rouge, and got comfortable in the leather seats as he backed out of the driveway. Immediately, he put his hand on the inside of my thigh, where it was the warmest.

"Where are we going?" I asked. I had noticed that, unlike other times, he hadn't told me where he was taking me. Every time I asked that day, he would avoid the question.

Looking at me quickly, he winked, making my pussy clench. "It's a surprise."

❀

"*Aaaaaaw*, baby!" I was jumping up and down like a little kid, smiling from ear to ear. "Are you serious?" I giggled uncontrollably, touched by his thoughtfulness.

Law looked down at me proudly, watching me unravel excitedly.

We were at an amusement park. I had told him some time ago that I had never been to one.

"But... Babe?" Looking around, I noticed that the park looked deserted. It was completely empty. "It looks closed."

"It is closed..." He smirked cockily. "To everyone but us."

I gasped, covering my mouth.

"It's not even the season for them to be open. I paid the owner to open it up for us."

Tears instantly came to my eyes. I was so tired of looking like a punk in front of Law. But he always had me crying for some reason. However, they were always tears of joy.

"C'mon." He took my hand and pulled me along towards the entrance.

Law's legs were so much longer than mine that I had to walk faster to keep up with him.

The night was magical. I felt like a Disney Princess or a Kingpins girlfriend in one of those hood books that Bianca is always reading. All of the staff treated us like royalty, and since Law had paid for it to open just for us, we didn't have to pay for anything. All of the games, rides, and even concession stands were comped. They had even installed heat lamps at each game and ride to ensure that we were nice and warm.

Law and I spent two hours playing all of the games. He had even ensured that he won me a lot of the big stuffed animals. By the time we were done playing, it took four of the staff to carry them to Law's car.

Then we rode every ride. Law was actually freaking out on some of them because he had never been on a roller-coaster. But he tried to act like he wasn't scared, playing it cool. I could feel his fear when we would go into the air because his grip on my hand would become tighter. It was funny to look over and see his gangsta ass on those rides with those locs and leather blazer with chinchilla fur around the hood and a mean mug.

"This was so nice, baby." We had decided to ride the Ferris wheel last. We were snuggled up with one another as it slowly turned. I looked over at him, and his dark eyes devoured me, holding me captive. "I love you."

Slowly smiling, he cupped my face and brought my lips to his. He then took my lips, initiating a filthy kiss that engulfed my needy body.

CHAPTER 18

ZOEY TURNER

Since the shooting, Lobo and I had spent a lot of time together. I had snuck him into the basement that night. As he'd slept, I had been on all the Chicago hood Instagram profiles trying to see if they would post about the shooting. By the morning, they had. Lobo had killed three men on that corner.

Lobo had left that morning but come back the next night. I knew that he wasn't there because he liked me. I felt as if he was only there because he wanted to be sure that I didn't go to the police. Most times, we were in motels. I would ask him why we never went to his place, and he gave me the same excuse that he lived too far and didn't want me at his trap house in the neighborhood.

When he would complain about spending the money for rooms all the time, I would sneak him into the basement.

"I'll holla at you later," Lobo told me softly as we stood at the back door.

"Okay," I returned, opening the door.

I hoped that he would kiss me, but he didn't. Lobo wasn't soft or caring with me at all. He merely fucked me. Sometimes he would take me to get something to eat, but mostly we picked it up on our way to go fuck. I was hoping that he would eventually open up to me so that he could help me get out of this situation. I was still working him, though.

I closed the door after him and hurried back to the bed. It was cold in the basement because it was the dead of winter and Zina's cheap ass refused to raise her heat above seventy degrees.

"*Shiiiit*," I shivered as I snuggled underneath the covers.

It was before seven in the morning, and Lobo and I had stayed up until two in the morning drinking and fucking. I was ready to close my eyes and go back to sleep, but I heard the basement door. Then I could hear Zina storming down the stairs.

"Fuck," I groaned. "Here we go."

She hardly ever came downstairs but to wash and talk shit when I did something wrong. I knew that she wasn't washing that early in the morning, so I closed my eyes, pretending to be asleep.

"Get the fuck out, Zoey."

Zina sounded so serious that my eyes sprung open in disbelief. "Huh?"

"Get *out*," she pressed through clenched teeth.

I stared at her blankly. "Stop playing, Auntie."

She stomped towards the let-out couch. She then ripped the covers off of me.

"I'm not playing with you! Get the fuck out! You gotta go! I told you to stop letting that nigga come into my house."

"This was the only time," I lied. "He was too drunk to drive home."

"So, I look stupid to you," she sneered. "The only goofy mother-fucka here is you. I can hear, Zoey. That nigga be here all the time. You got me fucked up. I told you he was trouble, but you so hard up for some dick that you're willing to put me and my kids at risk?!"

I blinked owlishly, not wanting to say anything that would make her really put me out.

"Get out, Zoey." She wasn't even yelling. She was so calm that I knew she wasn't playing games.

"Get out before I *help you* get out."

She was so pissed that I knew she was fighting to keep from putting her hands on me. Sighing, I stood and started to collect my things. "You know I don't have anywhere to go."

"Go with that nigga and let me know how that goes," she taunted me.

I bit my tongue. "Really?"

"Yes, really. If you gave a fuck about securing the place that you live *for free*, you would have given a fuck about it, but you don't. You think you too good to help out or listen to me. So, take your saditty ass on."

Zina had a lot of fucking nerve standing there looking at me like I was beneath her when she was way grimier than I could ever be.

My glare was icy as I shook my head. "You ain't shit."

Her eyes ballooned. "Me? *I* ain't shit? I took your fake bougie, broke ass in. You can't blame nobody but yourself for fucking your mother's husband."

"Bet." Then I scoffed, shaking my head. "Don't worry about it. I'll get my things and leave."

"Thank you," she spat and then stormed out and up the stairs. On the way, I could hear her murmuring more obscenities which were making my blood boil.

I hurriedly packed. It didn't take me long because I didn't have many things. I threw on some joggers, a shirt, and my coat. I stormed towards the back door, carrying all of my things with me, and slammed it after me.

Throwing my hood on, I walked up the gangway. I reached into my pocket for my phone and called Lobo, hoping that he hadn't gotten too far.

"Hello?"

"Lo! Can you come back and get me?"

"Why? What's wrong?"

"My auntie put me out. She knew you've been over here."

He clicked his tongue, and I frowned. But he said, "A'ight. I'm around the corner. Here I come."

I walked to the corner, and he was soon pulling up. I opened the back passenger door and threw my things inside. I then hopped into the passenger seat.

"Where I'm taking you to?" he asked, seemingly pressed.

"To your place. I don't have anywhere else to go."

He laughed dryly, which made my skin crawl. "Nah, shawty, you can't do that."

"Why not?" I asked, glaring at the side of his head. He wouldn't even look at me as he drove off.

"Look. I got a bitch, okay?" he said coolly.

"Are you fucking serious?" I snapped. "Do she know you been fucking and laying up with me?"

He scoffed. "Man, shawty, chill."

"Ain't no chill! You've been fucking me for weeks! With yo' lying ass! You can at least look out for me!"

"Okay, okay," he frowned, annoyed. "I'll get you a room."

ZURI TURNER

Law looked at me, chuckling and shaking his head.

"This isn't funny," I scowled.

He grinned teasingly. "It *is*. You have nothing to be worried about."

My pout deepened. "Yes, I do. My family is crazy."

Law clicked his tongue, waving off my anxiety. "Girl, c'mon."

Law opened his driver's door, and I groaned, opening mine.

Tonight was the monthly dinner at Dad's. Law insisted that he come because he wanted to meet my family. I told him that I would have preferred he met my dad when it was just us, but Law was persistent that he meet everyone.

I slowly climbed out of the car, regretting that I had allowed him to force me into this. Law was still laughing at me while he got Kingston out of the back seat.

"You better not judge me after you meet these motherfuckers," I fussed.

"Your dad sounds like he's cool."

"He's not the issue. My crazy ass sisters are. Well, Zadah, really."

"You already warned me about her. How she is has nothing to do with you."

I was still pouting. He closed the back passenger door and then stepped towards me, kissing my forehead.

He grabbed my hand and started towards the house. My legs were literally shaking. I knew that seeing Law would ignite pettiness in Zadah that would erupt from her mouth in pure ignorance.

I rang the doorbell and took a deep breath. I could hear my nieces and nephews inside playing. Soon the locks on the door were unlocking, and it opened.

"Hey, Z—" Zina's greeting stopped abruptly when she saw Law standing next to me. She had seen pictures of him on my social media because I posted pictures of us. A slick grin spread on her face from ear to ear, and then she smiled. "*Awwww*, shit! Law is in the building!"

Then she lightly pushed me to the side and grabbed his arm. "C'mon in, brother-in-law!"

I held my forehead in embarrassment, but Law laughed as he walked into the house. As I followed, I heard the house go completely silent. I hadn't told anyone that Law was coming because I wasn't ready for the interrogation.

Looking around the living room, I saw my father, Zadah, Treyvon, and the kids looking up at Law. My dad had heard of him, and I was sure that Zadah had seen him on my social media, but they didn't know that we were serious enough for him to come to dinner.

"Law, this is my dad, my sisters Zina and Zadah, and Zadah's fiancé, Treyvon." Then I took a deep breath, swallowing my fear. "Everybody, this is Law, my man, and... Kingston's father."

"The fuck?" Zadah spit.

Zina's eyes bucked dramatically, and then she started cracking up.

"Wait..." My father blinked slowly, staring from me to Law to Kingston. "So... you were cheating on Rashaad?"

My lips pursed together, and I nodded. I knew that if Law and I were going to be together, it wasn't fair to him that my family thought that Rashaad was Kingston's son. I had to be honest.

Zina's bellowing got louder. "Good for you, bitch!"

The entire room laughed, even Zadah and Law. The tension was then eased.

Law handed me Kingston and then went around the living room, shaking hands with the men and hugging the women. My eyes narrowed as I watched Zadah size him up, but that bitch kept her distance.

As he started to speak to the kids, the doorbell rang. I was closest, so I answered it.

Opening it, I was floored to see Zoey. We hadn't been face-to-face since Zadah had exposed her. My eyes sympathized with her. She didn't look like my Zoey anymore. She looked rough, unkempt, and dirty.

"Hi," she muttered, avoiding my eyes.

"Hi, Zoey." My heart was beating violently. I didn't know what to say or do. I wanted to hug her, but I also wanted to smack the shit out of her.

A gust of cold wind rushed by, landing an icy cloud on us, so I was forced to hurriedly step out of the doorway, protecting Kingston from the cold.

As she stepped into the house, she curiously eyed Kingston. I knew that she had most likely seen him on my social media. What had also kept me away from her was the fact that she hadn't even apologized or reached out for the sake of getting to know him. He was her brother and only other sibling, but she had the audacity to be too ornery with me to even acknowledge him.

She continued to ignore his existence, pulling her eyes away from him, and proceeded into the living room. Everyone fell silent again, but this was their first time seeing her since everything had happened as well. Law watched me sympathetically as I clung to Kingston as if he could support me through this tension.

"Hey, sweetheart." My dad lovingly kissed her on the cheek with a hug.

I looked at Zadah, watching her sneer at Zoey. Treyvon lowered his head, reluctant of the drama that we all felt coming. Surprisingly, Zina sneered at Zoey. I made eye contact with Zina and then walked by everyone into the kitchen. Law watched me longingly. Because of my stare, Zina knew to follow me.

"*Biiiitch*," she sang as she came in.

"Did you know she was coming here?" I asked her.

"No. I kicked her out this morning."

My eyes bucked. "For real?"

"She snuck that nigga in again. She had to go."

I sighed, shaking my head.

"So, maybe she is here to make up with you because she needs a place to stay," Zina suggested. "This is the best place for her to do it. She knows Dad won't let things get too far."

A part of me hoped that that was the case. I hoped that Zoey had finally come around to being the girl that I raised and would be kind enough to at least apologize. Even as I hoped that, I wondered how we would ever get back to where we were. Even the thought of that process was exhausting.

I grimaced, shaking my head. Of course, this shit would go down when Law was here.

Zina's eyes empathized with my being uncomfortable. I simply shrugged and left out of the kitchen. Zina was on my heels.

"I'm glad you're here, baby," my dad was telling Zoey as me and Zina walked back into the living room.

"I just wanted to come by to see everyone. I won't be here long," she told my dad, which got my attention.

I lingered back near the space that separated the dining room from the kitchen.

Even my dad's eyes narrowed. "You aren't staying for dinner?"

"*Naaah*," she said slowly. "I can't break bread with family that has babies by their *sister's fiancé*."

"What?!" my father barked, whipping his head towards Zina.

"The fuck?!" Zadah spewed, standing to her feet.

"Oh shit," I muttered under my breath as I recoiled. I gave Law a knowing look, and he just lowered his head, avoiding my reprimand.

I should have never let him talk me into this.

Zadah's face contorted into confusion as she looked between me and Zina.

"Yeah, Zina!" Zoey spewed.

Oh fuck...

My heart beat frantically as Zoey kept on, "While you were talking all that shit about me not being shit. *You* ain't shit! Tremere is Treyvon's baby, Zadah! I heard Zina talking to him on the phone about it!"

Oh God. I recoiled, shaking my head.

Zadah immediately took off towards Zina, knocking over cocktail tables *and* kids. Law immediately started to push the kids out of the way. As Zadah and Zina collided and started to attack one another, Treyvon stepped in, trying to pull them apart. I stood back, holding Kingston tight, glaring at Zoey. I was in disbelief at the pleasure on her face while she watched Treyvon unsuccessfully get in between Zadah and Zina as they tried to beat each other's faces into the floor.

"You stank ass bitch!" Zadah snarled as she tried to pull Zina's lace front off of her head.

"Fuck you!" Zina growled, attempting the same.

They continued to spit obscenities at one another while pulling off wigs. Zadah's shirt was in pieces, causing her titties to fall out. My dad, embarrassed, started to rush the kids down the hall and into the bedrooms, giving Law the opportunity to help Treyvon pull Zina and Zadah apart. He was easily able to snake his arm around Zina's waist and lift her up into the air. Her chocolate face was painted red with blood. As she spat violent threats at Zadah, blood flew from her mouth.

"Yeah, I fucked your nigga! That's my baby daddy too, bitch! How it feel, hoe?!"

"I'mma kill you!" Zadah screamed as she clawed her way out of Treyvon's grasp, but he successfully had a hold on her. He started to drag her towards the front door. That's when I realized that the door was wide open, and Zoey was gone.

Disappointment made my heart break. She hadn't come to make amends. She had come to start this shit and leave. That realization brought tears to my eyes. I was heartbroken that she was still so ornery and resentful that she didn't feel the need to simply say that she was sorry. Instead, she was intent on creating more chaos and breaking even more bonds that she needed.

Sobbing, I walked towards the front door. On the way out, I grabbed Kingston's car seat. Zina was still yelling threats and vulgarities at Zadah, who, once I was outside, could hear Zadah doing the same as Treyvon was forcing her into the car.

AANAN "LAW" WOODS

I wanted to follow behind Zuri, but I knew that if I let Zina go, she would run outside.

Luckily, their dad was coming out of the hallway. He rushed towards me, saying, "I got her."

I slowly let her go, and of course, she tried to rush past her father. But he was a big, stalky dude, so he had been able to stop her.

I rushed out of the door and made sure that it was closed tight behind me.

I could hear the muffled sounds of Zadah screaming, and then a car pull off. I looked around and saw Zuri in my car with her face in her hands.

I rushed to the car and hopped in.

"What did I do to her to make her hate me so much?" Zuri cried.

I could only hold her. There was nothing that I could say to make her feel better. I wanted to protect her from this, to make it better, but I couldn't. That was Zoey's job, and she was failing.

Zuri cried into my chest for a few minutes. When she pulled back, her makeup was smeared all over her face and my shirt.

"I'm so sorry, babe," she told me.

"Why?"

"You know what? I take that back," she sassed. "I ain't sorry about shit. I told yo' ass my family was crazy and not to come over here."

Laughing, I started the car. There was no way we were going back in that house that night.

As I backed out of the driveway, I told her, "Yeah, you did, but all families got that bullshit."

She looked at me with disbelief dancing in her tearful eyes. "That didn't scare you away?"

I scoffed with a smile. "Hell no."

She smiled, relieved, wiping her tears away.

"I know one thing, though." I smirked, looking at her.

She watched me reluctantly. "What?"

"I'll never call you bougie again. Y'all some *ghetto* motherfuckas."

◈

I had stopped at Harold's to get us something to eat before taking us back to Zuri's crib.

As she started to get out of the car, my cell rang. I didn't recognize the number, but it was a Florida area code.

"Go ahead and take the food in the house. I'll grab Kingston."

She nodded, taking the food that was already in her lap and getting out. I knew that my baby was exhausted from all the drama and Zoey's bullshit. Even her walk was weak.

I answered the phone. "Hello?"

"Hi. Is this Aanan Woods?"

I sat up, wondering who the fuck would know my government name. This didn't sound like one of those scam calls. "Yes, it is."

"This is Detective Conrad from the homicide division of the Palmetto Bay police department. Do you have time to talk?"

I grimaced and lightly pounded my hand on the steering wheel. Then I forced myself to sound unfazed. "Yes."

"I, unfortunately, have some bad news for you." He then cleared his throat. "We... um... We found a body of a female homicide victim two weeks ago. That body was positively identified as Whitney Price today."

I feigned sorrow. "Wow... O-okay."

I was relieved that her body had finally been found. I had purposely chosen not to get rid of her body altogether. I needed her body to be found eventually so that there would be a death certificate, which was needed for her policies to be paid out and for the properties to be transferred to the kids.

"I'm so sorry for your loss."

"What happened to her?" I played along.

"We are conducting an autopsy, but it looks like homicide. It appears that she was the victim of a home invasion and kidnapping some time ago. The home that she was living in had been vandalized."

"Are you sure that it's her?" I pressed to put the act on even more.

"Yes. She was positively identified by dental records."

"Wow." I then cleared my throat. "Okay."

"We don't have any suspects at this time. But we are working diligently on the case..."

I got out of the car, allowing him to run this shit down. He'd told me who to call at the morgue to fly her body to Chicago. But he had informed me that there wasn't much of her body left to have a funeral with.

ZURI TURNER

A couple of hours later, I was emotionally exhausted. Law had tried to get my mind off of what had happened by talking to me about any and everything, but I couldn't shake the sadness.

After we ate and I put Kingston down to sleep, we went into my bedroom to call it a night.

"Are you staying the night?" I asked him.

"I need to go home. Willow has been acting really clingy still. She misses her mom."

I pouted as I collapsed on the bed. "I understand."

"See?" he asked, smiling dramatically so that I would. "This is why we need to hurry up and move in together."

I giggled weakly. My inability to give him anything more made his shoulders sink. He walked toward me and grabbed my hand. I looked curiously at him as he pulled me up to my feet.

"What?" I reluctantly asked.

"Come here."

As he started to walk me towards the master bathroom, I had no strength to fight him. But I had no idea what he wanted. I prayed that he wasn't trying to have some sexy moment in the shower. I loved my baby, but my head wasn't in it at the moment.

I was forced to smile when I saw that the bathroom light was off. However, it was dimly lit with a multitude of candles. There was a bubble bath that had been ran. I could smell the lavender that he had added to the water. There was a glass of wine on the edge of the tub, along with my phone and AirPods.

I looked back at him, touched, as he leaned against the doorway.

"Relax. Take some you time," he said smoothly. "I got the baby."

My shoulders sank, warmed at his efforts. He coolly winked and then left the doorway, closing the door behind him. I started to strip, appreciative that after all the mayhem, I still had something to be happy about. Law was keeping his promise; he would always make sure that I had a smile on my face.

I heard the television come on in my bedroom as I finished stripping. Then my phone began to vibrate. I quietly groaned when I saw that it was Zina calling again.

Scowling, I sat on the edge of the tub and answered. I had ignored so many of her calls since I'd left my father's house. I didn't want her to continue calling while I was trying to obey my man and relax.

"Yes, Zina?" I answered quietly because I didn't want Law to hear me,

"Damn, you mad at me or something? I didn't do anything. Your damn daughter–"

"Zina, I don't want to talk about this shit. I am sick of you and Zadah's bullshit–"

"Wow. Really?"

"Yes. Zoey was wrong for telling, but you were wrong for even fucking Treyvon. It was going to come out eventually."

"That's some–"

"I'm done, Zina. Fucking done. I'm over all the drama. It's fucking exhausting. I need some space from all of it for a while."

"Damn. So, you need some space from me?"

"*Yes*, I do." And before she could say anything else, I told her, "I have to go, Zina."

Then I hung up and put my phone on Do Not Disturb.

I had to stop subscribing to my sisters' drama. Unfortunately, if that meant separating from them, so be it.

A MONTH LATER

CHAPTER 19
AANAN "LAW" WOODS

I t had been a month since that dinner at Zuri's pop's crib. Zoey had really fucked her head up, but she was finally getting back to her old self.

But I wanted to ensure that her smile was back on her permanently and that she knew that despite the disloyalty around her, she deserved the best.

"Hey, baby," Zuri greeted me with a smile as she opened the front door. I licked my lips as I stared at the Ethika sports bra and booty shorts that she was wearing. The bright colors popped off of her brown skin. The shorts were barely covering her ass. Her ample cheeks were hanging out of the bottom of them as she switched back and forth, hypnotizing me while walking through the foyer.

When she realized that I was lingering in the foyer, rather than following her to the living room, she looked back over her shoulder.

"What are you doing, babe?"

"Go pack a bag," I smoothly told her.

Her confusion was cute as her brows curled. "Huh?"

"*Go pack a bag.* We're going to the airport."

Chuckling nervously, she asked, "What?"

I slid towards her, closing the space between us, and held both of her hands. She slowly smiled, looking up at me with a curious grin.

"I want you to go upstairs and pack a bag."

"Where are we going?" She smiled.

I shrugged. "I don't know. We'll see when we get to the private jet."

Her eyes ballooned. "Private jet?!"

"Yeah. I booked us a private jet."

"Shut up," she said, play smacking my arm. "No, you didn't."

I bent down, kissing her forehead. "Yes, I did, baby."

Her eyes batted bashfully as she looked up at me. "Why?"

"You deserve a vacation."

"How long are we going to be gone?"

I shrugged a shoulder. "How long do you want to be gone?"

She flushed with admiration and pure joy. "What about Kingston?"

"I already called Marlene. She's on her way."

She took a step back, almost startled. "You're serious."

"As fuck."

I needed to show her what a real nigga does. Fuck taking her out to eat, to the movies, or going to bars. She could do that herself. I needed to give her what she couldn't give herself; back shots on a balcony in perfect weather with palm trees in the distance.

"THIS IS SO DOPE, BAE!" ZURI WAS GIDDY AS SHE CLIMBED THE STEPS of the jet. "This is *niiiice*," she said, mimicking Tiffany Haddish.

I chuckled, proud that I was able to put this smile on her face. She looked around the jet in pure amazement.

This jet was nice than a bitch. The Boeing Business Jet could sit up to twenty people, and had a full kitchen, two restrooms with showers, and a separate dining room. It looked more like a luxurious one-bedroom condo.

"Here, baby. Take some pictures of me.," Zuri spat excitedly.

I took the phone from her, teasing, "Oh, you need some pics for the gram?"

"Hell yeah," she boasted as she posed in a seat.

My baby looked beautiful. She was only in a pair of Fendi leggings with the logo and a matching tank top. She took off her Moncler coat now that we were on the jet. She had put on her makeup, and her hair was extra big and shiny.

I took quite a few pictures for her and even some videos.

"Would you like me to take a picture of both of you?" the flight attendant asked.

"Yes," Zuri answered excitedly.

I handed the flight attendant the phone, and we posed for a few pictures.

"Now, what would you like to drink?" she asked.

"I'll take a double shot of Glenlivet neat," I told her.

"I'll take the same."

My eyes whipped towards Zuri. "Oh, you drinking whiskey with your nigga?"

"Yeah, fuck it. It's a vacation."

"Oh, I'm about to get some pussy *pussy*."

The flight attendant laughed along with us.

Just then, the pilot emerged from the cockpit.

"So," he said with a smile, clapping his hands together. "Where are we going today?"

I looked over to Zuri. She still looked baffled at this entire experience. The whole time that she packed, she kept asking me if I were serious. She had packed a bit of everything, but it was all summer fits or swimwear, so, of course, she wanted to go somewhere warm or tropical.

"The Maldives," she finally answered.

I nodded, liking that answer. I had never been, but I had seen pictures on social media. That shit looked sexy as fuck. There was definitely going to be a lot of Backshot Mania popping in that moth-erfucker.

"Great choice." The pilot smiled. "Well, buckle up and get ready for takeoff. Once we are in the air and the seat belt sign is off, you can retire to the sky bedroom if you'd like."

Zuri's eyes ballooned animatedly. "A *bedroom*? There's a bedroom on here?!"

The pilot roared with laughter at her excitement. "Yes, there is a bedroom through that door right behind you."

She looked behind herself with her mouth fully agape. "Oh shit," she breathed.

❦

"YES, BABY! OH MY GOD," ZURI'S VOICE QUIVERED.

"I love you so much," I groaned.

She whimpered, throwing her ass back on my dick. "I love you too. *Fuck*."

The Backshot Mania had started as soon as we took off and escaped to the bedroom. The scent of her moist center wafting into my nose as I hit it from the back was making it so hard for me not to cum.

"Turn over," I demanded. I had to pull out to keep myself from bussing too early.

She was weak as she tried to roll over, so I assisted her by grabbing her by the waist and putting her on her back.

I then spread her thick thighs apart and dove between her phat lips. She opened her thighs even wider as her fingers laced in my locs. She began to feed me her peach savagely, grinding it into my face. Her moans of passion drowned out the roar of the jet's engine, encouraging me to devour her pulsating clit.

"Fuck," she panted. "Fuck, baby. I'm cumming."

I smacked her ass, and she let out a high-pitched exhale.

"C'mon," I demanded softly. "Give it to me, baby. Cum in my mouth."

"Shit!" she spat.

Her clit was throbbing in my mouth, so I knew that she was about to cum. So, I sucked with passionate finesse, holding her thighs apart so that her knees were touching the bed.

As I French-kissed her clit, my hand caressed her ass, writing poetry all over them as my tongue tasted the words.

"Oh God!" she screamed as her juices began to shoot down my throat.

Then I lifted to my knees and grabbed her waist. She was still recovering from that orgasm, still catching her breath, still quivering. But I didn't give her any time to recover. I brought that pussy to me and plunged deep into my home.

ZOEY TURNER

♫ *Whole lotta money in this safe, don't worry about us*
I got a bad bitch in my place, she don't care if I touch
We just fuck, but I can't say it, but she still my crush
This smoke gon' take me straight to space like I'm Elon Musk
Elon Musk, like I'm Elon Musk
This smoke gon' take me straight to space like I'm Elon Musk ♫

As Lobo pulled up on my mother's block, I sat up and turned down "Elon Musk".

"This is it right here," I told Lobo as I handed him the blunt and pointed to my mother's house.

As he took it from me, Lobo slowed down as he approached the house.

"She ain't here, right?" he asked, staring up at the large brick home.

"Nah. They went out of town. I just don't know for how long," I said, staring at the Jeep Cherokee in the driveway. "That's her nanny's car."

His eyes darted towards me. "Damn, your mama got it like that?"

"Not really. My stepfather did. She was just able to save up a lot of cash."

"That nigga, Law, be here all the time?" Lobo asked as he hit the blunt.

I nodded, staring at the house that I longed to still call my own. "Every night."

My mother hadn't changed the login information for the Ring app, so I still had access to it on my phone. Since Zina had told me about Law, I had been watching him come and go all day and night. He definitely had a bag because he was driving a 2022 Bentley Bacalar. I knew who Marlene was because I could hear her talking as she came in and out as well. Then, I saw Law and my mother leaving that day with suitcases.

"Damn, this a real lick. That nigga got a bag."

I nodded. "Mmm humph."

Lobo's eyes were wide with excitement as he continued to stare at the house, plotting.

After leaving my grandfather's house, I was so pissed. Everyone was still gathering like one big happy family without me. My mother had even moved on to yet another rich nigga, while I was struggling to feed myself. She didn't even care about my well-being. She even had a new kid and everything.

Once I'd left there and had to beg Lobo to get me another room for the night, I suggested to him that I let him rob Law. I knew that that would keep him in my good graces and get me a bag as well. After that, he started asking around the hood about Law. He had found out that after getting out of jail, Law had gotten right back on and was the plug for a network of hustlas in the city. So, Lobo was game to hit this lick with my help.

Fuck it; everyone else was taking what they wanted.

It was my turn.

"And you can still get in the crib?" Lobo asked.

"Yeah. I still have keys. I can let you in and even delete all of the footage from the Ring camera through the app as soon as you leave."

He smiled, pulling off. "Bet. So, all I gotta do is slip up in that motherfucka while they're sleeping and grab his ass. He'll take me to the cash to save his life, I'm sure. Shit, I should bring a homie with me to grab your mom's too, to ensure he gives up that bread." Then he looked at me with a questioning stare. "You good with that?"

I nodded. "Nah. I don't want anything to happen to her. You can take Law, though. I don't give a fuck what happens to him, as long as we get some bread."

Lobo grinned menacingly. "I got you. As soon as they get back from out of town, it's poppin'."

CHAPTER 20
ZURI TURNER

The Maldives had been magical.

I had to pinch myself every time I woke up and looked out onto the ocean. We had been there for two days and had hardly left our private villa.

We were staying in a two-bedroom private reserve on Soneva Fushi. It was like a luxurious treehouse. There was an ocean view, but the villa was also hidden away in a stretch of jungle. It was centered around a massive outdoor pool and waterslide. They had a private space with a steam and sauna room, gym, and study.

We had a staff that waited on us hand and foot. Every meal had been prepared by the finest chef, and there were two masseuses on the property to give us massages whenever we wanted.

"I don't want to go home," I moaned as I curled up with Law on the outdoor sofa.

We were watching the sunset while drinking and watching a movie in the outdoor theater that projected films on the house.

"What about Kingston?" Law asked, rubbing my back lovingly.

I frowned. "Who?"

He roared with laughter, throwing his head back.

My baby had been looking so good in that Maldives sun. He had gotten even more tan. He looked so regal walking on our private beach, shirtless in linen shorts with his locs falling down to his waist.

"We can send for Kingston and Marlene," he suggested.

"Don't tease me," I pouted.

"We have to go home tomorrow."

I feigned a sob.

"Marlene has work to do," he said, chuckling at my fake tears. "We can come back anytime you want, though."

I smiled up into his eyes. I know this nigga was so tired of seeing my teeth. I had been smiling into his face for two days.

"So, we have to leave in the morning?" I pouted.

"Yeah."

I sighed, curling into him. "Well, thank you so much for this. It was so nice and much needed, baby."

"It ain't over."

I looked up at him. "What you mean?"

His smile was so shy as he reached into his pocket. When he pulled out the black velvet ring box, I sat up slowly. It appeared to be an engagement ring, but I didn't want to get my hopes up since we hadn't been together that long.

Law was usually so confident, so hard. Now, he was timid, shy, and unsure as he stood.

"I know it's early, but nothing about the way that we have been doing things is conventional. I love you so much. I've never said this before in my life because it's never been true before now." My breath hitched. I brought my hand to my chest, touched by not only his sentiments but the sincerity in them. I fought to keep my cries of adoration silent as he continued, "But I can hardly tell my own heart from yours anymore. You own me. I'm yours."

Inhaling deeply, he lowered to one knee. I threw my hands over my mouth. I looked down at him with tearful eyes. My skin flushed with excitement. I could feel it tingling at the surface as I began to squeal.

He opened the box, and I could no longer sit still. I started to bounce in my seat, ogling the five-carat, three-stone engagement ring. The round, brilliant-cut diamonds danced in the orange hues of the setting sun.

"Will you be mine forever, baby?" he asked. "Will you marry me?"

I burst into tears, unable to speak. I threw my face into my hands, nodding. I felt him take my left hand and bring it away from my face. I forced myself to see through my tears as he slipped the ring on my finger.

Suddenly, applause could be heard approaching. I looked around frantically and saw Bianca, Ox, and Megan walking up to the back of the villa from the beach with their phones in their hands.

I finally found my voice, screaming, "Oh my God!"

I started jumping up and down, flailing my arms wildly. When Bianca started to run to me, I took off to meet her halfway.

"*Heeeeey*, bitch!" she greeted as we threw our arms around one another.

I was sobbing again as I hugged her tight.

We rocked from side to side as she said, "Congratulations."

As we pulled away, I saw Law shaking up with Ox. Me and Megan embraced. I was so happy to see them all. Megan and I had started to get really cool since we were always around each other now. She was really cool and was teaching me how to deal with a nigga in the game.

"Okay, enough of that crying," Bianca spat happily. "Where the drinks at?! It's a motherfucking party now!"

I looked over at Law, who was smiling devilishly at me. I ran up to him, throwing my arms around him.

"So, we *aren't* leaving in the morning?" I beamed.

He reached behind me, softly grabbing my ass. "No, baby. We aren't leaving in the morning."

"Unt uh. Don't call me 'baby'," I sassed.

He smirked with a grin, causing his brow to curl. "What am I supposed to call you then?"

Cheesing, I waved my ring in his face with so much pride. "Mrs. Woods... if you nasty."

AANAN "LAW" WOODS

Two days later, I was up bright and early because I was still accustomed to that from when I was locked up. I was standing on the patio, enjoying the weather and view for one last time and handling business.

This trip had been surreal. The smile that had been on Zuri's face was unexplainable. But I had been grinning too. I would never have imagined being in such a magical place as the island we had escaped to. A lot of niggas got money and thought that living it up in Miami was the dream. But this shit gave me higher heights to aspire to. My family deserved a home like this to escape to whenever they wanted. And I was going to get it for them.

As I relaxed on an outdoor sofa, I was making a few calls to solidify the plans for Whit's body. I had decided against having a funeral for the sake of my kids. They were already under the impression that she was gone. They were too young for me to put them through the trauma of explaining that she was dead. So, I had decided to allow the funeral home to cremate her. I would then save the ashes for them and explain to them that she was dead when they got older.

Hearing the balcony door slide open, I looked up and saw Ox stumbling out. Two days of partying and nonstop smoking and drinking had left us all feeling and looking like shit.

I chuckled. "Damn, dawg, you a'ight?"

"*Shiiit*," he sang lowly as he collapsed on the couch next to me. "Megan had me up all night. She wanted to fuck all over this island."

I tossed my head back, laughing.

Ox gave me a serious stare as he said, "You good, fam?"

"Good with what?"

"Proposing to Zuri."

"You think it was too fast, huh?"

"Hell nah. I see the way you look at her. I'm a married man too. I remember the feeling I had when I wifed my shorty up. But as men, we're forced to handle a lot of shit while dealing with a lot of new emotions. I'm just making sure my dawg good."

"I'm good, man. It's new to me, but I know I want her in my life. As soon as I found out Kingston was mine, it was just confirmation that no matter how long we've been at this shit, it was time to put a ring on it. We can take our time getting married, but I want that ring on her finger to let her and the world know that she's mine."

Ox nodded proudly. Then he yawned dramatically, stretching.

"Man, I'm tired *as fuck*. I ain't never drunk this much in my life."

I chuckled, saying, "We leave this afternoon. It's all good. Why you up this morning if you so tired?"

"My phone was blowing up. Niggas got murked this weekend in the hood."

I scoffed, shaking my head. Jail had been a good vacation from this bullshit. I had totally disconnected from the streets, so if my brother hadn't heard about it, neither had I. I had always been two steps ahead, protecting myself at all costs for the sake of Ma and my kids. Yet, now that I had proposed to Zuri, I couldn't imagine putting her through the pain of losing me to prison or the grave.

"Some of our people?" I asked.

"Hell nah. Just some niggas I grew up with."

"Man, sorry to hear that."

It was sad how nonchalant Ox was as he shrugged. He was so immune to death that it wasn't fazing him. I guessed that I was the same.

"That shit comes with the game," Ox said with a sigh. "Most of us either gonna end up dead or in jail."

That was facts. We were willingly living a very dangerous game, but that shit was eerie as hell. At our age, we were considered old heads. Not many hustlas made it to see thirty years old. I was constantly feeling as if I was running on borrowed time, and at any moment, my luck was going to run out.

CHAPTER 21
AANAN "LAW" WOODS

It had been a long day of traveling and going through customs. It was after midnight by the time that we were tiredly ambling through the front of Zuri's crib.

Zuri let out a deep sigh of relief as she locked the door.

"I'll carry these upstairs in the morning," I groaned, setting our suitcases along the wall in the foyer.

"Okay," she yawned.

She started to pad up the stairs, and I followed. Days of drinking, smoking weed, fucking, and partying had me worn out. Luckily, Marlene had sent Zuri and me a text message when we landed that Kingston was asleep and she would stay overnight in the other guestroom to tend to him if he woke up during the night so that Zuri and I could get some rest.

When we got up the stairs, Zuri surprisingly walked past her bedroom.

"Where are you going?"

"To go get Kingston," she said as if I should know. "I want him to sleep in the bed with us."

I chuckled, grabbing her elbow. "Don't wake that lil' nigga up. You crazy?"

"But I miss him," she pouted.

And she actually pulled away and kept walking to Kingston's room.

"Zuri!" I whispered her name through gritted teeth.

Her thick, short legs started to move faster, so I took off, catching up with her. I grabbed her around her waist and picked her up. She giggled quietly while I carried her into the room.

"I wanna sleep with my baby," she said as I put her down in the room.

I closed and locked the bedroom door. "Girl, if you pick him up, you'll wake him up. If you do, you gonna be here by yourself because I'm going to the crib. I need some sleep."

Her mouth dropped playfully, but she knew better than to play with me.

"Fine," she spit with a smirk. "I'm going to take a shower then."

I nodded and then collapsed on the sofa in the room with a relieved grunt.

Something was telling me to go home to my other kids, but I had ignored it, figuring that I would get some sleep at Zuri's and pick my kids up from my mom the next morning.

You're always supposed to listen to your gut, though.

That motherfucker is always loyal to you and never steers you wrong.

ZOEY TURNER

I thought that when we turned onto my mother's block I would feel bad. But as I saw that Bentley and my mother's Porsche in the driveway, I saw how lavish her life still was. She was living comfortably with no consideration for my well-being. So, I wasn't going to consider hers.

"So, when you unlock the door, just go back to the car and wait. Once I get in there and up my hammer on him, he's going to cooperate. I'm going to take him out of the house and make him drive to where most of his bread is. Once you see us pull off, go back to my trap spot and wait on me. Okay?"

I nodded.

Lobo's eyes were wide with greed as he pulled over a few feet away from my mother's house. "You ready?"

"Yeah."

I was game. I knew that Lobo wouldn't hurt my mother. This wasn't about her; this was about Law's bread, and we wanted some.

Turning the engine off, he told me, "C'mon."

It was three o'clock in the morning. The block in the affluential neighborhood was quiet and still. Yet, the hustle and bustle of the main streets in the heart of the city were only a few miles away.

Random sirens blared in the distance, drowning out the sounds of us creeping out of the car and up the sidewalk.

Since I had access to the Ring app, I had already gone into it and turned off the notifications so that my mother's phone wouldn't get notified when the motion detector alerted.

My hands weren't even shaking as I unlocked the door quietly. Lobo secured the bandana around his mouth, and he then threw his hood over his head.

Once the door was unlocked, he motioned with his head towards the car. As planned, I left the porch and went to the car. I slipped into the driver's seat and went back to the Ring app. I deleted the footage of us entering the house and then turned the camera and motion detectors off.

AANAN "LAW" WOODS

As I stirred, I realized that I had fallen asleep on the sofa.

"Fuck," I groaned.

I had been in a deep ass sleep. I nearly felt drunk as I tried to get my shit together and get in the bed with Zuri.

As I stood, I heard a noise downstairs that didn't sit well with me. This time, I followed my gut. I crept to Zuri's dresser and grabbed my hammer. I took the safety off, ready to blaze as I inched towards the bedroom door.

The house was quiet and dark. So quiet that I was able to hear movement in the foyer.

"What the fuck?" I mouthed.

My grip on my hammer got tighter as I eased out of the doorway into the hall. I pressed my body against the wall as I crept down the hallway so that I wouldn't be seen.

Once at the top of the stairs, I took a moment to listen and watch. I narrowed my eyes, trying to see through the darkness.

As soon as I saw the silhouette of the hoodie and gun in the person's hand, I aimed and fired.

The gunshot ricocheted loudly through the quiet of the house like an explosion. He took off towards the front door, and I followed. As soon as he hit the front door, I was on his heels. I wanted this bitch ass nigga to know not to ever pull it at this crib again. I figured it was some young shorty on some thirsty shit. Only the young niggas did shit like jack cars and run up in cribs. I had been one of them. So, I kind of felt sympathy for him. I had planned on beating the fuck out of him and schooling his young ass.

"Aye!" I barked, startling him.

He turned around, aiming his hammer at my head. As soon as the streetlights hit his face, I saw that this wasn't a young shorty.

Anger washed over me. I already knew that this motherfucker would shoot me.

So, I shot first.

I emptied the clip.

I let that bitch breathe.

ZOEY TURNER

"Oh my God. Oh my God. Oh my God," I chanted hysterically as I watched Law chase Lobo out of the house.

"This stupid motherfucker," I gritted. "How did he fuck this up?"

The engine was still running. My hand was on the gear shift. I threw the car in drive so that I would be ready to pull off when Lobo hopped in.

But then Law shouted. "Aye!"

I gasped and held my breath.

Lobo turned and aimed his gun at Law.

"Fuck!" I shouted; eyes ballooned with fear.

Then Law did the same. But he started pulling the trigger and never stopped.

"Shit!" I shouted as Lobo's body slumped to the ground in the middle of my mother's front yard. "Fuck! Fuck! Fuck!"

I made a U-turn and took off.

I wasn't about to stick around and be connected to this shit.

"What the fuck?" I began to unravel, not knowing what to do. "I gotta get the fuck outta here."

I had to leave.

Fuck it.

Then it dawned on me.

I was going to go to Lobo's trap house, find whatever money was there, take his car and leave. I didn't know where I was going to go, but at least I would have the means to get there.

I did ninety all the way to the trap spot. My heart was beating out of my chest. I didn't even wonder if Lobo was alive. I was too busy trying to make sure that my mother would never find out that I had anything to do with this. While at a red light, I went to the Ring app and turned my mother's camera back on and her notifications. Then I deleted the app from my phone.

About fifteen minutes later, I was pulling up in front of Lobo's trap house. Because it had been my plan to go there anyway, Lobo had given me a key. I was digging in my pocket for it when I heard cars approaching at high speeds down the street. I looked in the rearview mirror and saw two police cars barreling toward me. I figured that they were speeding to a call and opened the driver's door.

"Put your hands up!"

Startled, I froze, looking back. Officers were running toward me with their guns drawn.

"Get out of the vehicle with your hands up! Now!"

My lips began to tremble with fright. I wondered how they had associated me with Lobo breaking into my mother's house so fast.

"Fuck," I gritted.

I put my hands out of the car first and then slowly stepped out.

Then, I was rushed by two officers. The others approached the driver's side of the car.

"Zoey Turner?" one of them asked, approaching me with his hand on his gun.

Shit. "Y-yes?"

"Place your hands behind your back."

"For what?!" I exclaimed.

"You have the right to remain silent—"

"What am I being arrested for?" I cried.

Ignoring me, the officer took my wrist into his hands and placed my hand behind my back. Then he took the other and did the same. "Anything you say can and will be used against you in a court of law—"

"You're supposed to tell me what I'm being arrested for!!!"

"You have a right to an attorney. If you cannot afford an attorney, one will be appointed for you."

I gritted, giving up trying to get any answers out of these motherfuckers.

"Where is Lobo?"

I blinked rapidly, confused. "Huh?"

"*Where. Is. Lobo?*" he reinforced.

"He's not in the car," I heard an officer say as he left the passenger side.

"Check the house," one of them ordered.

"What am I being arrested for?" I asked again.

The officer looked down at me, grinning with a taunting smirk. "You and Lobo were caught on Ring camera footage on 63rd and Michigan at the time of the robbery and shooting that resulted in those murders on 63rd and Indiana. You're being arrested for felony murder. Any other questions?"

My face immediately went slack, and my knees went weak. I nearly dropped to my knees, but the officer holding onto my elbow drug me back up, laughing as I crumbled into pieces of despair.

ZURI TURNER

The gunshot woke me out of my sleep.

I gasped when it sounded like it was so close.

I sat straight up. Looking around the room, I saw that Law wasn't on the couch sleeping anymore, and my bedroom door was now opened.

I jumped out of bed and flung open the drawer of my nightstand. Then I snatched out the pistol that Law had bought me. As I ran out of the room, I took the safety off.

"Law! *Laaaw*!!" My scream was curdling as I ran through the house.

"Zuri?!"

Gasping, I remembered that Marlene was in the house. My eyes darted down the dark hallway towards my baby's room. "Stay in there, Marlene!"

"What's going on?!" Marlene asked frantically.

"Stay in the room!" I demanded.

I nearly slid down the stairs, running down them so fast. Fear consumed me when I saw that the front door was open. Just as I was about to continue down the stairs, I heard Law bark, "Aye!"

I then started to take my time, creeping down the stairs. I held the trigger tightly, remembering everything that Law had taught me about firing guns.

Then multiple shots rang out right outside of my front door. They were so close that I ducked, feeling as if I could possibly get hit.

When they finally stopped, I started to cry out again. "Law!!"

"I'm good, baby."

I immediately started crying with relief. I stood up and took off out of the house.

Barefoot, I ran out onto the porch and froze when I saw the body in the yard.

"What the hell happened?!"

"That nigga was inside the house."

"Are you serious?!"

"Call the police, baby?"

Looking around, I saw lights coming on in neighbors' houses. "My phone is upstairs," I said slowly, staring at the bloody body in my yard.

"Here." Law reached in his pocket and tossed me his phone.

With shaking hands, I called 9-1-1.

"9-1-1, what is your emergency?"

"I need an ambulance. There was an intruder in my house, and he was shot."

"Is he alive?"

"No," I said, peering at his bloody corpse. Holes riddled his torso with gunshots so fresh that they were still smoking amongst the cold, brittle night. "He isn't breathing."

CHAPTER 22
ZURI TURNER

The police were at my house for hours after that. I was worried that, with his background, Law would be arrested. However, since he hadn't been charged with any felonies, his gun was registered and legal.

That body was in my yard until nearly ten o'clock that morning. It was amazing to me how long it took the coroners to come. As my neighbors started to come out of their homes for work and school, they saw the police, yellow tape, and body draped on my lawn and started to gather around my house. After answering too many questions, I retreated into the house to get away from them.

I was clinging to my baby as I sat beside Bianca on my couch. Bianca had come over when Law finally left to go see his kids, and Marlene left to get the hell away from all the drama. She was really shaken up, but luckily, she didn't blame me for what had happened.

Bianca and I looked like we had been run over by buses because we still hadn't gotten any rest from the trip.

"I still don't understand how that footage got deleted like that."

So many strange things were unexplainable to me and the police.

There had been no forced entry. And when the police had asked for my Ring camera footage of the hours the shooting had occurred, it had been deleted.

Bianca opened her mouth to speak, but then my cell rang.

I looked down at it in my lap and groaned when I saw that it was my sister.

"Is that Zina again?" Bianca asked.

"Yes," I groaned.

She had been calling me all morning, but I had been serious when I told her that I was done with her and Zadah's drama and getting some space.

"Anyway," I said, sending her to voicemail.

"Does anyone else have access to the app?" Bianca asked.

"Rashaad and Zoey had it on their phones."

Bianca then reluctantly gave me a telling look.

"*Nooo*," I said slowly.

"I'm just saying."

"Rashaad is in jail."

"I ain't talking about him."

My eyes narrowed, wondering where she was going. But then she smirked, tilting her head dramatically.

"Why would Zoey...." My words trailed off as I began to wonder.

"You said that she was on bullshit when she came by your father's house. Maybe she wasn't done."

"So, she would send some nigga in here to rob me?"

"Zina said she was hard up for money."

I shook my head slowly. "I know that she has been doing some foul shit lately, but she ain't no street chick. What would she know about some shit like that?"

"You didn't know that she knew anything about fucking your husband, but she did that too." Then she lifted her hands in surrender. "Just sayin'."

Hairs stood on the back of my neck. I tried to consider it but couldn't even fathom it.

My phone rang again.

"Fuck!" I cried out in irritation.

Looking down into my lap, I saw that it was Zina again.

I snatched it out of my lap and answered, "What, Zina?"

"Hello, *sister.*"

"What do you want, Zina?" I groaned.

"I just called to tell you to check on your stank-ass daughter."

"I don't have time for this shit right now, Zina!"

"I'm not trying to be messy," she assured me. "This is important. That nigga that she was sneaking in my house was killed last night."

"Was she with him?"

"I don't think so. I just see posts about it from people in the hood on social media. Looks like he was shot trying to break into somebody's crib. I told that *wench* to stop fucking with that loser ass—"

"I gotta go, Zina." I hung up, holding my head in my hands.

"What?"

"I think the guy that broke into my house was Zoey's friend."

Bianca shook her head, smirking as if she knew she was right but hated that she was.

"Zina said that he was killed last night trying to break into somebody's house."

"Shit," Bianca breathed, sitting back. "I didn't want to be right."

"Can it just be a coincidence that her friend was killed in the same way last night that this guy was?"

Bianca's brow rose dramatically. "That'll be one hell of a coincidence, Zuri."

A FEW DAYS LATER, THINGS GOT EVEN EERIER.

I was in the nursery feeding a wide-eyed Kingston.

I hadn't had to do much investigation to find out if Zoey had anything to do with the robbery. The police had been able to quickly identify the robber as Lobo, Zoey's friend, since he had an extensive record. Since there had been no forced entry and the footage was erased from the Ring camera app, I knew it was Zoey.

Since learning that the day prior, my daughter was now dead to me. She wasn't a street chick, but she lived in Chicago. She knew how people lost their lives so easily during robberies. She had put me and Kingston's life at risk, not only Law's, just for the sake of coming up. For that, I could never forgive her.

"He's starting to look like his daddy." Marlene smiled as I bottle-fed Kingston in a rocking chair.

I nodded, agreeing with a grin. Now that he was getting older, he was definitely starting to get more features. He had Law's heavy-lidded eyes, almond-colored skin, and full lips.

"Thanks for coming back, Marlene."

She looked down at me, smirking as if I should have known better. "Girl, gunshots don't scare me, chil'. And, clearly, that was an isolated incident."

My eyes shied away, embarrassingly. I had been honest with Marlene about Zoey being involved because I wanted her to be comfortable in my home. Since the robbery, Law had ensured that all of the security measures in the home were increased, starting with changing the locks.

I was now living in a fortress.

My phone began to ring. Since I had my AirPod on, I double tapped it to answer without reaching for the phone as it sat in the window seal.

"Hello?"

"Hi, Zuri."

My eyes narrowed, hearing the familiar voice. "Michelle?"

"Yes, it's me."

I sat up a little, alarmed. I hadn't heard from Rashaad's secretary since I had quit the County.

"Is everything okay?" I asked.

"*Ummm*," she moaned reluctantly. "I don't know."

Then she paused, making my heart beat wildly. So many outlandish, ridiculous things had happened that I was now literally planning for the worse.

Then she sighed and said, "Word has been coming over from the Women's Division that Zoey is locked up over there."

Immediately, my body slumped with regret. "Oh God."

I wondered what the hell she had done now. Though she was dead to me, I hadn't told the police about her involvement with Lobo. Since he had been killed during the robbery, I knew that if they knew about Zoey, she would be arrested. Lobo had already suffered the consequences of trying to rob us. I prayed that that was enough to keep Zoey from ever doing some foul shit like that again. She was dead to me, but I could not be responsible for sending her to jail.

Concerned, Marlene stood close by.

"So, I looked it up before calling you to make sure, and she is in the system," Michelle went on. "She's been held on felony murder charges."

"Murder?!" I shouted, causing Kingston to jump out of his skin.

I stood and handed him and his bottle to Marlene.

"Yes," Michelle said reluctantly. "I read the report, and she was seen on Ring camera footage getting into the driver's seat when the shooter got out and ran towards the scene of the murder. Then he came back, and she drove off. She was denied bail."

"*Oh. My. God.*" I held my forehead, shaking my head slowly. I felt sick to my stomach. It was turning violently as I tried to wrap my head around this shit.

"I went over there to check on her. She's a mess. I asked her if you knew that she was in there, and she said that she didn't want to call you."

"Okay... Okay, Michelle. Thank you."

I had no more strength.

None.

"I'm sorry, Zuri."

"Thanks for letting me know," I told her before hanging up.

"What's going on, Zuri?" Marlene asked.

"It's my daughter." I felt like my throat was closing. I couldn't breathe. The person that I had raised, the person that had all of my heart; I felt like she was gone. Like she was dead. I had lost her.

"Is she okay?" Marlene asked.

"I don't think so," I said with delusion.

I didn't know what I was feeling. I wanted to cry but couldn't.

I didn't have any more tears.

Absolutely none.

◈

MY HEART SANK WHEN ZOEY ENTERED THE VISITATION ROOM A FEW hours later. Looking at her was like watching a stranger. I didn't know this woman. All of the glitz and glam was gone. Her face was bare and still beautiful. It was the new hardness in her eyes and her deceitfulness and lies that made her ugly. She was wearing oversized blue scrubs. She looked dirty and tattered, unlike the spoiled little girl that I had raised.

Yet, for the first time, she looked at me with relief. The distress and need made her look like my little girl again, in need of her mother's love.

When I stood, she actually raced towards me and wrapped her arms around me so tight that I could feel her fear.

I closed my eyes and hugged her back. That's when my tears returned. I felt so guilty, like I had done this to my child.

I could see the impatience on the CO's face, so I forced myself to let her go.

We sat down at the table, giving one another longing gazes.

I reached over and held her hand.

"Thank you for coming, Ma. Thank you so much. I need a lawyer. They're threatening me with forty years."

"Did you know he was going to kill those people?"

"No. I promise I didn't. He pulled over and told me to get in the driver's seat. I didn't know what he was going to do. Now they're charging me with first-degree felony murder because he had robbed the guys before he killed them. And they can't charge him."

I lowered my head. First-degree felony murder was the most serious crime that a person could be charged with.

I wanted to lecture her. I wanted to tell her that she should have listened to her aunt, that she should have listened to me and gone to college. But to beat her down at a time like this would be useless. Those were lectures that I had given her time and time again before and had gone through one ear and out the other.

"They can't charge Lobo because he is dead, *right?*" I pressed.

Using his name made her tense up.

My eyes bore into hers, anger boiling over as I thought about our potential deaths, had my man not been a trained killer. "Law is the person that killed him, but you know that, right?"

She recoiled with shame, pulling her eyes away from mine.

I raised an angry brow as I watched her guilt unfold rapidly. "Can I ask you a question?"

"Yeah," she muttered reluctantly.

"You let that boy into my house and deleted the footage from the app, right?"

I already knew the answer, but I wanted her to be a true adult for once.

Shrinking, she started to nervously ramble. "He made me do it, Ma. I didn't have anybody else. Zina had kicked me out, and I didn't have any money or a place to stay. He was the only person that I had in my life that would help me out, so I felt like I had to listen to him."

"How did he even know about Law?" I pressed, narrowing my eyes.

Her eyes shied away from me again.

"You told him, right?" I pressed.

She was too embarrassed to answer, but I knew the truth.

Looking at her, I knew that no matter how enraged I was with her, I had to give in to my motherly instincts. I blew a heavy breath, saying, "I'm going to get you a lawyer."

She sighed with relief. "Thank you so much—"

"Don't thank me," I cut her off with such a stern expression that her eyes enlarged, and she swallowed hard.

"I'm only getting you a lawyer because I wouldn't be able to live with myself if I just leave you in here with no help. But that is all I have for you. You are going to get time for this; there is no way around it. And I'm not going to be putting money on your books, accepting calls, sending letters, or visiting you in whatever Federal prison that they haul you off to; none of that shit. I'm done." Her eyes started to well with tears as I went on, "I've spoiled you. I ruined you. So, I have to help you get out of something that I feel like I had a hand in doing. But I wash my hands of you. You are a hazard to my life. I'm leaving you to learn the lessons that I couldn't teach you."

I then stood because I felt myself breaking down. I had never experienced a breakup so hurtful. It felt like death to walk away from her startled doe eyes, but I had to.

I had to let go. It was time. I was no longer subscribing to the drama that Zoey, Rashaad, and my sisters insisted on ruining their lives with. My heart was indeed broken. Rashaad and Zoey had left it in a condition that couldn't be fixed. Yet, God had given me Kingston and Law, who was mending it back together in an even better condition than it had been in before it was broken. I had never been a super religious person, but as I walked out of that prison, I had to realize that, while the people in my life were breaking me, God was putting me back together. Along with Law and Kingston, He had also given me

Marlene, a mother figure that I had missed, and Bianca, who was becoming like a sister to me.

God had taken the shattered pieces of my life and mended that which was broken, making it strong enough to hold all the blessings He was pouring into me. He had not only restored what was lost but had restored it *abundantly*.

A MONTH LATER

ANNAN "LAW" WOODS

Looking over at Zuri completely unraveling in the passenger seat was so funny.

"Stop laughing at me," she whined.

"Are you seriously over there scared of some kids?"

"I don't want them to hate me."

"They won't. I promise."

That hadn't been any help to her. She was still freaking out, biting her nails and wildly staring out of the window.

It had been almost a month since I had proposed to Zuri. Though we had met one another's families, we wanted them to meet each other now that we were engaged. So, Zuri, Kingston, and I were heading to Ma's for dinner. Zuri still wasn't fucking with her sisters, so she had only invited her father and Bianca. Reese, Shay, and the kids were meeting us there as well.

As I pulled onto Ma's block, Zuri started to look flushed.

I reached over and placed a supportive hand on her thigh. "It'll be cool, baby. I promise."

She nodded nervously and took a deep breath. I loved her even more for being this nervous about meeting my kids. That meant that she cared how they received her, and that meant a lot to me.

We parked and climbed out of the car. Zuri was literally wringing her hands as she followed me up the steps while I carried Kingston.

Before I could even ring the bell, Ma was opening the door.

"Hey—"

"Gimme my baby," she blurted, stepping out onto the porch and taking Kingston from me.

"Really, Ma?"

"Boy, c'mon in here." Then she motioned for us to follow her into the house. "Hey, Zuri."

"Hi, Gloria."

I looked down at Zuri, smiling at the fact that she was so nervous that her voice was shaking. I grabbed her hand to give her some support, and she clung to it.

"Hey, daddy!" Serenity came running to the living room. She collided with my legs, hugging them.

I reached down, hugging her back. "Hey, baby."

Once she noticed Zuri, she started to bounce her eyes between her and me, all while running my way.

"Where is your brother and sister?" I asked her.

"In the kitchen."

"Tell them to come here."

"August and Willow, daddy wants you!!" she screamed.

Laughing, I told her, "Girl, I could have done that." Then I reached down and pinched her cheek.

As she giggled, she still looked up at Zuri, eyes full of curiosity.

Willow and August ran into the living room, and their curiosity rose as soon as they saw Zuri.

Smiling, I told them, "Come here. I want you all to meet somebody."

They inched towards us, still eyeing Zuri.

"I want you all to meet my fiancée, Zuri."

Willow frowned. "What's a fiancée?"

"We're getting married." Both her and August's eyes widened. "She is going to be my wife and your stepmom."

Being five, Serenity was confused as hell. But Willow and August understood.

Zuri bent down, extending her hand out. "Hi. Nice to meet you guys."

August shook her hand. "Hi."

Surprisingly, when she stuck her hand out to Willow, she hugged Zuri.

Giggling in shock, Zuri said, "Well, hi, Willow."

"Hi. You're pretty."

Ma was sitting on the couch holding Kingston and looked on with tears in her eyes. August rolled his eyes, taunting his sister's dramatics.

Zuri was smiling from ear to ear. Finally, her nerves were gone. "Thank you."

The way that Willow was clinging to her pulled at my heart. I knew that it was because Willow had been missing her mom's presence. Even though my mom and Shay had been overcompensating for Whit's absence, it was nothing like a mother's love.

"*Moove*, Willow!" Serenity whined, pulling on Willow's leg. "I wanna hug too!"

Willow sucked her teeth. Zuri reached and pulled Serenity into their hug. "You can have a hug too."

Willow looked up at her with wide eyes. "My daddy bought me a big dollhouse. You wanna see it?"

"Yeah. Where is it?"

Willow took Zuri's hand, pulling her out of the living room towards the stairs to take her to the second floor, where the playroom was that Ma had in the house for her grandkids.

"Wait, y'all gotta meet your brother."

August's mouth dropped. Then he slowly started to smile. My smile met his.

"I got a brother?" he asked with excitement.

"Yeah. He's over there."

The kids' eyes bounced over to Kingston, and they ran towards him.

"I wanna hold him, Grandma!" Willow said.

August pushed her out of the way. "I wanna hold him first!"

"Aye, y'all stop fighting!" Ma urged. "Sit down, and you all can take a turn holding him."

They quickly sat down, even Serenity. My mother carefully placed Kingston in August's arms first. And the way that he proudly looked down on his brother brought a tear to my eyes. But I was too much of a real nigga to let that bitch fall.

⊗⊗⊗

Ox tilted his head, giving me a sarcastic sneer. "You sure about this, bro?"

An hour later, everyone had made it. My family was getting along great with Zuri's dad, Rodger, and Bianca. Once the food was almost finished, Ox, Reese, and I dipped off into the backyard to smoke a blunt. It was cold as hell, being the middle of February. So, we were hiding behind the furs on the collars and hoods of our leathers as he smoked quickly.

"Yeah, I'm sure. I'm out the game." I nodded, feeling so much relief.

Reese looked over at me, smiling with approval.

It was time. That attempted robbery had put things into perspective for me. Even though it hadn't stemmed from my dealings in the game, I wasn't willing to put Zuri, my kids, or my family in danger. That included removing myself from the game.

Now that Whit's death was on record, all of her assets had been split evenly amongst our kids. However, since they were kids, I was the trustee. Therefore, I had access to the 1.9 million she had made from the buildings she had sold, and I was the owner of the ones that she hadn't.

"No trade backs this time, nigga," he grinned.

Reese and I laughed as I heard Ma yell out, "Y'all come on in here and eat!"

"Bet," Ox said, rubbing his belly. "A nigga starving."

I followed Ox through the sliding balcony door. We walked into the kitchen, and the enticing aroma of fried chicken teased us. Bianca, Shay, Megan, and Zuri stumbled into the kitchen, laughing as if someone had just told a joke. I grinned at the sight of them already getting along so well. I was even more convinced that Zuri was the one. She had been the missing piece to the picture of my family, and she fit in so perfectly.

The kids filed in as well, along with Rodger.

Everyone sat down at the table in front of the feast that Ma had laid out buffet style. I remained standing in front of my seat next to Zuri.

"I wanna sit by Zuri!" Serenity insisted when Willow tried to sit on the other side of her.

"Unt uh! This is my seat!" Willow spat.

"Neither one of y'all are sitting beside her. Gone over there with the rest of the kids," Ma fussed.

Ma had set up a separate table on the other side of the dining room for all of the kids. Willow and Serenity pouted as Zuri playfully puckered, sympathizing with them.

As everyone got comfortable, I announced, "I want to say something before we start eating."

Everyone halted, looking up at me curiously. I laid a hand on Zuri's shoulder, and she smiled.

"The way that me and Zuri met was unconventional, but it was meant to be because I believe that your soulmate is not someone that comes into your life peacefully; they come and shake shit up so that you can *see* them..." Zuri looked up at me, grinning from ear to ear. Her slanted eyes were sparkling with tears. "You fit so perfectly into a space that had been left open for you. Anyone before you was a playmate," I told her. "But you are my soulmate because you have my soul. I used to dream about having this peace, this love. And now, my reality is better than my dreams. You're a dream come true, baby. Thank you for accepting me and my kids. And I'll spend the rest of my life showing you how much I appreciate you."

Overwhelmed, Zuri stood and cupped my face. As we kissed, everyone in the kitchen started to egg us on dramatically.

"I love you," she spoke into our kiss.

"I love you too, *Mrs. Woods*."

A YEAR LATER

EPILOGUE

Law and Zuri had only been able to wait another year before they committed themselves to one another before God.

"I'm so glad them motherfuckers finally knocked out," Law groaned.

Zuri laughed at his frustrated exhaustion as he plopped down on the bed in one of the master suites of the mansion.

That Friday night had been hectic. They had arrived with the kids at the Airbnb in North Carolina early that morning. Marlene was along with them. After a year of working for Zuri, Law had hired Marlene full-time. She was a wonderful maternal figure in their household that lovingly nurtured all of their children while Law was busy managing his many real estate investments and new, flourishing trucking business. Now that Kingston was over a year old, Zuri had decided to go back to work. However, instead of clocking in for someone else, Law had helped her open her own counseling facility on the Southside of Chicago for rehabilitated felons.

That afternoon, their family had begun to trickle in as well. First, Gloria, Reese, Shay, and the kids had arrived. Then Rodger, Zina, and her children. Stacy, her kids, and her nurse, Gabriella, followed. Ox,

Megan, Bianca, and her boyfriend, Prophet, whom she had been with for six months, had flown in together. Prophet was a part of Ox's crew, whom Bianca had met while partying with the crew one night. He had loved Bianca's bubbling personality and had never left her side since the moment she had forced him to take shots with her in VIP.

Zadah and her kids weren't in attendance because Zadah and Zuri's relationship had yet to be repaired. Zuri and Zina's relationship slowly began to mend as time went on, however. Zina's efforts at bettering herself had aided in their relationship re-blossoming. Rodger was so disgusted with Zina and Zadah that he had scolded them like they were fifteen and had distanced himself from them as well. Hurt that she was potentially losing her father and Zuri, Zina had started to change her ways. She had enrolled in nursing school. She was getting her RN and wanted to focus on Pediatric nursing. She was a great mother to her children. Treyvon continued to be an involved father to Tremere. However, he had left Zadah three months after Zoey had revealed his truths. Zadah had wanted to keep him, but he felt as if that was only because she wanted to feel like she had something over Zina. He could no longer take her drama, so he left her and canceled the wedding.

Reeling, Zadah continued to cause drama that eventually ousted her from the family. She had moved her and her children to Vegas and rarely visited.

Since Law and Zuri were getting married that Sunday on the grounds of the estate, a rehearsal dinner had been that evening, prepared by one of the best chefs in North Carolina. Then the elders and the children were sent to bed while the others had an after-party at the indoor pool that they had taken golf carts to because it was on the opposite end of the estate. There had been a lot of drinking, drugs, and bald-headed hoe shit that lasted until three in the morning.

"What time do I have to get fitted tomorrow, bae?" Law asked groggily.

Zuri yawned as she padded around the room, collecting her pajamas and toiletries so that she could shower. "Ten o'clock."

"*Fuuuuck*," Law groaned.

"I told you to get a tux in Chicago. But *noooo*."

"I wasn't trying to be lugging that shit through the airport like you were with that dress."

"Well, now yo' ass gotta get up early." Zuri playfully shrugged as she entered the bathroom.

Once in the bathroom, Zuri was forced to hear the rampant thoughts in her head. She often thought of and worried about Zoey. Frightened of the years that she was facing had she taken her case to trial, Zoey had taken a plea deal of fifteen years. Zuri feared that she would break one day and foolishly began to take care of Zoey again while she served her time. However, Zoey had sent many hateful letters to her mother, enraged that she hadn't been helping her financially. So, Zuri knew that, even though Zoey had been dealt the worse hand, she was still spoiled and entitled. On a weekend like the one that was happening presently, with so much family around, Zuri missed her first love.

Though she was about to marry the love of her life, Zuri often thought of Dom and kept him close to her heart. Shortly after returning from the Maldives, Law insisted that Zuri be the bigger person and give Dom's parents the insurance money, despite Robyn's constant harassment. So, she did, which ended the lawsuit.

Law's body flew back on the bed. He could feel himself falling asleep before he would be able to shower off the day and chlorine. Even his locs were soaking wet because Bianca had been trying to teach him how to swim. Even in his delirium, he smiled weakly, still in disbelief that he was about to marry his soulmate. He loved the fact that his family was there and wished that Unc could have been there. He and Unc had established an even closer bond in the past year. They talked every day, sometimes twice a day. And, despite Unc's refusal, Law was keeping his commissary full. He had even hired a lawyer to try to appeal Unc's initial case since it could have been seen as self-defense or temporary insanity, but the appeals continued to be rejected. Unc had become a father figure to him, so he'd wished that he could be free. But he was appreciative of Unc's presence, even if only verbally, along with Rodger, who he had a blossoming father-son relationship with as well.

"*Baaaae*," he heard Zuri call out.

"Yeah?"

"I need a big towel. Somebody stole the ones out of here."

"Where are the extra ones?"

"My dad said there were some in his room."

Groaning, Law forced himself out of bed. He ambled out of the room with one eye open, but he didn't complain. He loved Zuri like feigns loved dope, and needed her like a fish needed water. He would do anything for his soul, but only because every day, she showed and proved that she deserved it.

Luckily, Rodger's room was at the end of the hall. So, Law had reached the doorway soon. He had only knocked to announce his entry but hadn't waited for approval. Assuming that Rodger was fast asleep, he quietly opened the door.

"Oh God!" he heard a familiar voice shriek.

He froze, fighting to realize what he was seeing in the darkness. Figures scurried around on the bed as if they were wrestling in a frenzy.

The light was on in the adjoining bathroom, and the door was opened a bit. Therefore, he could see his mother's dreadful face.

"Ma?!" he bellowed. "What the fuck?!"

Law ran his hand along the wall, trying to find the light. Finally, his hand found the switch and turned it on.

"Y'all fucking serious?!" Law's baritone voice bellowed throughout the quiet, sleeping house. His anger echoed like an infuriated beast.

Gloria cringed, covering her naked body with a sheet as Rodger stood, naked, wide-eyed, and covering his genitals with his hands.

"Oh my God!" Law cringed, bending down, sick at the sight before him.

"What's going on?" Bianca's voice could be heard coming down the hall.

"Oh *gaaawd*," Gloria said, but with a laugh.

"You laughin', Ma?! You think this shit funny?!" Law snapped, taking long strides towards her.

"Law, let me explain," Rodger pleaded.

Halting his steps, Law gave Rodger a deadly glare. He took a deep breath, closing his eyes. "Rodger, I swear to God, don't say a fucking thing to me right now."

Gloria started to beg him. "Law, please calm down."

Law's eyes popped open, and he narrowed them at her.

"I'm grown as hell," Gloria started, but then dramatic boisterous laughter could be heard in the doorway.

Bianca stood in the doorway with her bonnet and sleep shirt on, cackling to the point that she was on her knees, falling to the floor. "*Heeeeeelll* nah!"

"What the fuck is–" Zuri had run up frantically, t-shirt and leggings thrown on in such a frantic that one of the legs was barely pulled all the way up. "Daddy?!"

Zuri's repulsion only made Bianca bellow with laughter so hard that she was gasping for air. "I think I just peed on myself!" Bianca cackled.

Law secretly thanked God that Ox, Megan, Reese and Shay's bedrooms were on the other side of the estate.

Bianca's high-pitched laughter continued to pierce the air as she fell apart on the floor in the doorway.

"Bianca, would you shut the fuck up before you wake the kids?" Gloria said through clenched teeth. "And get in the bed, Rodger."

Rodger carefully inched over to the bed, keeping his hands over his genitals and his bare ass facing the wall.

As he climbed into the bed and slid under the covers, Law slowly unraveled.

"Ma," he said so calmly that it was frightening to everyone except Bianca, who was still hooting. Zuri just stood behind him with her mouth cartoonishly agape.

"Law," Gloria said, slowly trying to rationalize with her annoyed and incensed son. "We've been meaning to tell you–"

"*We?*" Law winced, making Bianca bellow again, who now had tears in her eyes.

"Yes, *we*," Rodger said. "We've been seeing each other since a little after the dinner you had at her house."

"But-What..." Law couldn't find the words, so he just groaned. "*Uuuhhh!*"

"Oh, Law, grow up!" Gloria spat. "I'm grown. I can have a man. I deserve to get some too. Everybody else around here is in love and fucking."

Zuri doubled over. "Oh my God."

"Ma!" Law barked.

"*Aaaaaaahhhh!*" Bianca screeched with laughter.

"Bianca, if you wake up Kingston, I'm beating yo' ass," Gloria threatened.

Gloria was in her fifties, but she was still young in mind and body and was very much from the streets. So, Bianca took her seriously. She sucked her lips in, sitting Indian style on the floor, with humored tears streaming down her face.

"I gotta get the fuck out of here," Law muttered, turning to leave.

"Law, wait," Rodger insisted.

Through clenched teeth, Law told him, "Rodger, I'm *not* talking to you while you're in bed with my mother with your dick out, bro."

Zuri gave her father reprimanding eyes. He returned with sympathy laced in his, but she turned to follow her man.

"Move, bitch," she said, pushing Bianca out of the doorway and then closing the door.

Bianca fell out laughing again, laying out in the hallway, as Zuri scurried behind Law, who was taking long, angry gaits towards their room.

Once inside, she closed the door and inched towards him as he plopped down on the bed.

"You okay?" she reluctantly asked.

"My mama was just fucking." He still was in pure disbelief.

Zuri pouted, sympathizing with him as she stood in front of him. "I know, baby."

"She was naked." He was even still cringing.

"I know." Bending down, Zuri put her arms around him and rubbed his large back. "She *is* grown, though."

"We're step-siblings."

"No, the fuck we not!" Zuri spat, laughing.

Looking at her, Law finally smiled. Laughing as well, he leaned over, grabbed her waist, and pulled her onto his lap. "Come here, sis."

"Don't call me that," she glowered, slapping his shoulder.

Holding her, he buried his face into her chest. She put her arms around him, bringing her bear of a man closer to her. She could feel his heart slow from a rapid pace to a calm one as she held him tight.

Law hadn't been being dramatic when he'd said that he needed her. Zuri was always able to soothe the monster, to calm his storm. Likewise, he had and would always protect her, not because she was weak, but because she was important. She was vital to his existence, and he and his children would never be the same without her. Because Zuri knew that, she was eagerly ready to dedicate her life to Law in two days. Yet, she had already done so emotionally. He had come into her life and shown her that the most violent storm could produce the most beautiful and loving rainbow. And he had proved to her that sometimes you have to risk getting your heart broken just one more time so that it can break wide open.

THE END!

Don't miss another release from Jessica N. Watkins! Text the keyword "Jessica" to 25827 to receive text message notifications of future releases by Jessica N. Watkins!

ABOUT THE AUTHOR

Jessica N. Watkins was born April 1st in Chicago, Illinois. She obtained a Bachelor of Arts with Focus in Psychology from DePaul University and Master of Applied Professional Studies with focus in Business Administration from the like institution. Working in Hospital Administration for the majority of her career, Watkins has also been an author of fiction literature since the young age of nine. Eventually, she used writing as an outlet during her freshmen year of high school, after giving birth to her son. At the age of thirty-two, Watkins' chronicles have matured into steamy, humorous, and gritty tales of urban and women's fiction.

Jessica's debut novel *Jane Doe* spiraled into an engrossing, drama filled, and highly entertaining series. In August 2013, she signed to SBR publications, which ignited her writing career with the *Secrets of a Side Bitch* series.

In 2014, Jessica began to give other inspiring authors the opportunity to become published by launching Jessica Watkins Presents.

Jessica N. Watkins is available for talks, workshops, and book signings. For bookings, please send a request to authorjwatkins@gmail.com.

Instagram: @authorjwatkins
Facebook: missauthor
Twitter: @authorjwatkins
Snapchat: @authorjwatkins
Website: LitByJess.com
Amazon: www.Amazon.com/author/authorjwatkins

OTHER BOOKS BY JESSICA N. WATKINS:

PROPERTY OF A SAVAGE (STANDALONE)

WHEN MY SOUL MET A THUG (STANDALONE)

SAY MY FUCKING NAME (STANDALONE)

RIDESHARE LOVE (STANDALONE)

EVERY LOVE STORY IS BEAUTIFUL, BUT OURS IS HOOD SERIES (COMPLETE SERIES)

Every Love Story Is Beautiful, But Ours Is Hood

Every Love Story Is Beautiful, But Ours Is Hood 2

Every Love Story Is Beautiful, But Ours Is Hood 3

WHEN THE SIDE NIGGA CATCH FEELINGS SERIES (COMPLETE SERIES)

When The Side Nigga Catch Feelings

When the Side Nigga Catch Feelings 2

IN TRUE THUG FASHION (COMPLETE SERIES)

In True Thug Fashion 1

In True Thug Fashion 2

In True Thug Fashion 3

SECRETS OF A SIDE BITCH SERIES (COMPLETE SERIES)

Secrets of a Side Bitch

Secrets of a Side Bitch 2

Secrets of a Side Bitch 3

Secrets of a Side Bitch – The Simone Story

Secrets of a Side Bitch 4

A SOUTHSIDE LOVE STORY (COMPLETE SERIES)

A South Side Love Story 1

A South Side Love Story 2

A South Side Love Story 3

A South Side Love Story 4

CAPONE AND CAPRI SERIES (COMPLETE SERIES)

Capone and Capri

Capone and Capri 2

A THUG'S LOVE SERIES (COMPLETE SERIES)

A Thug's Love

A Thug's Love 2

A Thug's Love 3

A Thug's Love 4

A Thug's Love 5

NIGGAS AIN'T SHIT (COMPLETE SERIES)

Niggas Ain't Shit

Niggas Ain't Shit 2

THE CAUSE AND CURE IS YOU SERIES (PARANORMAL COMPLETE SERIES)

The Cause and Cure Is You

The Cause and Cure Is You 2

HOUSE IN VIRGINIA (COMPLETE SERIES)

House In Virginia 1

House in Virginia 2

SNOW (COMPLETE SERIES)

SNOW 1

SNOW 2

JESSICA WATKINS PRESENTS

Want to be notified when the new, hot Urban Fiction and Interracial Romance books are released? Text the keyword "JWP" to 22828 to receive an email notifying you of new releases, giveaways, announcements, and more!

Jessica Watkins Presents is the home of many well-known, best-selling authors in Urban Fiction and Interracial Romance. We provide editing services, promotion and marketing, one-on-one consulting with a renowned, national best-selling author, assistance in branding, and more, FREE of charge to you, the author.

We are currently accepting submissions for the following genres: Urban Fiction/Romance, Interracial Romance, and Interracial/Paranormal Romance. If you are interested in becoming a best-selling author and have a FINISHED manuscript, please send the synopsis, genre and the first three chapters in a PDF or Word file to jwp.submissions@gmail.com. Complete manuscripts must be at least 45,000 words.

Made in the USA
Las Vegas, NV
09 January 2024

84138500R00184